good

dt

S0-BAS-565

"You're the kindest man I ever met."

"I guess that's close to being sexy," Travis said ruefully.

"Even better."

Travis lowered his head and brushed his lips softly against hers. Anne wanted to smile with joy at the idea that such a simple caress could leave her desiring so much more. She wanted nothing more than to throw herself into Travis's arms and bury her face against his neck, inhaling the clean fragrance of his skin and absorbing his inner strength. She had been alone with her secrets for so long that the need for someone to share them with grew every time she was with him.

"I feel safe with you," she whispered. "You don't know how much that means to me."

ABOUT THE AUTHOR

Linda Randall Wisdom is a well-known name to readers of romance fiction. Long-term service in personnel, marketing and public relations gave her a wealth of experience on which to draw when creating characters. Linda knew she was destined to write romance novels when her first sale came on her wedding anniversary. She lives in Southern California with her husband and a houseful of exotic birds.

Books by Linda Randall Wisdom

HARLEQUIN AMERICAN ROMANCE

Don't miss any of our special offers. Write to us at the following address for information on our newest releases.

Harlequin Reader Service
901 Fuhrmann Blvd., P.O. Box 1397, Buffalo, NY 14240
Canadian address: P.O. Box 603,
Fort Erie, Ont. L2A 5X3

CODE
OF
SILENCE

LINDA
RANDALL
WISDOM

Harlequin Books

TORONTO • NEW YORK • LONDON
AMSTERDAM • PARIS • SYDNEY • HAMBURG
STOCKHOLM • ATHENS • TOKYO • MILAN

For Corinne Meyer,
my honey of an editor,
who may crack the whip at times,
but—darn it—
the book always comes out better!
Thanks for keeping me on the right track.

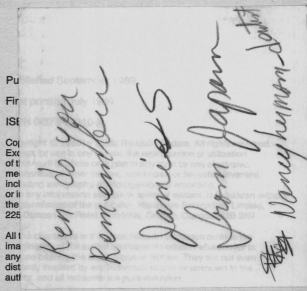

Published September 1990

First printing July 1990

ISBN 0-373-16310-

® are Trademarks registered in the United States Patent and
Trademark Office and in other countries.

Printed in U.S.A.

Prologue

So much blood. She looked down at her trembling hands, not even noticing when her numb fingers released the gun. Dazed, she watched it drop to the carpet. She couldn't stop staring at the man lying on the floor before her, a large spot of red flowering obscenely on his white shirt. *So much blood.* He couldn't still be alive with such a horrible wound in his chest, but she was afraid to go closer and make sure. Her face still burned where he had struck her; she hadn't been about to give him a chance to go after her again. She clenched her hands in front of her, finding them slippery with sweat. Fear coursed through her veins. Thunder rumbled outside, and lightning shot white-hot through the darkened room.

"Mommy! Daddy!"

The tiny voice was enough to pull her back to the present. She turned and stared at the little girl standing in the doorway, her heart-shaped face puffy from the bruises marring the pink skin that was shiny with tears.

"Mommy," she whimpered, holding up her arms for comfort.

"Everything's fine, honey." She ran over and picked her up, holding her tightly. She cradled the child's face against her breast to hide the horrifying sight behind her and swallowed the hysterics that threatened to burst forth at any moment, as the enormity of what she had just done hit home. It hadn't been so much that he had struck her in a drunken rage, which was nothing new; it was that he had attacked their little girl, and she had honestly feared he would kill the child. She was only grateful that she'd been able to stop him before their daughter was badly hurt. She wasn't going to allow her to suffer the way she herself had all these years.

What was she going to do now? She should call the police, tell them she had just shot her ex-husband. But that would bring in the entire Sinclair family, and she wouldn't have a chance of revealing the truth then; as if anyone would believe her. Joshua Sinclair hadn't liked her from the beginning. Shooting his only son would surely give him cause to have her shut away for the rest of her life. A terrified cry bubbled up her throat. For a moment she visualized police cars surrounding the house, then remembered the nearest neighbor was a mile and a half away and that the thunderstorm overhead had probably made it impossible to hear the shot.

She concentrated on remaining calm in what appeared to be an insane situation. Maybe he wasn't dead, she told herself. In that instant she made her decision, aware that if she was successful, there would be no turning back. Carrying her daughter, who had wrapped her legs around her waist, she raced down the hall and entered the first room on the right. She set the girl on the bed, but the child promptly began crying again and held up her arms.

"Shh, it's all right." She laid a finger across her lips, then spoke urgently. "Honey, I want you to take off your nightgown and put on some play clothes."

"Are we going somewhere?"

She threw open the closet door and pulled out clothing. "Yes, we are."

"Is Daddy going with us?" Her daughter's voice was muffled by the nightgown she was pulling over her head.

The mother saw the red haze descend over her eyes again. "No."

She quickly pulled open dresser drawers, tossing clothing onto the bed next to a tote bag she had found in the bottom of the closet.

"Honey, you need to get dressed as quickly as possible." Her tone was urgent, yet without the panic she felt deep inside. "Can you do that for me?" She paused, looking around at the frilly room decorated in yellow and white, filled with more toys than one child could play with in a lifetime. Was she right in taking her away from all this luxury when she had no idea what her own future held? Not to mention if she herself were caught? No, she couldn't allow herself to think that way. She had to succeed, for her daughter's sake, more than her own. She took several deep breaths to calm the hysteria that still threatened to burst out. She had to keep her wits about her. Time was of the essence. She would break down later.

I have to keep thinking that I can do this. I have to find the courage, she ordered herself, zipping up the bag after filling it with clothing and a few toys. *Contrary to what you've been led to believe, you are a strong person. Do this for Nicola. Don't let her down. She needs you.* She used the back of her hand to wipe the tears from her cheeks.

"Mommy, where are we going?" the little girl whispered as her mother pulled her outside through the sliding glass door in the master bedroom. Lightning flashed again across the sky. Anne breathed deeply. She wanted nothing more than to collapse and allow someone else to sort out this mess, but she couldn't do that because without proper representation, she would be found guilty and be locked up.

"We're going away, honey. Far away." How was she able to keep her tone so collected, considering the raw state of her nerves? She put her daughter into the car and returned to the house to make a quick phone call to the police. Saying she had heard a gunshot, she gave the address and hung up, before they could question her further.

When she returned to the car, Anne looked down at the delicate features of her daughter, marred now by an ugly bruise on one cheek. She blinked back the tears. How could someone so young be forced to suffer because a man felt he had the right to punish, no matter how petty the grievance or how small the victim? The sight of the bruise that he had inflicted on Nicola earlier strengthened her resolve to get them far away, where she would never be hurt again.

Her brain was already clicking away, deciding what steps had to be taken. Once she left the house, there was no turning back; her life would never be the same again. She was grateful that she had picked up her dry cleaning on her way to see Nicola, so she had some clothing to take with her without stopping at her apartment first. Now she would only stop at the automated banking teller to withdraw cash. No charge cards for this trip. "We're on our own now."

THE LARGE NEWSSTAND was known for carrying major newspapers from all over the country. The blond woman wearing oversize sunglasses scanned the papers until she spotted the one she wanted. She found it difficult to appear matter-of-fact when she visualized a policeman around every corner, waiting to arrest her. She hurriedly paid and returned to the small motel down the street, where a tired little girl was still sleeping. She let herself in and headed for a table next to the grimy window. She quickly leafed through the newspaper until she found what she had been looking for.

Lloyd Sinclair, heir to Sinclair Manufacturing, is listed in stable condition after a shooting incident in his home eight days ago. Anne Sinclair, his ex-wife, is being sought for attempted murder and the kidnapping of their four-year-old daughter, who was the object of a bitter custody battle. Any information as to their whereabouts should be reported to the local authorities.

She laid the newspaper on the table and moved away to stare at herself in the mirror. The dark blond hair rinse did nothing for her coloring, but it did change her looks. Now she should do something about the color of her eyes. She'd seen an ad in the paper for colored contact lenses. She had some jewelry with her, and could sell it a piece at a time when she needed to. Anne thought of the driver's license and social security card in her wallet and wondered what to do about them. Something else to consider as she descended into an uncertain future.

She looked back at Nicola, who had put so much trust in her during these last bewildering days. Little did she know that her mother was wondering if she could take care of herself, let alone a child. But her decision had been made more than a week ago, and she couldn't back down now. The girl turned over, rubbing her eyes with bunched fists.

"Mommy," she whimpered. "Are we going home today?"

"I'm afraid not," Anne murmured. "From now on, our home will be wherever we are."

Chapter One

"Dad, it's not fair. Tell her, okay?"

Travis looked up from the newspaper he was trying so hard to read and smiled at the pleading expression on his daughter's face. "What's not fair? And who am I supposed to tell that to? Honey, did you take shorthand in your speech class? Because it would be nice if you spoke in complete sentences, then I wouldn't have to ask so many questions."

"Nikki Davis. Her mom won't let her come to my birthday party." The child bounced on the chair, her two braids dancing around her shoulders. "Talk to her mom, *please*. Nikki has to come."

Travis sighed and put away his newspaper. It was obvious he wasn't going to be allowed to read it this morning.

"Susie, did you ever stop to think her mother might have a very good reason for saying no?"

She grimaced at his logic. "Not Nikki's mom. She never lets her do anything fun. After school she has to go straight home, and she can't go anywhere on the weekends."

He looked skeptical, by now used to his daughter's elaborate explanations. "Honey, aren't you exaggerating just a bit?"

"No, I'm not!" Her hazel eyes sparkled with youthful indignation. "Her mom practically keeps her a prisoner."

He sighed. "Okay, who exactly is this monster of a mother?"

"Mrs. Davis works at Lorna's as a waitress," Susie replied. "And they moved here just after Christmas, so Nikki doesn't know all that many kids, and I figured my party would give her a chance to know them better."

Travis couldn't help smiling. If nothing else, his daughter was generous to a fault. As far as she was concerned, the entire world should be friends, and she worked hard at doing her share.

"So will you talk to her? Please?" she pleaded, looking at him with what he privately called her "waif" look. He knew he could never turn her down when she looked at him like that.

"All right, I'll talk to Mrs. Davis." He held up his hand to halt her squeals of excitement. "But if she says no, that's it, Susie. There will be more than enough guests to make your seventh birthday memorable, and I'm sure this Nikki will soon make plenty of friends on her own." He stood up and dropped a kiss onto the top of her head before striding out of the kitchen. In the hallway he stood in front of the large wall mirror, adjusting the gold sheriff's badge on his shirt, then set his tan Stetson on his head.

"I gather Susie was adding a few more gray hairs to your collection," a woman's voice broke in.

"Hey, I'm still the best-looking guy in Dunson, lady," he said with a grin, sketching a salute at the reflection of the tall woman standing behind him. "And this badge just adds to the appeal. Women just fall at my feet. They see me as a western Superman fighting for truth, justice and the American way. But I'm still an all-around humble kind of guy."

She gave a most unladylike snort; but then Maude Hunter never had considered herself a lady.

"If the badge adds to the appeal, it's because you never bothered to get that broken nose of yours fixed, which only makes you look like a good-looking thug."

Travis shook his head. "I got this distinctive nose running for a very important touchdown during the homecoming game," he recalled fondly. "And later on I got Karen Peterson in the back seat of my '58 Chevy."

Maude sighed. Her son's exploits as high school football star and sex symbol were legendary. "And now you're the sheriff of a small town, whose most exciting moment was when Sy Williams dropped his pants in front of the Thursday Afternoon Ladies Club. I'm sorry to tell you this, but your only appeal is in the fact you're single."

His lips twitched in an answering grin. He knew she was kidding, but it was a game they enjoyed playing. "From what I heard, that was the liveliest meeting they'd had in more than thirty years." He glanced down at his watch. "Susie, if you want a ride to school, you better be outside in thirty seconds!" he bellowed.

"Coming," she sang out.

Five minutes later Travis ushered his daughter into the dark blue Cherokee parked in front of the large ranch house. After dropping her off at the school, he headed for the sheriff's office located next to the city hall.

Cal, Travis's deputy, sat at the front desk, engrossed in keeping the contents of a jelly doughnut from sliding onto his lap.

"Hi ya, Travis." His words were muffled as he talked around the doughnut. "It's been quiet."

"What else is new?" Travis said dryly, picking up the weekend report. "Cal, I thought you were giving those up."

The young heavyset deputy looked sheepish as he finished the last bite of the sugar-dusted confection.

"Yeah, well, I stopped by to say hi to Mary Ellen, and she had just finished filling these with raspberry jam." He looked as if his explanation said it all.

Travis picked up a large earthenware mug decorated with the words Number One Dad in red, filled it with coffee and carried it into the tiny cubicle he called his office. His favorite joke was that if he turned around, he'd bump into himself.

He sat at his desk looking over the weekend report, which was pretty much like the previous ones over the past few months. No criminal activity, nothing.

"So why am I here?" he muttered. He knew why. His sheriff's salary was being put away to pay for a new bull his ranch badly needed. That was the only reason he had taken the job in the first place. The previous sheriff had died and the town council had asked him to take over, since Travis was one of the few people with any kind of criminal justice experience, thanks to a stint in the navy's military police. As he read the report, he was vaguely aware of the phone ringing and Cal's low rumble.

"Travis." The younger man appeared in the doorway. "Wilma just called. Zeke's at it again."

He groaned. "Damn, you'd think he would have learned by now. Well, you better get out there before Wilma carries through her long-term threat and shoots him in the family jewels. As if Zeke would even think of fathering a child this late in life."

Cal nodded. This was nothing new to them. Zeke Carlson had a bad habit of sneaking off and visiting the widow Lassiter. His wife had tartly informed him that an eighty-four-year-old man had no business sniffing around other women. His reply was always the same; he was old, not dead.

"And if Wilma has that scattergun of hers out, take it away and bring it in," Travis ordered. "I don't want her to

go ahead and use that sawed-off shotgun on him. Oh, Cal."
He held up a hand to halt the other man's exit. "Do you
know a Mrs. Davis working over at Lorna's?"

Cal frowned. "Mrs. Davis doesn't ring a bell, but Lorna
did hire a new waitress named Lee, who works there during the day. Why?"

"No special reason. Her daughter's in Susie's class."

"I don't know that much about her," Cal admitted.
"You want me to find out?"

"No, I think I'll just head on over there myself," Travis
decided. "You go on out and talk to Wilma."

Cal puffed up with pride at the thought of being given an
important assignment. "I'll do you proud."

"Just bring back the gun."

Travis spent the rest of the morning doing the paperwork that never seemed to end, and talked to the deputy
who patrolled the town streets. Cal returned later with an
old-fashioned scattergun cradled in one arm, and the news
that Wilma was now threatening to either divorce her wandering husband or castrate him.

"Sure hope it's the former." Travis stood up and slapped
his hat onto his head. "I think I'll head on out to lunch."

The restaurant was a short distance from the office, and
apart from one of the taverns that only served dinner, was
the only eating place in town. Lorna, a heavyset woman of
indeterminate age with brassy blond hair and faded blue
eyes, kept the interior homey looking with red gingham
curtains and matching tablecloths. Travis walked in, greeting friends, and immediately headed for the end of the
counter, sitting down on one of the stools and setting his
hat on the empty one next to him.

"Travis, you sly one." A woman's hand, its nails pol-
ished a lethal-looking red, covered his shoulder. "Come on
over here to one of my tables. I'll see you get extraspecial
service."

"Sally, if you weren't happily married to a man who's four inches taller and definitely outweighs me, I'd sure be tempted." He grinned rakishly.

The blond waitress chuckled. "Will doesn't mind my flirting, as long as I don't touch." Looking up when someone called out her name, she wrinkled her nose at Travis and sauntered away, swinging her hips in a sultry motion.

Travis looked down toward the other end of the counter, where a petite woman stood taking an order from the town's only plumber.

She looked to be in her late twenties. Her tiny figure was clothed in a red knit pullover top and jeans, the usual uniform for Lorna's waitresses, and her shoulder-length brown hair was brushed back from her face and tied with a red ribbon. Her features were expressionless and her voice was low.

"Mornin', Travis." A dark-haired man in dusty denim overalls stopped for a moment before leaving.

He looked up, smiling a greeting at the man and at the same time seeing the waitress turn in his direction. For the briefest moment her eyes widened, then a polite mask seemed to slide over her face as she walked toward him.

"Sheriff." Her low voice, with the barest hint of a Southern accent, didn't reveal any of her initial trepidation. "What would you like?"

"Oh, a cheeseburger with the works, fries and coffee. I'll wait until my meal for my coffee." He smiled up at her. "You're Mrs. Davis, right?"

She nodded stiffly, then fear clearly took over again. "Is it my daughter? Has something happened to her?" She held her order book in front of her, her pen clutched between her fingers.

"No, nothing's happened to Nikki," he hastened to assure her. "Although I am here because of her. Actually, it's on behalf of my daughter, Susie."

"Susie Hunter," she murmured. "Yes, Nikki's mentioned her. I believe they're in the same class."

"Well, I'm afraid Susie's convinced her life will be over if Nikki can't come to her birthday party next Saturday," he explained, with an easy grin and the tone of a parent well used to a child's exaggeration.

She shook her head, offering a slight smile. "I'm sorry, but we have plans for that day."

"Are they something you might be able to change? It's all fairly normal. We have a barbecue at the ranch and a general all-around brawl, but a well-supervised one." He kept smiling.

She realized he wasn't going to allow her to get away with a vague excuse. "Well, let me think about it. I'll put your order in," she murmured, moving away.

When Lee slapped the order onto the counter in front of Lorna, the older woman grinned broadly.

"I see you met our sheriff," she commented.

"He's here because he would like my daughter to attend Susie's birthday party," Lee mumbled, picking up an order and wondering why she even bothered to explain.

"Well, isn't that nice he came by to deliver the invitation personally." Lorna used the metal spatula to turn over a sizzling hamburger patty on the grill. She slapped one finished patty onto a bun and added the usual fixings.

Lee wasn't about to agree. As far as she was concerned, men were a species she could do without.

A few minutes later she set the food and coffee in front of Travis. "Would you like anything else, Sheriff?"

He opened a bottle of catsup and tapped a portion next to his French fries. "Just your consent that Nikki can come to Susie's party. You're also invited. The parents are always more than welcome," he added when he noticed her hesitation. "Look, if she's grounded for some reason you don't want to talk about, I won't press the issue. After all,

Susie's been punished more than a few times in her short life."

"No, that's not it." She told herself it wasn't his charming smile that was making her change her mind. It was more the memory of Nikki's tear-filled eyes.

"She'll be able to run and scream to her heart's content," he cajoled her. "I guarantee you'll get a very tired kid in return. And how many times does that happen?"

"I . . ." What could she use for an excuse? "Next Saturday?"

"Yes."

She nodded before she lost her nerve. "What time should she be there?"

"One o'clock. If you'd like, I can pick her up."

"No," Lee said hastily. "I'll drive her out."

Travis sensed this wasn't a time to push. "Fine, we'll see you then."

She nodded stiffly and moved away.

He watched Lee out of the corner of his eye as he ate his hamburger and drank his coffee. Sally halted long enough to refill his cup and ask about Maude and Susie.

Travis drew a rough map on a napkin and gave it to Lee when he paid his bill.

"Please plan on staying, too," he urged her. "I think you'd enjoy yourself. You'd also get to meet a lot of the parents of kids from Nikki's class."

A thin smile was her only answer as she accepted the napkin.

Lee watched him leave the restaurant and couldn't help but fear what would happen next. From the moment she'd seen the khaki uniform and gold badge, she'd felt as if her body was held in a gigantic vise that was squeezing the life out of her.

She ordered herself to calm down before her anguish was revealed on her face. After all, he was the law and might wonder why she was afraid of him. She had to be careful. She turned away, picking up a damp rag to wipe down the counter. She figured if she kept busy, she'd forget how much her feet ached. She had worked as a waitress on and off for the past three years, but she had never got used to it. Still, she was usually lucky enough to find a position that let her work her own hours, so she could be home with Nikki in the late afternoon.

Lee already regretted saying Nikki could go to the party. She hated herself for denying her daughter those all-important friendships during the time when a girl needed so badly to belong to a group. And she hated herself for not being able to tell Nikki the truth behind her admonitions. All the girl knew was that because of their gypsy life-style, making friends was painful. It appeared that Susie Hunter was proving to be an exception.

Lee spent the rest of her shift serving customers, wiping off tables and taking inventory in the storeroom until it was time to leave. Since the small house she rented was only a few blocks away, she walked whenever she could to save gas, and in a town this size it was easy to do.

Lee enjoyed the crisp, early-spring day as she walked down the sidewalk. She recalled the morning she and Nikki had arrived in Dunson, Montana a couple of months ago. She had only meant to stop for gas and some breakfast, but after driving through the small town with its friendly populace she'd felt as if she had come home. She had meant to travel another couple of hundred miles before looking for another place to settle in, but Lorna's need for a waitress had prompted her to stay. While rentals certainly weren't the norm in such a small community, she found an available house, when a retired couple wanted to move south but didn't want to sell their home. It was as if fate had meant Lee to stay there.

"Three years," she whispered, unlocking her front door and entering the tiny living room. As always, her eyes swept through the room to see if anything looked out of order. Nothing appeared unusual, not the oatmeal fabric-covered couch, the two dark gold easy chairs or the lamps. There were no personal mementos scattered around. The house might look more sterile that way, but it was easier if they had to leave in the dead of night. "Please, God, don't let this town be my downfall. Don't let him find me."

Glancing at the clock and realizing Nikki would be home from school soon, she hurried into her bedroom and exchanged her top for a dark blue sweatshirt with three ducks dancing on the front; it had been a Christmas gift from Nikki the previous year. She brushed out her hair, pinning it up in a loose knot.

"Mom?" a young voice piped up, just as the screen door slammed.

"No, the Easter bunny," she teased, walking into the kitchen just as her daughter opened the refrigerator door and withdrew a milk carton. "How was school?"

Nikki wrinkled her nose. "Mrs. Lansing wants us to make up posters about the four basic food groups for Parents' Night. Can you believe it?"

"Sounds healthy."

"But that kind of thing is for little kids," she informed her mother with all the maturity of a seven-year-old, sometimes going on thirty, as Lee would say teasingly. "We should do something more serious. Mom, she is so boring."

"Something more serious? What do you have in mind, *War and Peace*?"

Nikki rolled her eyes but said nothing.

"Susie's father came to see me today," Lee remarked casually.

The girl's eyes widened. "Because of the party? Are we going to have to leave here?"

Lee wanted to cry at her daughter's saddened tone. How many times had they crept out of a town in the middle of the night because someone had shown even a trace of interest in either mother or daughter? While Nikki might not know the reason behind their constant moves, she'd grown to accept them.

While Lee had thought large cities were safe, she quickly discovered they weren't. There'd been Kansas City, where a nosy neighbor had read about Anne Sinclair in the paper and begun to take too close an interest in Nikki and herself. So she'd decided a small town would be better—until Homer's Run, Nebraska, where the school had wanted more information on Nikki's past than Lee was willing to give. She had gone as far west as Flagstaff, Arizona, only to leave late one night because of a renewed television story about Lloyd Sinclair's shooting that was accompanied by an appeal for Anne Sinclair's apprehension, and as far east as a small Vermont town, where a detective had shown up, looking for her. And with each move, Lee had felt her stomach tear into tiny pieces.

She couldn't remember the last time she'd had a peaceful night's sleep. She was so afraid of the moment when Nikki would be old enough to ask for the truth. What would happen then? Would her daughter turn against her for what she had done? Or would she be able to search her memory, recall the truth and understand why Lee had done what she did?

"Sheriff Hunter came to convince me to allow you to go to his daughter's birthday party," she said quietly.

Nikki's mouth opened and closed, but nothing came out. She obviously feared the worst.

Lee smiled. "I said you could go."

She ran over, hugging her mother so tightly that Lee laughingly complained her ribs would surely crack.

"I love you, Mom." Nikki's words were muffled against her mother's shirtfront.

Lee grasped her shoulders and drew her back, so that she could gaze down into the tiny, heart-shaped face so like her own.

"And I love you so very, very much." Her voice broke. "And I'll always be here for you."

Nikki squealed. "I'm gonna call Susie." She raced out of the kitchen.

Lee chuckled as she picked up the discarded milk glass and rinsed it out.

"If the daughter is anything like the father, no wonder Nikki wants her as a friend," she murmured, thinking of the sheriff who had watched her so closely. Even as emotionally scarred as she was where men were concerned, she had to admit he was a nice-looking guy. Determined to put Travis Hunter out of her mind, she left the kitchen to finish her housekeeping chores.

"NOTHIN' ever happens around here," Cal groused, standing in the doorway of Travis's cubicle.

Travis cocked an eyebrow. "What about this morning with Wild-eyed Wilma, or are you looking for a major crime wave?" He was aware that Cal sometimes had enough trouble with hotheaded Wilma, and doubted he could handle a real criminal. Travis wondered if even *he* could; it had been many years since those busy days in the military police.

The younger man reddened. "Hell, you know what I mean. All we ever get around here are the Saturday night drunks. It's nothin' that would put this place on the six o'clock news."

Travis nodded, understanding Cal's frustration. "Television makes our job look glamorous and dangerous all at the same time. Instead, we have kids cutting school or skinny-dipping in old man Wilson's pond, not to mention breaking up the teenage lovers parked out on back roads. Yeah, it isn't anything we'd get medals for, but if trouble ever did show up, we'd be here to protect the townspeople. That's what counts. If you want the big action, you're going to have to go to the city, and to be honest, I don't think you'd be happy there."

Cal nodded. "Yeah, you're right, but it can't stop a guy from hoping that something exciting might happen around here."

Travis chuckled as he stood up. "Tell you what. If any big-time cattle rustlers come around, I'll let you handle the case."

"You can joke about it, but you never can tell."

"That's true, but I've lived here all my life, and hardened criminals don't usually show up in Dunson." He patted Cal's shoulder as he passed by. He nodded at the other deputy as he entered the office. "Hi, Marv, all's quiet."

Marv grinned. "Tell me something new."

As Travis drove home, he wondered if he wasn't living in one of the most boring towns in the country. After his travels in the navy he had wondered if he wouldn't return home and feel dissatisfied with the ranch. Surprisingly, he hadn't. He liked living in a small town. And with all the gossip and crazy intrigue that went on, he really couldn't call it dull. He sped down the side road leading to the house and parked in the rear.

"You're late." His mother stood in the open doorway.

"Cal was talking about his dream of solving the crime of the century." He climbed out of his truck and slammed the door.

Maude shook her head. "That boy shouldn't watch *Miami Vice*. He has enough ideas as it is."

"Dad!" a high-pitched voice squealed, just before a small body propelled itself at him. "Thank you, oh, thank you! You're the best dad in the world!"

He started laughing as he lifted Susie into his arms. "I am, huh? I think I want to preserve this moment for the next time you tell me how horrible I am when I order you to clean up your room."

Susie grimaced at his teasing as she was lowered to her feet. "You know what I mean. You made Mrs. Davis let Nikki come to my party."

He shook his head. "Whoa there, kiddo. I didn't *make* her do anything. I merely talked to Mrs. Davis, assuring her the party will be properly supervised and she would have nothing to worry about. The end decision was still hers."

"But you don't understand. She never lets Nikki go anywhere. It's as if she's afraid something would happen to her if she didn't go home straight from school."

Travis's mind backtracked again to Lee Davis's first reaction to him. "She's a single parent. You may not realize it, but I worry about you, too. The only difference is, I know your grandmother is here when I'm not. So why don't you lighten up a bit, okay?"

"And wash your hands for dinner," Maude interjected.

"I don't care how you did it. I'm just glad she's coming." Susie loped out of the room.

Travis turned to his mother. "What is so special about this Nikki?"

Maude shrugged. "You know Susie, she takes everyone under her wing. Nikki Davis is her latest project, although I feel it's more than that, this time around. Susie seems to feel she doesn't have any fun, so she's determined to liven up her life."

"Some would say Susie has a very generous streak in her. I'd call it pushy." Travis hung up his hat.

"She obviously felt it was for a good reason." Maude began setting covered dishes on the table. "So what is Nikki's mother like?"

"Someone easy to forget. Nice looking, but nothing to write home about."

"That's not saying very much. You still haven't told me *about* her."

Travis shrugged. "Brown hair, brown eyes, a little over five feet tall, very thin, that's it. As I said, nothing memorable." Except the most delicate features he had ever seen on a woman. Almost as if an old-fashioned cameo had come to life. He hoped she would also come to the party, because he was curious to learn why she'd first acted as if she were afraid of him.

Maude watched her son across the room, a slight smile crossing her face. Travis might say the woman was easily forgettable, but she had an idea he wasn't listening to himself. Her son had been restless lately. Maybe a new woman in town was just what he needed.

"I'll be very interested in meeting the mysterious Mrs. Davis," she commented, all too casually.

Travis shot her a sharp look. "You're never interested in meeting anyone new."

"True, but I'm also allowed to change my mind. Now go wash your hands for dinner. It's my poker night, and I don't intend to be late."

AFTER NIKKI WENT to bed, Lee turned on the small television set to an old movie and sat curled up on the couch with yarn she was crocheting into an afghan, but her mind wasn't on either the film or her task.

When Nikki had asked her if they were going to have to leave town, she'd almost said yes—all because Nikki's new friend was the town sheriff's daughter.

The town sheriff. She leaned back her head, her eyes closed in a weariness that was more emotional than physical—a tiredness that came from keeping secrets that grew heavier and more dangerous with each passing day—secrets that left her suspicious of everyone she came into contact with, especially the sheriff, no matter how kind his eyes were.

"A nice-looking man who could easily sign my death warrant," she murmured to herself.

Chapter Two

"See, I told you everyone would wear jeans to the party, Mom," Nikki wailed, looking out the car window as they approached the Hunter ranch. "Susie said we'll be able to ride horses. You have to wear jeans when you ride a horse." She spoke as if it was a hard-and-fast rule.

Lee sighed. "Whatever happened to frilly dresses and Pin the Tail on the Donkey?"

"Nobody wears frilly dresses in Montana," she informed her mother as if she had lived there all her life.

"I'm discovering that," she said dryly.

"Are you going to stay? Susie said some of the parents do," Nikki continued.

"I don't know yet." Just looking at the cars parked on the hard-packed dirt in front of the house made her body tense. Not to mention the idea of spending a few hours in the sheriff's house. Why couldn't he have been a dentist or plumber? Then she wouldn't feel as if the dark cloud continually following her was now threatening to descend and smother her.

Lee parked the car, barely stopping before Nikki was out and running. Lee followed her daughter's trail, intent on telling her she would return for her later.

"Lee, glad to see you decided to stay," Travis said genially, holding out his hand in greeting. "The adults are keeping a safe distance from the kids. It saves wear and tear on the sanity. Come on over and meet the others.''

She held back. ''No, really, I wasn't—''

If he heard her weak attempt at turning him down, he ignored it as he cupped her elbow with his palm and guided her toward the rear of the house. She looked up at him with huge eyes when he touched her, but he had no idea how much self-control she had to exert not to pull away from him. ''Everyone, this is Lee Davis. Carol Talbot, John and Rita Carter,'' he went on, introducing her to the other parents, who were sitting on the deck overlooking a large barn and several corrals.

''I was just going to explain that I'd be back later for Nikki,'' Lee managed to say with a weak smile.

''Nonsense.'' A tall, gray-haired woman stepped out onto the deck. ''I'm Maude Hunter, this ruffian's mother. And I would guess the pixie out there is yours.'' A smile softened her normally stern features. ''Susie performed a rapid-fire introduction. Your daughter has beautiful manners. She actually called me ma'am.''

''I try.'' Lee felt tongue-tied, facing this dominant personality. Now she knew where Travis had inherited his own forceful appeal.

Maude nodded. ''We'll talk later.'' It sounded more like an order than a mere polite phrase.

''Her bark is much worse than her bite,'' Travis murmured, sensing Lee's unease. He gestured toward a large coffee maker that stood on a table near the door, along with a platter piled high with pastries. ''Help yourself. We're all very casual around here.''

Seeing she wasn't to be given a chance to leave, Lee poured herself a cup of coffee but resisted food. She knew her churning stomach wouldn't accept anything solid. She perched on the edge of a chair, listening to the conversation flowing around her, but soon learned she wasn't to be just an observer, as she had hoped.

"Travis, I heard Zeke was out cattin' around again." Dave, the father of a freckle-faced Stuart, grinned. "I'm surprised Wilma hasn't given him a butt full of buckshot yet."

"She would have this last time, but I had her shotgun taken away," Travis told him, then went on to explain to Lee the story of the eternally unfaithful Zeke.

She smiled, but it didn't quite reach her eyes. "It appears he has a habit that's difficult to break."

"You haven't been here very long, have you?" Carol questioned Lee.

She smiled briefly. "A few months."

"More people move out of Dunson than move in," Jim commented. "We don't have all that much to offer new residents."

"Small towns are nicer," Lee said tersely. She could have said she felt safer there rather than in the city, even though she could lose herself more easily in the latter. But in this small town she also felt more vulnerable. "At least here I wouldn't have to worry about Nikki joining a street gang."

"That's true," Rita agreed. "We've never had that problem here. Of course, Travis probably has something to do with that!" She laughed. "But we want to hear about you."

Lee fought down the panic that had begun to claw its way up her throat. She kept telling herself that everyone was merely being friendly, but they were so damn curious about her!

Rita smiled. "Where did you live before you arrived here?"

"Kansas City," she replied, lying without hesitation.

"How long have you been divorced?" Carol asked.

"Four years." At least that was the truth.

"Does your ex-husband ever see Nikki?"

"He died not long ago." A lie she wished was true. She could feel the acid burning her stomach. It took every ounce of courage she had to sit there and politely answer their questions. "He had a heart attack."

"You poor thing. You've really had it rough, haven't you?" Carol commiserated. "Don't you have any family at all?"

She willed herself to remain calm, but it wasn't easy. What would they think if she told them about her mother and father, the two people who put up such a pious front in public, and who were so emotionally abusive behind closed doors? "No, no family," she replied quietly.

One of the other women spoke up next. "At least you have Nikki," she said. "Children are such a comfort, aren't they?"

Lee's smile felt stiffer by the moment. "Yes, they are." She forced herself to relax the hands that lay clenched in her lap.

"Didn't your husband have any family?" someone else asked.

"Where are you from originally?"

"How do you like Dunson?"

Lee felt as though the questions were rolling around in her head like so many marbles. It might have been simple curiosity on their part, but it was pure agony to her. She'd always been able to deal with nosy people, but how could she be rude to ones who were so sincere? Still, she couldn't stem the panic in her body. In the end, it was easier to smile and excuse herself, saying she wanted to go to the corral to watch the children.

It hadn't taken her long to realize that this group of people was close-knit, but willing to allow in newcomers. And while they asked questions like a district attorney, they were equally willing to talk about themselves.

"I say the guy doesn't have a chance." Jim was arguing amiably with Travis about a court case that was making headlines all over the country.

"Why not? He's in the right. Everyone knows that," Travis argued back.

"So he's in the right. The other guy has the clout and the expensive lawyers. Who do you think will win? The one with the power. Come on, you've been around long enough to know better. Get your head out of the clouds."

Travis grinned. "I still like to think that the law will back the right person, okay?"

He perched his hip on the deck railing, his position enabling him to watch Lee at the corral without her being aware of it. Today her hair was left loose, its ends curling under, just above her shoulders. He noticed she wore little makeup except for a pale peach lipstick. Her tan slacks and off-white polo sweater were nothing special, almost as if she preferred to blend into her surroundings. His instincts told him that she sat there looking cool and composed, but wasn't that way inside. Every now and then he'd swear a flash of fear darkened her eyes. He just wished he knew why. There was definitely more to this woman than met the eye. Her skittish reaction to him prompted him to wonder if she hadn't had a good marriage; that would have been an excellent reason for a divorce. His attention shifted when he noticed his mother's sharp gaze was fixed on him. He smiled blandly, but knew she had caught him staring at Lee and would be sure to question him later. Slowly he straightened and walked down to the corral to stand behind Lee. Before he could say a word, she tensed, clearly sensing his arrival, and moved away as if she were merely shifting her weight.

"Don't mind them," Travis said softly. "A town this small doesn't get new residents very often, so they'll pounce on anyone new, first chance they get."

"I guess I'm not used to it," she murmured, her head bowed.

Travis caught the faintest hint of a light, spicy floral scent in the air. For the longest time after his wife died, he had been convinced he wouldn't be attracted to another woman. Although "intrigued" would be the proper word where Lee was concerned.

Maude spoke up. "Travis, don't you think we should start the barbecue now?"

"Sounds about right." He moved back to the deck, somewhat reluctantly.

"That is one frightened woman."

Travis turned his head at his mother's pronouncement. "Who's the cop here?"

"Reading someone's actions has nothing to do with police work," Maude scoffed. "She answers questions, but says little or nothing. She remains separate, even as she sits in the middle of a group. I also noticed her daughter says little, which you have to admit is unusual for a child that age."

He stared at his mother. "You interrogated her?"

Maude showed no remorse. "Of course not. I merely wanted to get to know my granddaughter's new friend."

"Yeah, sure." He accepted the platter of hamburger patties she held out.

"It's a sad day when a man won't believe his own mother," she muttered, returning to the kitchen.

Left alone, Travis once again looked down at Lee in the corral. As if sensing she was being watched, she turned her head, looking toward the house. For a brief moment their eyes rested on each other, then Lee slowly turned away.

Dangerous, her brain warned her as the group was led to lunch by a band of shouting, hungry children. Several tables had been set up, with one off to one side for the adults.

"These hamburgers aren't from one of your cows, are they?" Jim joked. "This isn't Ivy, is it? She used to follow everyone around, remember?"

"Oh, Dad, that's gross!" moaned his daughter Stephanie.

"James, you've never lost that sick sense of humor, have you?" Maude said, filling the children's glasses with lemonade. "Of course, I can't think of any other four-year-old who would walk into church wearing only his underwear, because he claimed it was too hot for clothes. I will admit you did it with flair."

All eyes turned on the man who shifted uncomfortably in his seat.

"Maude, don't you ever forget anything?" he muttered.

"No. Why do you think so many people are afraid of me?"

"Mom thinks she's the perfect example of the crotchety old lady everyone is intimidated by," Travis confided to Lee.

"We'll dispense with the 'old,' thank you very much," Maude said tartly.

Travis saw the barest hint of a smile touch Lee's lips, then just as swiftly disappear. He wondered what it would take for her to display a real smile that would light up her face and eyes. He watched her glance at him again, then her gaze skittered away when she found him looking at her again.

Lee's appetite was gone, but she forced herself to finish her food, to converse naturally, to do anything to give an appearance of normalcy. She knew it should be second nature to her by now, because lies had become so much a part of her life over the past few years. She looked at Nikki sitting at the other table, laughing and talking with the other children, and felt pleased that she looked so happy.

"Come on," Susie called to her playmates, jumping up from the table and running off.

Nikki immediately followed her friend, but stumbled and would have fallen if Travis hadn't caught her. His teasing words about not being so much in a hurry froze on his lips when he noticed how she abruptly backed away from his helping hand, looking just a bit fearful, her eyes wide.

"Are you all right?" he asked gently, thinking her fright came from almost falling.

She nodded, the motion jerky as she backed away, not allowing her gaze to leave him until she was several feet distant.

After that little incident, Travis wasn't surprised when Lee and Nikki were the first to leave the party.

"Thank you for having me," Nikki whispered, refusing to look at Travis as he walked them out to the car.

"I'm glad you could come." He smiled at Lee in a reassuring manner. "You see, we're not so bad. Well, not as bad as we could be."

Without saying another word, Nikki scrambled into the car.

"She—ah, she has trouble making friends," Lee said, thinking she should explain her daughter's obviously rude behavior. "Susie has been great in trying to get her out of her shell."

"What about her mother? Does she have the same problem?"

"Her mother has enough going on between her job and being a mother." Lee smiled coolly. "Thank you for having us."

"I'm glad you came. And I'm sure we'll be seeing each other again. In a town this size it can't be helped," he said with a chuckle.

As Lee drove off, she could see Travis in the rearview mirror standing in the driveway.

"Did you have fun?"

"Yes." Nikki paused. "Susie's dad is real big."

Lee now understood her reserve. One thing she had been grateful for was that Nikki had been too young to appear to remember her father's violent nature, though she couldn't ignore the fact that the child suffered from nightmares. "He just seems that way to you, honey, because he's a tall man and you're still a little girl."

Nikki's lower lip trembled. "He's not tall, Mom, he's big."

Once they arrived home, Lee told Nikki to take a bath before getting ready for bed. An hour later she showered quickly and retired with a book, but soon fell asleep.

Her sleep was restless, though. Lee was Anne again and back in Texas. In the house where she had spent so much time keeping up appearances.

LLOYD, IMPECCABLY dressed as usual, was pacing the length of the living room, his classically handsome face marred by the fury etched on his features.

"Did I say you could give her a party?" he demanded in the voice that could ooze honey or spit acid. "She's too young to appreciate one."

She stood before him, feeling like an errant child with her hands clasped in front of her. "I didn't realize I had to ask your permission, Lloyd." She kept her voice bland, because she knew better than to further antagonize him when he was in this mood.

He spun around, spearing her with icy eyes. "Dammit, Anne, it's my money you're wasting here," he snarled.

"It's her third birthday—the first one she'll really remember. She should have something special."

"Give her another teddy bear and she'll be happy."

"Lloyd, we're not talking about a tremendous cost here. Just a cake, ice cream, some games and a few friends over," she pointed out, still keeping her voice soft so as not to agitate him. "They'll be gone and any mess cleaned up before you get home from your golf game. It will be as if they weren't here."

"You got the last part right, because they won't be here. You want the party so badly, you get off your butt and earn the money for it. Otherwise you cancel it," he ordered in the tone that brooked no disobedience.

Anne took a deep breath. "It's too late. The invitations have already gone out and the cake has been ordered. I honestly didn't think it would upset you this much."

When he stared at her, she felt the waves of anger rolling across the room and choking her. "Upset me? You do nothing but aggravate and embarrass me. What do I have to do to get you to listen to me?" He advanced on her. "I don't care if that party is in five minutes. I want it cancelled, do you hear me? For once in your life, do what I say!"

She heard him and knew what was coming next, but had no way of stopping it. Curses, shouting and then the pain. Bruises she would have to hide from the outside world.

"No," Lee moaned, thrashing around in bed. *"No!"* she screamed, jerking upright.

Her eyes flew open and she breathed deeply to still the stampede in her stomach. She could feel the sweat trickling down her back and between her breasts, and the pounding in her head from the trauma her nightmare had caused.

"Mom?" Nikki stood in the doorway, wide-eyed and very frightened. "You screamed."

"Everything's fine." Lee held out her arms, and the girl sprang onto the bed and into them.

"It was one of your bad dreams again, wasn't it?" Nikki asked, snuggling as close to her mother as possible.

"I'm afraid so. Probably from mixing the chocolate cake with the hamburger." Lee felt the fear slowly drain from her body as her daughter's body heat warmed her.

They huddled together for the rest of the night, Nikki subconsciously protecting her mother from the past, Lee hoping to keep the nightmares at bay. But she knew they'd return again, no matter how far or for how long she and Nikki ran from the past.

"WHAT ARE YOU GOING to do about it?"

Travis looked up from the cigarette he had been contemplating. "I know, I said I'd quit, but I'm weak. What can I say?"

Maude shot him a look of frustration as she sat in the chair next to him. "You know very well what I mean."

"She's an interesting woman," he admitted.

"This from the man who stated he would remain a single parent, because he didn't care to get involved again." She sipped from the glass of whiskey she held in one hand.

He drew on his cigarette. "She seems to be a classy lady, and I think she needs a friend." Travis looked out over the darkness, hearing the sounds of horses nickering among themselves.

"Maybe she does, but are you sure that's what you're looking for?" Maude inquired bluntly. With that she rose slowly to her feet and walked into the house. "You're not getting any younger, you know."

"Interfering old woman," he muttered, a slight grin on his face.

"I told you to knock off calling me old!"

WHEN LUNCHTIME rolled around, Lee wasn't surprised to see Travis walk in and seat himself at the counter.

"Mornin'," he greeted her with a broad smile as he set his hat on the empty stool next to him.

"Sheriff," she repiied, unable to resist returning his smile as she filled his glass with water. Why did one of the nicest men she had ever met have to turn out to be a lawman?

"Travis," he corrected her. "I only expect to be called Sheriff when I'm on official business. Right now, I'm just a guy who's hungry for some of Lorna's beef stew and dumplings."

She nodded and moved away.

Travis turned to speak to several of the other men present, then gave Lee a thank-you smile as she placed a cup of coffee in front of him.

"I know you didn't ask for any, but I've heard that sheriffs only drink coffee," she explained shyly.

He lifted the cup to his lips, pleased she had made the special effort, even though she still showed a wariness around him. "You're right. I probably drink too much of it, but I wouldn't know how to begin the day without a cup, even when it's as lousy as Cal's. Thank you."

A moment later Lee returned with Travis's bowl of stew, topped with fluffy dumplings.

"You going to Parents' Night on Thursday?" He threw out the question just as she prepared to leave him. He really wished he knew what to talk about with someone as skittish as Lee, because he wanted to receive a real smile from her. He didn't know what he'd have to do, but he'd find out.

She shrugged. "I hadn't thought about it one way or another."

"You should. It's one of the town's big nights. I'm talking wild here. The teachers tell us how great our kids are and how they're positive they'll be our future leaders," Travis intoned. "See what fun you can have there?"

She nodded. "Oh yes, it sounds like a barrel of laughs."

"So I'll see you there?" he asked.

Lee braced her hip against the counter, looking as if she was prepared to stay for more than thirty seconds, which was what Travis had hoped for. "I admit Nikki has talked about her art project, so I'm certain she'll want me to go and see it."

He smiled. "Then I'll see you there."

Lee stared into Travis's warm brown eyes, unconsciously noting the gold flecks sparkling in the dark depths. She wasn't sure how he had so neatly trapped her into a decision, but with his friendly manner he had done it. Because of one man she found it difficult to trust any other, although she worked hard not to instill that distrust in her daughter. She turned to pick up the coffeepot and refilled Travis's cup.

"Yes, I'll be there. You better eat your food before it gets cold," she said huskily before moving down the counter to greet a new customer, aware that Travis's eyes were on her every step of the way. What she didn't know was that her lips were curved in a faint smile, and that he was the cause.

"Tell Lorna she's outdone herself, as usual," Travis told her, leaving a tip by his plate. He paused, looking at Lee with a searching gaze. His mouth opened, wanting to tell her that she should wear her hair a bit fluffier, rather than skinned back in that ponytail. Instead he merely smiled again and stood up. She dropped her tip into her apron pocket and smiled at him. He again noticed that her smile still failed to reach her eyes.

"Don't let Lorna overwork you," he advised lightly as he placed his hat on his head and left the restaurant, lighting a cigarette as soon as he was outside.

Travis's afternoon was uneventful as Cal recounted the gory news of a killing spree in Chicago he'd read about in the newspaper, and of the later high-speed chase that had eventually caught the killers.

"You wouldn't be happy there," Travis told him. "They'd make you go on a diet."

"No Mary Ellen Coffman," he muttered.

"And no Mary Ellen," Travis agreed. "But don't let that stop you from dreaming. None of us would get very far without our dreams."

"Such as you, hoping you'll have enough saved up for a new bull before the next election rolls around," Cal guessed.

Travis nodded. "You got it. Come election year, I'm hoping to gracefully step down and allow someone else to pin on this badge."

"Since I prefer to remain the ever-faithful deputy, I don't know who they're going to find to replace you."

"Stan Richards would jump at the chance."

Cal grimaced. "He'd declare martial law within a month."

"And the streets will be safe to walk again," Travis laughingly intoned. "Yep, Stan would be just what this town needs."

The deputy eyed him slyly. "Rumor has it you're stopping by Lorna's for lunch because of the new waitress."

"The new waitress's daughter goes to school with Susie," Travis pointed out. "The lady's also new to the town, and doesn't seem the type to make friends easily."

"And you're a friendly guy."

Travis leaned back in his chair, his hands clasped behind his head. "Sure am. Hell, I'm Mr. Personality."

"Well then, one thing I know, Lorna's lunchtime business is gonna increase, 'cause everyone's interested in a possible new romance." Cal rubbed his hands in anticipation. "Yes sir, the bets are going to be flying high."

"Cal, gambling's illegal."

"Then it's a good thing I'm a member of the law. That way, if I get caught, I can just go ahead and arrest myself."

Chapter Three

Mom, you can't wear that!'' Nikki wailed, flopping onto Lee's bed.

"Honey, you're going to wrinkle your clothes, lying like that. And what is wrong with this? It's a perfectly good dress.'' She indicated the navy dress with a red leather belt.

"It's bo-ring.'' Nikki slid off the bed. "Why don't you wear that yellowish dress?'' She disappeared into the depths of Lee's closet until she found a dull gold soft wool dress. "This one.''

Lee's fingers flexed as she resisted the urge to touch the soft wool. She had forgotten all about it, although she had carried it with her all this time. It had once been her favorite dress. She started to shake her head, then caught the pleading look in Nikki's eyes.

"Well, if you want me ready in time, you'd better let me get dressed.'' She pulled the dress off the hanger, keeping her face averted to hide her smile. She knew exactly what her daughter was doing. From the beginning Nikki had been extremely vocal in expressing her opinion of Lee's new hair color, saying it made her look too drab.

Twenty minutes later, Lee was dressed and following an excited Nikki out the door. She found herself experiencing a few butterflies of her own at the idea of moving among so many people.

"YOU LOOK PRETTY," Nikki whispered as they entered the brightly lighted school building.

"You're only saying that because you chose the dress," Lee said lightly. "Now, where to first?"

"The assembly hall." Nikki's head bobbed right and left as she greeted other children.

"Nikki!"

They both turned to see Susie charging down the hall dragging her father with her, while Maude sauntered slowly after them.

"Tommy Myers said hi to me!" Susie whispered, grabbing Nikki's arm.

Nikki's eyes widened. "He did?"

Travis grimaced over the girls' heads. "I'd had no idea they started talking boys so young. All I cared about at that age was horses and baseball."

"With me it was dolls," Lee confided.

Travis's eyes swept over her dress, noticing how the dull gold color of the sheath complemented her skin tones, and how the dark brown leather belt accented a tiny waist. He was no judge of women's clothing, but the dress and belt appeared to be of excellent quality and not something a waitress making minimum wage could afford.

"Then you two haven't lived until you've heard all about Tommy's good points," Maude interjected. "It appears he's a seven-year-old hunk."

Travis nodded. "That explains everything then. I just wish Susie would wait a few years before she decides boys are better than her horse—say twenty or thirty." He stood in the crowded hall looking relaxed in jeans, an earth-tone plaid shirt and rust-colored V-neck sweater. Tonight he didn't look at all like the town sheriff, but Lee still didn't feel calm.

"Where do I find your classroom?" inquired Lee, tugging at her daughter's hand.

"First is the principal's speech of welcome to the parents." Travis lightly tapped Susie on top of her head. "C'mon, kiddo, let's see if the esteemed principal has finally come up with a new speech this year, or if he'll again talk of children being our greatest assets in life."

"That speech is older than I am," Maude said dryly. "Morton probably learned it from his father." She turned to Lee. "His father was principal here and his grandfather before him."

Lee opened her mouth to protest being swept along in their company, then just as quickly closed it. She was astute enough to know that an argument on her part would only arouse suspicion. She nodded and walked down the hall with Travis walking beside her, the two girls and Maude ahead of them.

Lee was aware of every step they took and every stare directed their way, not to mention whispers of speculation. For a long time she had worked hard to remain in the background, but with Travis she had been set at center stage. She felt even more uncomfortable as they entered the large assembly hall and took seats near the front.

Lee looked around at the off-white painted walls, the stage with its deep red velvet draperies, the old wooden theater seats. She leaned toward Travis.

"I have an idea that no matter what town a person is in, I bet all school assembly halls look the same," she murmured. "If I didn't know better, I'd swear this was the same hall from my old school, even down to the gold tasseled tiebacks on the drapes, and seats needing new padding."

"Maybe it's part of the blueprint for every school," he replied with a grin. "In fact, it looks the way it did when I attended here and that was more years than I'd care to count."

"I'm certainly glad someone else is admitting their age." Maude gave her son a telling look.

The principal, Morton Ellis, stepped up to the podium.

"Good evening." His greeting hummed over the microphone. "And welcome to Parents' Night." He went on in a drone, his speech obviously one he had given many times. As he went on about the children being assets, Lee ducked her head to hide her smile.

Travis leaned over to murmur in her ear. "He'll also talk about our need to nurture them."

The principal spoke slowly. "And we must nurture them, so that they'll grow tall and strong."

Lee coughed to cover the laughter bubbling up her throat.

Travis cleared his own throat, pleased he'd given her a reason to laugh, because the sound was music to his ears. He wanted to hear it more often.

"I told you, it never changes," he muttered.

Mercifully the speech was kept short, and the members of the audience were invited to visit their children's classrooms and meet the teachers.

"Mrs. Lansing is nice, but boring," Nikki told Lee as they walked down the hall, the girl pulling on her mother's hand so that they were ahead of the Hunter family. "At least Mrs. Spenser lets us do what we want. I like her."

The classroom was set up with the children's names on each desk. Mrs. Lansing stood at the front of the room, talking to the parents. Lee went forward, introducing herself to the woman. It didn't take her long to realize Nikki was right—she doubted the teacher had ever had an original idea in her life. Lee thought of her years in college and the dream of becoming a teacher; until a dark prince had swept into her life and carried her off.

"Do they ever work on one large project together?" Lee asked the woman, remembering her stint as a student teacher. "Or even work individually on something that could later be put together? I know of one class that de-

:ided to build a model of their state capitol. It was also a wonderful way for them to study history.''

Mrs. Lansing smiled thinly. ''The way you talk, some-one would think you were a teacher at one time. Besides, you have to remember the children are only in the first grade, Mrs. Davis. They certainly can't take on something so ambitious.''

''I'm a parent concerned that her daughter receives the best education possible. Besides, age has nothing to do with what's inside a child's imagination when it's given full rein,'' Lee argued.

Travis stood off to one side, his arms folded across his chest as he listened to Lee's discussion with Mrs. Lansing. He liked her idea of working more closely with a child. While it was well-known Mrs. Lansing was an excellent teacher in the basics, she wasn't long on imagination. The class projects were the same every year and showed little individuality, because the children's input wasn't encour-aged.

Lee's gaze wandered for a second and caught Travis lis-tening to her with intense concentration. Horrified at the idea that she had brought such attention to herself, she mumbled an excuse and searched out Nikki, suggesting they look in at her art classroom. There, Lee was pleased to meet a teacher who encouraged her students to be creative and innovative.

''Nikki shows a flair for the unusual,'' Janice Spenser told Lee, her slender hands moving restlessly as she talked. ''She especially enjoys creating collages.'' She gestured to-ward one on the wall, which was a large piece of colorful poster board, covered with bits of fabric, lace and trims. ''She calls it New Wave Fashion.'' She smiled, turning her head when someone called her name. ''Excuse me. If you have any questions, please feel free to ask.''

"Think they're allowed to express their individuality in here?" a low voice asked from behind, once Lee was alone.

She didn't turn around. "Judging from some of these portraits of life on other worlds, I'd say they're more than allowed." She gestured toward one drawing, depicting a plaid planet with its inhabitants color-coordinated. "Sometimes I wonder where they get their ideas."

Travis grimaced at the neon colors used in one picture. "Judging from this, I'd say late-night television."

Carol approached them. "Lee, how nice to see you again. Hello, Travis. Did you two come together?" Her bright eyes darted from one to the other.

"No, I'm afraid this strange man keeps insisting on following me around," she confided, showing more animation than she ever had before, as Travis was quick to note. "And if he doesn't stop doing it, I'm going to be forced to call the sheriff."

"You'd have better luck calling his mother," Maude observed from behind them with a chuckle.

Carol giggled. "Dial 911," she advised, then walked away.

"Well, well, the lady has a sense of humor." Travis cocked his head to one side, pleased to see Lee's cheeks turn pink. "I have to say you're full of surprises. I wonder how many more there are. I think it's going to be interesting to find out." He reached out and lightly grasped her arm.

Lee ducked her head, trying unobtrusively to move away from his touch. "Sometimes I just forget myself."

"Please, do it more," he encouraged.

Nikki and Susie stood across the room, watching their parents. When they joined the girls, Nikki looked pensive.

"Can we go home now?" she asked in a stiff voice. Her tiny face looked pale and pinched with tension as she stared up at her mother.

Lee looked surprised at her request, since Nikki had been the one so eager to come in the first place, but she couldn't miss the pleading look in her eyes, and guessed that the reason for it had something to do with the way her daughter had kept demanding her attention all evening.

"I thought we could stop by the drive-in for a soda," Travis suggested, sensing the silent communication between mother and daughter, but not the reason behind it.

"Yes!" Susie squealed, pleased with the idea of staying up past her bedtime. "Come on, Nikki, it'll be fun. I hardly ever get to stay up this late." She looked up at her father under coyly lowered lashes.

"No." Nikki kept her eyes on Lee's face. "I just want to go home, Mom. Please."

"All right," she murmured, turning from her daughter to Travis. "Thank you for the invitation, but I think Nikki has discovered she's more tired than she thought she was. So we'll just say good-night here." She looked at him sharply as he followed them out of the room.

"As the law in this town, the least I can do is see you to your car," he explained smoothly.

"From what I've heard, the crime rate here is extremely low," she said dryly, walking swiftly down the hall, but Travis easily kept up with her as they exited the building.

"Smart move," he complimented, noticing she had parked under one of the lights in the parking lot.

"A woman alone learns very quickly how to protect herself," Lee replied, unlocking the car door and ushering Nikki inside.

Travis placed one hand on the car roof and the other on top of the door, stopping Lee from getting inside.

"For some reason, Nikki doesn't want to go with us," he said softly, his expression solemn. "Now I can't imagine it has anything to do with Susie or my mother, so it must be me. I've never thought of myself as a monster."

Lee took a deep breath. "As I said before, I think she's just tired. Good night, Sheriff."

"I told you, the name's Travis. And what about the mother? Does she see me as a bad guy, too?" he asked quietly, moving just a shade closer.

Lee looked down at the ground, but all she saw was his highly shined boots. She discovered a light woodsy scent in her nostrils—something sharp and tangy, not cloying like the expensive cologne Lloyd always wore. "No," she whispered, slowly lifting her head to look into the dark eyes that were warm with kindness. "Travis."

He stepped back, as if satisfied just to hear his name on her lips. "Good night. Drive safely."

Lee drove off, one eye on her daughter, who sat as close to her as was possible with her seat belt on. Their lives were taking some very abrupt turns and right now, she wasn't sure what to do. Her first instinct was to run, but something was stopping her. Perhaps because no matter what, she still felt safe in Dunson. But she reminded herself that it wasn't a good idea to fall into complacency, because the vultures were still out there, ready to pick her bones clean.

"Is THAT COFFEE still good?" Maude asked, entering the kitchen that was lighted only by the light burning over the stove.

Travis shrugged as he sipped the hot liquid. "Must be. This is my third cup."

"That's only because it's the only thing that gets you going in the morning. Did you eat anything?" she asked, opening a cabinet door and pulling out a frying pan.

"Not yet. I was hoping you'd wake up and take pity on me."

"I'm your mother, Travis, not your wife."

"I know, but only mothers take pity on a starving man." He watched her pluck eggs and bacon out of the refrigerator. "Especially when the starving person is their favorite son."

"You're my only son," she reminded him, then added casually, "Susie told me she wouldn't mind having Nikki for a sister."

Travis choked on his coffee and began coughing, until Maude administered a firm slap between the shoulder blades.

"Damn!" he gasped. "Kill me, why don't you!"

"This is purely Susie's idea."

He picked up a napkin and wiped his mouth. "And not a new one, either. As for the lady in question, I'd say she has a few secrets. No one like her chooses to settle in Dunson. She's much too intelligent to work at a low-paying job, unless she prefers to keep a low profile. Besides, I'm perfectly happy playing the role of a swinging bachelor."

Maude raised an imperious eyebrow. "Swinging bachelor? I can't remember the last time you went out on a date, not to mention indulging in an affair."

Travis looked wild-eyed at the latter suggestion. "Mom, you're supposed to protect your darling boy from such things. Besides, I told you Lee Davis isn't my type, and you agreed." For a brief moment the image of her glowing in the gold dress flashed before his eyes. He caught his mother's suspicious gaze and relented. "Okay, she might be my type, but I don't think she's in the market for a new husband. And I'm no expert on women's clothing, but that dress didn't look like something off a discount rack. She's a woman of many contradictions."

"The belt was real lizard skin, which is not cheap, and you're right about the dress. Now she could have bought it at one of those stores that feature designer clothing at a reduced price, but for some reason I don't think so. I've done enough sewing to recognize quality fabric, and that dress was top of the line."

A smile touched his lips. "You sound the way Cal does, when he's dreaming of a major crime wave hitting town and he gets a chance to solve it."

Maude dished bacon and eggs onto a plate and set it on the table.

"Speaking as a woman who notices things, I'd still say she's running from something," she pronounced, pouring a cup of coffee for herself.

"And being a nosy old broad, you'd love to know her so-called secret."

"Don't call me old." She looked at him with what he laughingly called her Queen Elizabeth manner.

"Then don't play detective." He waved his fork in her direction. "If the lady turns out to be a new Bonnie Parker, I'll take care of it, okay?"

Maude drew herself up to her full height. "I am not speaking of Lee in the negative sense, Travis. She seems like a very nice person, but not the kind to put down roots in Dunson, as I told you before." Her dark eyes, so much like her son's, were serious. "There's something about her that reminds me of a lost kitten thrown out in the rain. She'll just head on, looking for a dry place."

Travis rose to his feet, carried his dishes to the sink and rinsed them off. On his way out he paused long enough to drop a kiss onto the top of her head.

"You know, Mom, you're a regular old softie," he murmured. "What you'd really like to do is take Lee and Nikki under your wing and protect them from all the imagined horrors in the world. But don't worry, I won't give your secret away." He strode outside.

Maude watched him leave. "Deep down in these old bones I feel their horrors just might be more real than we can imagine. And if so, they won't be ending anytime soon." She looked out the window. "A storm is coming, Travis. And I don't mean just the weather."

TRAVIS SIGHED as he gazed into the occupied cell.

"Dan, when are you going to give up these nights of drunken debauchery?"

The man seated on the cot looked up at Travis with bloodshot eyes.

"Hell, Travis, if it wasn't for my fines, you wouldn't have these luxurious surroundings for your guests," he drawled. "Not to mention you have excellent room service."

Travis shook his head at the man whom he had grown up with and who owned the ranch next to his.

"All this gets you is an evening of brawling, a night in jail and a lousy hangover in the morning. Is it really worth it?"

"Sure."

Travis shook his head again. "You're killing yourself by degrees, old buddy. I don't want to see you in here for a long time." He walked away.

"You say that every month," Dan called after him. "Do me a favor, when you come by next time, think up something new."

Cal was waiting for Travis in his office.

"Marv said Dan dropped the fine off when he first came to town," Cal told him. "He told Marv he thought he'd pay in advance for once, so he'd save time."

Travis raked his fingers through his hair. "All because he fell in love with the wrong woman. Funny, I never thought he'd take the easy way out. Of course, I guess we should be glad he only gets drunk once a month, when he sends out the alimony check." He picked up the report lying on his desk and scanned it quickly. "You feeling all right, Cal?"

He frowned at the sudden question. "Yeah, why?"

Travis lifted an eyebrow. "I didn't see any doughnuts on your desk."

Cal flushed. "Mary Ellen told me if I didn't lose a few pounds she wouldn't see me anymore. She said it was for my own good. And all because she started reading those fitness magazines. Hell, Travis, I'm no Arnold Schwarz-enegger and I don't want to be."

No matter how much he tried to visualize it, Travis couldn't see Cal as another Conan, either.

"She just wants you healthy, that's all." Travis smiled at the younger man. He knew a lot of law officers wouldn't want Cal as their deputy. But he knew for a fact that Cal was methodical with the paperwork and was excellent when dealing with children. Cal was also one of the finest trackers Travis had ever known, and he couldn't imagine having anyone else by his side during a crisis.

"Let him stew in there a couple more hours before you let him out," Travis told him. "Also tell him the fine will be stiffer next time, and his incarceration will be extended for an additional twenty-four hours every time he's arrested for drunk and disorderly conduct."

"I'll tell him," Cal replied.

After that Travis spent the morning visiting the local businesses, a practice he had begun when he first took over the position of sheriff. At each store he asked about any security problems they might be having.

"If I could get the kids to buy the magazines instead of standing around and reading them, I'd be a happier man," Lonnie Stevens, pharmacist and owner of the town's only drugstore, declared. A man in his seventies, he had a smile for everyone and was known to open his store in the middle of the night for an emergency.

"Well, Lonnie, I'm afraid that other than setting the magazines behind the counter, you don't have much chance," Travis told him. "After all, I used to be one of those kids you yelled at."

The older man chortled. "You never read them, you only looked at the centerfolds."

Travis shrugged. "Yeah, I was into art then." He finished the cup of coffee the druggist had poured him a few minutes before.

"How's Susie doing? Maude hasn't been in for any more earache medication, so I figured she was over it." Lonnie slipped his hands into the pockets of the white smock he wore.

"So far, so good." Travis put his notebook into his jacket pocket. "At least she isn't getting us up at 2:00 a.m. I'm grateful for that."

"Say, I heard you've been hanging around Lorna's new waitress," the older man said slyly. "That you even were together at the school's open house."

Travis rolled his eyes. "Her daughter is good friends with Susie. As for me, between Susie and my mother I have more than enough female influence in my life."

"It's not the same, boy. After all, your mother's influence didn't stop you from looking at those centerfolds, did it?"

He grinned. "Mom's favorite saying was 'Always look and don't touch.' So I looked a lot."

Chapter Four

"Mrs. Davis, I'm afraid Nikki had an accident on the playground and injured her arm. Now, please don't worry, nothing was broken, but we did want the doctor to look her over." The principal's voice was sincerely apologetic. "Our nurse took her to the clinic, where she's being treated."

From the moment Lee heard those words, panic overtook all other feeling. A hurried drive to the small medical clinic assured her there was no serious injury, although Nikki would have to be kept in bed for a few days. She called Lorna to explain the problem, and the older woman gave her the time off. She drove Nikki home and settled her in, staying with her until she fell asleep. Then Lee wandered into the kitchen with the intention of making herself a snack, and finally settled on a glass of milk and a couple of graham crackers. How long she sat there, thinking of everything that could have happened to Nikki, she had no idea.

"Mom?"

Lee looked up to see her daughter standing in the doorway, staring at the box of graham crackers with a hungry look.

"I suppose you want peanut butter on your graham crackers?" she asked with a smile.

Nikki nodded as she walked over to the table and hoisted herself onto the chair. Her eyes were slightly puffy from crying and from the pain medication she had been given earlier.

"I didn't get any lunch." Her lower lip pushed out a bit.

"How does your arm feel?" Lee spread the chunky peanut butter on two graham crackers.

She wrinkled her nose. "It hurts. I wish I could have had a cast. Then everyone could have signed it. When Kirk broke his leg, all the kids got to sign his cast, and Mrs. Spenser drew a picture of a horse on it."

Lee smiled wryly, relieved there hadn't been a cast.

"I don't suppose you'll be all that unhappy that you'll have to stay home for a couple of days," she told her daughter.

Nikki's eyes lighted up. "That means I get out of my math test."

"I'm sure your teacher will give you a makeup test." She smiled at her daughter's downcast expression. "And of course, just because you have to stay at home, it doesn't mean you can't keep up with your homework and studying."

"Oh, Mom!"

"Oh, Mom!" Lee mimicked her wail, as she poured a glass of milk and set it in front of her. She looked up when the doorbell rang. "I wonder who that can be," she muttered, wiping her hands on the front of her jeans as she walked to the front door.

"Hi," Travis greeted her, standing behind Susie, who held a large stuffed animal in her arms. "I hope you don't mind that we stopped by to see how Nikki was doing."

"Oh, no." Lee stood back. "In fact she just woke up." She led them back to the kitchen, where Nikki was still munching on her crackers, her bare feet swinging back and forth. "Honey, you have visitors."

"Susie!" Her face broke into a broad smile when she saw her friend—the smile dimmed when she saw who stood behind her.

"Nikki, what do you say?" Lee prompted.

"Hello, Mr. Hunter," she muttered in a low voice.

"Nikki." He smiled warmly as if nothing had happened.

"This is for you." Susie held out the large toy pelican with a fish in its mouth. "I hope you feel better soon." She appeared to be reciting a rehearsed speech.

Nikki squealed with delight and hugged the toy against her chest. "Mom, can we go in my room?" she appealed, staring at Travis with wary eyes.

Lee nodded. "Just be careful with your arm. And put some slippers on your feet." After the girls ran out of the kitchen, she turned to Travis. "Ah, won't you sit down?" She gestured to the table. "I'm afraid we're not exactly equipped for company. Would you like some coffee or milk?" She flashed a weak smile.

Travis's smile was a great deal brighter, in an attempt to put her at ease. "No, thanks. I've had so much coffee today that I'm practically walking on the ceiling, and I gave up milk on my tenth birthday, when I informed my mother I was old enough to drink something a bit stronger."

"What did she say?" she asked curiously, already drawn into the story.

He chuckled. "She handed me a cup of coffee that was so strong it could suck the fillings out of your teeth. I immediately switched to juice. My fledgling male ego wouldn't allow me to go back to milk."

Lee sat at the table, clasping her hands in her lap. "It's—ah—it's very nice of you to bring Susie over here and to bring Nikki a gift."

He took off his hat and set it on the adjoining chair before sitting down. "No problem. Susie was pretty worried about Nikki getting hurt and wanted to see for herself that she was all right." He eyed her critically. "Although you look a little the worse for wear."

Lee shrugged. "Receiving a call from the school that your daughter has injured herself from a fall on the jungle gym can turn any red-blooded mother's bones to jelly. I'm feeling a lot more stable now."

He nodded. "I remember when Susie decided to take a dive off the top of the slide about two years ago. I probably aged fifteen years before the doctor said she was all right."

Lee smiled, this time more warmly than ever before. "You're a very caring father," she said softly.

"I'm a father panicking at the idea of his daughter turning into a teenager, who goes out with boys driving fast cars and eventually decides some pimply-faced guy with a squeaky voice is better than her old man," he confessed ruefully. "Crazy, huh?"

She shook her head. "Not really. Fathers aren't the only ones to have those fears. Nikki already prefers devouring old issues of *Glamour* and *Cosmopolitan*, asking what they mean about the rights of women and one-night stands. I feel as if she isn't going to have a real childhood." A strange dark light entered her eyes for just a moment, then disappeared, but not before Travis noticed it. She stared down at the table. "I don't want her to miss out on that," she whispered, then shook herself, returning to the present. "Well, how did we get off the subject so quickly?"

"We didn't. We were just picturing ourselves as grandparents." Travis attempted to keep his voice light.

"Mrs. Davis." Susie stood in the doorway. "Nikki wants to know if she can have some juice."

Lee turned and smiled at the girl. "Would you like to have some, too?"

Susie looked at her father, who gave a slight nod. "Yes."

"Yes, please."

She grinned at her father. "If I'm getting the juice instead of you, how come you're saying please?"

"Smart-mouthed kid," he muttered, not looking angry at all. "You take after your grandmother."

"She says I take after you."

Lee poured juice into two paper cups and handed them to Susie.

"Your mother appears to be a strong-willed person," she commented, returning to the table.

"Substitute 'stubborn as a mule,' and I'll agree with you wholeheartedly," he said. "My dad died when I was eight, and Mom was left with a ranch to run and a wild kid to herd. I'd say she's done great on both counts. I'd say you had a similar problem, although Nikki's a lot tamer than I was."

Lee's face turned a delicate shade of pink. "I haven't done anything special."

"I'd say you've done a heck of a lot more than you give yourself credit for." Travis pushed back his chair and stood up. "Consider it a trained observation from the local law," he joked, turning away to pick up his hat and missing the way her face whitened. He walked out of the room, setting his hat on his head as he spoke again, louder this time. "Come on, Susie. We've got to get going. If we're late for dinner, your grandmother will nail both our hides to the barn door."

"It was very nice of you to stop by," Lee said politely, following him to the door.

"No problem," he assured her with a smile, glancing to the side when Susie ran out, with Nikki following at a slower pace.

"Mom, could Susie spend the night sometime?" Nikki begged, sidling up to Lee and hanging on to her waist. "Please?"

Lee looked helplessly from the two expectant children to Travis, who was grinning. "Nikki, it isn't polite to ask like that," she scolded. "You're putting Sheriff Hunter on the spot, just as badly as you're putting me."

"Why don't we adults discuss it sometime when the two pair of big ears aren't around?" he suggested, ruffling his daughter's hair with his large hand.

"Thank you for my pelican, Susie," Nikki said after a subtle prodding from Lee.

Her friend beamed. "You're welcome. I hope you get to come back to school soon. I'll call you tomorrow and tell you what happened."

After the front door closed, Nikki hung tightly on to her mother's waist with her good arm. "Mommy," she mumbled. "I like having a friend."

"I know you do, honey." Lee hugged her back. "Now, why don't you sit on the couch with a blanket and pillow and watch TV, while I fix us some dinner?"

She brightened instantly. "Yeah! I'll bring Elmer with me."

"Elmer?"

"My pelican. We decided he looked like an Elmer." With that, Nikki ran toward her bedroom.

"Don't run!" Lee warned. "I don't want you to bang your arm against anything so I have to take you back to the clinic." She laughed softly and shook her head. "I should know well enough by now not to bother, because she'll do exactly what she wants."

"DAD, NIKKI'S LIKE ME, isn't she?" Susie suddenly declared during the drive to the ranch.

Travis glanced at her, puzzled by her question. "If you're asking if she's a girl, yes, she certainly is."

She put on a long-suffering look. "No, what I mean is, she doesn't have a dad while I don't have a mom, so she's a half orphan, too."

He wondered where her line of thought was taking her. "Yes, I guess so."

Susie nibbled on the tip of one finger. "She doesn't even have a picture of her dad, like I have one of Mom in my room. I asked her if she remembered him, and she looked kinda scared."

Travis shrugged, used to his daughter delving into subjects others might prefer to leave alone. "She might not remember him and that bothers her. Perhaps that's a subject better left unspoken," he advised.

"She doesn't have very many toys, because they move around a lot," Susie went on. "And Nikki is afraid of making friends, because she never knows when they'll move again. That's why she wasn't very friendly with me when she started school."

He sighed. "Susan Elizabeth Hunter, we have to discuss your nosy manner."

"Grandma says you never learn anything unless you ask," she protested.

"There's a difference in asking polite questions and asking impolite ones. We'll discuss the difference tonight right after dinner." He turned off the main road onto the paved one leading to the ranch.

"After dinner? What about TV?"

"Trust me, it will still be there tomorrow night. Tonight, we're going to do something entirely different. We're going to talk."

"How's your little girl doing?" Lorna asked, watching Lee wipe off one of the tables that had just been vacated.

She smiled. "At least she's back in school now, and I'm grateful for that. She enjoyed lying around watching TV for the first day, and after that she found the enforced inactivity boring and was more than ready to return to school today. Susie Hunter promised to look after her and make sure she didn't try anything too difficult.''

Lorna chuckled. ''That Susie is something. She's just like her mother, always willing to help out someone.''

Lee drew the damp rag over the table again, although it was already clean. ''What was her mother like?'' She deliberately kept her voice casual.

The older woman looked at her for a moment, but only saw a bowed head. ''Julie was one of the kindest and warmest people around. She always said that she had so much that she just had to share it with others. Travis used to tease her, saying if a needy person wanted the ranch, she would have given it to them. That girl had a heart of gold and there wasn't a mean bone in her body. Why, she didn't even like to gossip. Said all it did was hurt others. It near killed Travis when she died.''

''How did she die?'' Her question was a low-voiced murmur.

Lorna sighed. ''One of those senseless car accidents. She'd driven into Helena to do some shopping, and some kid who was high on drugs ran into her. Wouldn't you know he didn't have a scratch on him? Such a shame someone so full of life had to go so young.'' She shook her head, recalling the tragedy that had struck the tiny town. ''How did your husband die?''

Lee's eyes were unseeing. ''An accident,'' she whispered, still pushing the rag over the table, as if she were trying to rub the surface free of some unseen stain.

''Too much of that happening nowadays,'' Lorna commented, taking several blueberry pies out of the oven. ''It's a shame the good people have to go so young, isn't it?''

''It's not only the good,'' Lee murmured under her breath, straightening up from her task. She kept her face averted from Lorna, fearing her tortured thoughts might be mirrored in her eyes. She looked up, relieved, when a customer entered the restaurant, calling out a greeting to the other diners and seating himself at the counter.

"Hi, darlin'," he drawled, flashing a gap-toothed grin at Lee. "Give me a steak that's still mooin', a bunch of hard-fried eggs and plenty of coffee."

"You got it." She smiled in return, happy that life was now back to normal.

"Look, Wilma, no matter how mad you get at Zeke, you just can't go after him with a shotgun," Travis said, feeling all his patience leave his body as he faced the stern-looking woman.

She crossed her arms in front of her, her stiff demeanor indicating she would do as she pleased. "Travis, I have known you since you were toddling around in a droopy diaper," she stated in her no-nonsense fashion. "If you think just because you're wearing that tin badge you can dictate to me, you've got another think coming. I just want Zeke to know he can't continue cattin' around at his age. And if he keeps on tryin', he's just going to miss some important parts of his anatomy."

Travis smothered his groan of frustration. "Wilma, you're talking about doing something illegal. And as an officer of the law I would have to lock you up if you did it. Now why can't you and Zeke just settle this between yourselves in a less forceful manner?"

She pounded the top of the kitchen table with the flat of her hand. "Because that old coot won't listen to anything less forceful! Now why don't you worry about real criminals instead of Zeke's and my little upsets?"

Travis munched on another peanut butter cookie that Wilma had brought out when he stopped by. "Because ight now, you and Zeke are the only criminals I have," he explained mildly.

"Pish tosh!" She waved a hand dismissively. "We're no more criminals than you are. This is just called one of those marital disputes."

"We're not talking one of your soap operas here." Travis felt as if he were beating his head against a brick wall. "Wilma, all I'm asking is that you quit chasing Zeke around town waving that gun."

She eyed him slyly. "If I agree to lock the gun up in the cabinet, will you quit harpin' on it?"

He sensed a trap here and knew he would have to choose his words carefully. He reminded himself that they didn't own another gun and felt safe enough to say, "You'll lock the gun away?"

She nodded.

"Then I'll quit harping on it," he promised.

Wilma looked extremely pleased as she bustled around the kitchen, pulling a brown paper bag out of a drawer and filling it with cookies. "Here, you take some of these home. Maude never did learn how to make good peanut butter cookies. Hers were always too crunchy. Proper ones should be chewy with crushed peanuts on top."

Travis accepted the bag and prepared to leave the house, Wilma standing on the front porch.

"I don't want to see that gun out of the cabinet again," he reminded her.

She smiled warmly. "It won't be, Travis. 'Course, I didn't promise that if Zeke goes sniffin' around that woman again, I won't dig out my granddaddy's buffalo-skinnin' knife." She turned away and walked into the house.

Travis's eyes bulged. "Wilma!" He ran back up the steps.

The older woman peeked around the screen door. "Just funnin', Travis," she assured him, her faded eyes twinkling. "I swear, your face turns a strange shade of purple when you get upset. You should watch that. It might have something to do with your blood pressure. That's not something to fool around with."

"If I have problems with my blood pressure, it's because of you and Zeke making me crazy," he muttered, unsure whether to put his fist through the wall or heave a sigh of relief. In the end he thought about the bottle of whiskey he kept in the bottom drawer of his desk for emergencies. Right about now, that idea sounded a great deal more palatable. He walked down the cracked and broken sidewalk, determined to get to the sheriff's station as soon as possible; then he glanced across the street and noticed a familiar small figure loaded down with grocery bags.

"What are you trying to do?" he demanded, walking up to her.

"Augh!" a voice yelped in frightened surprise as its owner bent to keep hold of a bag that was threatening to slip out of her arms. Travis grabbed hold of it.

"Don't you think you've taken on more than you can handle?" he asked.

"I was doing all right." Her face reddened at her lie as another bag tilted badly to one side; Travis grabbed hold of that one also.

"Sure you were," he teased gently. "I can't believe you're doing all this for the exercise."

Lee grimaced. "The car wouldn't start this morning, and the cupboards were bare."

"You should have just done enough shopping to get you by until you had your car looked at," Travis scolded. "Come on, the station isn't very far from here. I'll drive you home."

"Oh, no, I couldn't have you doing that," she protested. "I can handle everything, if you'll just be kind enough to stack those bags on top of these."

He took her arm, not missing her subtle attempt to move away from him. "Kindness is driving you home, so don't argue with the law."

Since Travis had already turned away, he didn't see her eyes widen with fear as she stared at the neatly pressed khaki pants and the shirt bearing the metallic star. For a moment she had forgotten the meaning of his uniform.

"Of course," she murmured, rearranging the other two bags before one of them spilled its contents onto the sidewalk. "The law rules."

Travis looked down, puzzled by her cryptic remark.

"How's Nikki doing?" He shortened his steps to accommodate her slower pace.

A faint smile warmed her face. "Just fine. The swelling has gone down, but she's still following the doctor's orders by being careful," Lee explained.

When they arrived at the station, Travis suggested they go inside first, so he could check on messages before he drove her home.

"I can make it fine from here," Lee protested, a hint of panic in her voice.

"It will only take a minute," he promised, steering her inside.

From the moment Lee stepped inside she began counting in her head. None of it calmed the fear that was racing through her body. Her eyes swept the large room, dissected by a long counter and several desks, and landed on the row of Wanted posters stapled against a wall. A brown-haired woman kindly offered her some coffee, but she could only mutely shake her head.

"Why don't you put those heavy bags down and take a seat?" the woman suggested. "The sheriff shouldn't be long."

Lee gingerly lowered her body to a stiff-backed chair, one of the bags slipping to the floor next to her. She wanted nothing more than to run out of the building. Only the knowledge that Travis would run after her and demand an explanation kept her glued to the uncomfortable chair. She swallowed, but the lump in her throat refused to be dislodged. The longer she sat there, the more nervous she felt. She was convinced that the walls were slowly closing around her until there would be no escape.

"Ready?"

Lee yelped, her body jerking like a puppet. She looked up, her dark eyes huge in her face.

Travis hunkered down next to her, one of his large hands covering her fingers. He was stunned to find them ice-cold to the touch. "Hey, are you okay?"

She nodded mutely. "I—I guess I was off somewhere and didn't hear you coming. I was startled, that's all."

His brow furrowed with concern. He sensed it was much more than that, but knew this wasn't the time to pursue it.

"Okay," he said finally, straightening up. "Let's get you home." He led her outside to the parking lot, where his Cherokee was parked. Within minutes her shopping bags were set in the rear and Lee was ensconced in the passenger seat.

Once Travis was sitting behind the wheel he took a long and hard look at the tiny woman huddled next to him. The jacket she wore looked more suited to cool late-summer evenings than the chilly days that heralded spring in this part of the country.

"You should have worn something warmer," he chided, switching on the engine. "You could have easily turned into an icicle by the time you made it home."

"It isn't that cold," Lee argued.

"Maybe the air isn't, but the wind chill factor can get you every time." Travis turned on the heater and adjusted the vents until they blew directly onto her. "All right?"

"I was all right before."

He smiled. "You're a stubborn little thing."

Her eyes flashed danger signals. "Don't make me sound like somebody's puppy or kitten."

Travis continued grinning, enjoying her show of defiance, pleased that her previous wariness had disappeared.

"Okay, I get the hint. No more teasing you about your height."

All the same, Lee was relieved the moment they reached her house. She informed him she could handle the bags, but he made a point of carrying them into the kitchen and setting them on the counter.

"You should be flattered. I don't do this for just anyone," he told her. "Even my mother doesn't get this kind of special treatment."

"I don't want to take you away from your work," she persisted, standing by helplessly as he deftly emptied the contents of each bag onto the counter. She stood to one side, her hands clenched tightly at her sides. "Please, I can do that."

Travis stopped, hearing something akin to alarm in her voice. He turned around, looking at her stiff posture.

"You're right, I do have some things to do," he said quietly, pushing himself away from the counter.

Lee followed him to the door a bit too quickly. "Thank you for your help," she intoned.

Travis opened the door and turned his head. "If you need anything, give a call, okay? As for your car, Jim Scott's a good mechanic, and his prices are more than fair."

Lee nodded. "I will." *Please, just leave,* she whispered in her head.

She stood in the open doorway, watching Travis walk to his truck and drive away with a casual wave of his hand. The minute he was out of sight, she made a dash to the bathroom, where she was violently ill.

Chapter Five

"Mary Ellen can't break up with me! We've been going together since the third grade," Cal moaned, collapsing into his chair, which uttered a squeaky groan of protest.

Travis traded looks with Myrna, the office clerk. They'd been through this before, and were certain it wouldn't be the last time.

"You mean the two of you have gone together and broken up on a regular basis since the third grade," he corrected.

"I wouldn't worry, Cal," Myrna consoled the younger man. "You two will be back together in no time."

He shook his head, looking like a mournful sheepdog. "She's met someone new. Well, not new. Brad Jackson came back to see his folks, and they ran into each other at the drugstore and he asked her out."

"Brad Jackson, the heartthrob of the class of '78?" Myrna asked. "My, my, he is a hunk, isn't he?"

Cal now looked like a wounded puppy.

"Cal, it isn't as if the two of you have a commitment," Travis said carefully. In all the times his deputy had gone through separations from the girl he loved, he had never looked this pitiful.

"But it was always understood," Cal argued.

"Honey, nothing is understood unless it's put down in writing or said out loud," Myrna pointed out, putting an arm around his shoulders. "Now you just go out and find someone else who will appreciate you, instead of keeping you on a string the way Mary Ellen does. She doesn't deserve someone as good as you. There's plenty of girls out there who would jump at the chance of going out with you."

He looked up, his hazel eyes showing hope. "You think so?"

"I know so. Now buck up. Show Mary Ellen that she doesn't mean that—" she snapped her fingers "—to you."

He sat up and straightened his shoulders. "You're right." He stood up and adjusted his belt over his bulging belly. "I'll take the morning patrol, boss." He walked out of the station, looking like a new man.

"Talk about a transformation. I'm impressed." Travis saluted Myrna.

"After raising three sons who went through problems with girls from day one, I can handle this kind of thing in my sleep," she replied, stacking the reports that needed to be typed. "That Mrs. Davis is a mousy bit of a thing, isn't she?"

Travis cocked his head to one side, surprised by the abrupt change of subject. "I wouldn't exactly call her mousy," he mused, recalling the swift flash of temper she had displayed toward him.

"Well, she's got a pretty enough face, but she doesn't do anything to set it off," Myrna went on. "You'd think she didn't want anyone to notice her."

"Maybe she doesn't." Travis wondered where the conversation was leading and feared he knew. "She likes to keep to herself."

"She shouldn't," Myrna pronounced stoutly. "She has a child to look after and needs a man around to help."

He leaned across the counter and tapped the tip of her nose with his pencil. "Sorry, Myrna, this is the eighties, where a woman doesn't need a man to survive."

"Maybe so, but she needs someone to look after her, no matter what manner she puts on for the public. Your mother would agree with me on that."

"Since she never thought of remarrying all these years, she might not," he said lightly.

Myrna was undaunted. "Still, she'll agree some women need a good man." She eyed him keenly.

Travis groaned, now seeing where the conversation was leading. "Oh, no, leave me out of this." He held up his hands in protest. "Just because a single woman comes to town doesn't mean that we'll end up as the ideal couple. I'm perfectly happy as I am."

Myrna fixed him with the snapping dark eyes that saw more than most people did. "Then why did you drive her home that day?"

"Her car was on the fritz, and she had more groceries than any one person should have to handle!"

"Then I'm surprised you haven't followed her the last two times to the store to drive her home." Myrna smiled smugly.

His brows drew together. "What do you mean, the last two times? She didn't say all that much about her car, but I doubt the problem could have been that extensive for her to be without it all this time."

Myrna raised her eyes heavenward. "Did you ever stop to think that she might not have been able to afford the repairs? Travis, Lorna pays decent wages, but that doesn't mean they cover unexpected car repairs. I've seen that girl walking home from the store twice more since the day you drove her home. I stopped and offered her a lift, and she refused both times, polite as you please."

Travis let out a rough gust of air. "I should blast you and my mother for your snoopy natures, but after all this time I don't think it would do any good."

"We've always helped out others in this town. I don't think this is the time to stop that practice." Having said her piece, Myrna returned to her work.

"And they wonder why I won't remarry," he muttered, hiding in his office.

"Mom, ARE YOU awake?" Nikki's loud whisper penetrated the gray fog surrounding Lee.

She opened one eye, seeing her daughter's face close to hers. "I am now." She turned her head and stared at the clock on the small table next to her bed. "May I ask why you are waking me up at six-thirty on a Saturday morning, when I can sleep late?"

"Someone is trying to steal our car," Nikki explained, pulling at her mother's covers.

Lee laughed. "Honey, it doesn't run, so if they want to steal it, they're more than welcome to it." Then she realized exactly what Nikki was saying and that the car, even immobile, represented a modest level of security. She pushed aside the covers and shrugged on her robe.

"I used a chair and turned on the heat before I came in here," Nikki informed her with the pride of a seven-year-old.

Lee checked the thermostat and quickly adjusted it from 85° to 68°. She curled her toes against the cold floor, and decided to return to her bedroom for her slippers before confronting the car thief.

"Honey, you're not just saying this to get me up, are you?" she asked her daughter. "You did see someone around our car?"

She nodded. "A man. A tall one. He's looking into the car's insides, so I couldn't see his face."

Lee's mouth turned dry. Could someone have found her? Fearing the worst, she hurried into the living room, her slippers now forgotten, and peered out between the drawn curtains. All she could see was a denim-covered rear end. Faint sounds of metal striking metal could be heard. Taking her courage in both hands, she opened the front door and ran outside.

"What is going on here?" she cried out, stopping at the front of the car. "What are you doing?"

The body straightened up and dark brown eyes peered down at her shocked features.

"Just making sure everything is all right," Travis replied, looking unperturbed, as if he made it a practice to study her car's engine. "Hi, Nikki. Sorry I didn't bring Susie with me, but knowing her lazy weekend habits, she's still in bed." He looked down at Lee's feet. "You should get something warm on your feet. Your toes are beginning to turn a becoming shade of blue."

Lee blushed, realizing she was standing in the middle of her driveway, wearing nothing more than a robe. And knowing how nosy some of her neighbors were, they were already probably wondering what was going on between the town's newest inhabitant and the sheriff at such an early hour. "You still haven't told me what you're doing here."

Travis straightened up, wiping his hands on a greasy rag. "That's easy. I'm here because your car is out of commission, and you can't make a practice of walking to the grocery store in this cold weather. They may call this spring, but that doesn't mean we're having warm weather yet."

Lee felt her life going out of control with this man. "I'll take it to the mechanic on Monday, I promise," she said desperately.

He nodded, his expression grave. "Lee, do you have any idea what's wrong with it?"

She shook her head.

"For one thing, your battery is shot. That's why it won't
art. And your brakes are nonexistent," he added.

Lee blanched. While she knew little about a car's inner
orkings, she knew what Travis spoke of amounted to very
pensive repairs. Repairs she couldn't afford, unless she
ld the last of her jewelry; pieces she had kept for an ex-
eme emergency. Yet this was an emergency.

Travis hid the sympathy he felt, because he knew that was
e last thing Lee wanted. He knew he had already taken a
ance by looking at her car without her permission, but he
d an idea that was the only way someone as prickly as she
as would accept any kind of help.

"Thank you for the diagnosis," she said stiffly. "I'll be
re to tell the mechanic what you said."

He stood up, shaking his head. "Lee, your nose is grow-
g longer with every word you say," he said gently. "You
n't have the money for the repairs, do you?"

She stood up as tall as she could, looking regal even in a
be with her nose and lips turning as blue as her toes.
You have no need to worry about me, Sheriff. I've taken
re of myself for many years and survived. I'm sure I can
ndle this problem."

Travis made the mistake of grinning broadly. "You sure
ve a passel of pride for someone so small."

Lee breathed deeply, unable to believe one person could
ad her so easily. She wrapped her arms around her body
d stared down at her bare feet, which were rapidly turn-
g into ice cubes.

"Come on, let's get some coffee." Travis placed a hand
a her shoulder.

Shrugging away his touch, she marched back into the
ouse.

"I don't have any coffee made," she informed him
ughtily.

"Then would you like me to make the coffee, while yo
either put on some slippers or warmer clothes?" Withou
waiting for an answer, he strode into the kitchen. "Nikk
do you mind helping me?"

The little girl looked at her mother with a startle
expression. "I have to get dressed," she mumbled, run
ning into her room.

Travis couldn't miss the look on her face, but he merel
smiled and shooed Lee out of the room.

"Don't worry. I can find everything myself," he assure
her.

Lee escaped to her bedroom and changed into jeans an
a sweater in record time. After pulling on two pairs o
heavy socks and running a brush through her hair, she re
turned to the kitchen, inhaling the aroma of perking co
fee.

"Just in time," Travis announced, setting out two mug
He took one of the kitchen chairs, turned it around and sa
down, bracing his arms on the back. "Now we can talk."

She was instantly wary. "Talk about what?"

"Your car." Travis watched her pour cereal into a bow
and add a little milk before carrying it and a glass of juic
into the living room, where Nikki was watching cartoon
From where he sat, he could see the little girl look up at he
mother and seem to be reassured by Lee's smile.

When she returned to the kitchen, she took the chair d
rectly across from his.

"The repairs sound extensive, but they aren't," he wen
on. "In fact, I've done stuff a lot more complicated tha
that. All you need to provide is the parts, and I'll provid
the labor."

Lee shook her head vehemently. "I can't let you d
that."

"I can be just as stubborn as you. If I had an extra ca
to loan you, until yours could be fixed, I would." He sippe

his coffee and found it rich and strong, just the way he liked it. "Lee, out here neighbors help one another in times of trouble. Now I have a hunch that you're not used to our ways, and you're trying to use your pride as an argument. It won't work. Look, let me figure out the parts you need and get them. And if you're trying to come up with another argument, let me remind you about your daughter. What if there was an emergency in the middle of the night? We only have the one ambulance, and if it's already out on a call, you might not have a way to take her to the clinic."

Lee bowed her head, silently admitting defeat. Travis was right about her pride; she didn't want anyone's help. She couldn't allow herself to get close to anyone. But if something did happen to Nikki, and she couldn't get hold of anyone else, she would blame herself for the consequences. She reminded herself that she had no choice but to accept his help. She needed the work done; she couldn't deny that.

"All right," she agreed in a low voice, aware she didn't sound grateful, but had trouble doing so after being bullied in such a subtle manner. Her head snapped up, and she looked him squarely in the eye. "But I will pay for the parts, and I want to repay you for your time."

Travis nodded. He glanced down at his watch. "Fair enough. We don't have a parts store here in town, but the next town over does. I'll head over there when it opens. Until then I'll go back out to my place." He looked at Nikki, who was pushing the bowl and juice glass onto the counter. "Would you like to go back with me and see Susie?"

She spun around. For a brief second, happiness flared in her eyes, only to be instantly dimmed as she realized what his question implied. "No."

"No, thank you," Lee prompted gently.

Nikki hunched her shoulders. "No, thank you," she whispered, slipping away.

Travis looked startled by the little girl's abrupt refusal. "Funny, most kids think I'm a real pushover," he mused, smiling at Lee.

"She's very shy around adults," she explained. "And she hasn't been around men all that much."

Travis thought about the girl running with the other children at the party, and couldn't equate the laughing, happy girl with the fawnlike one in this house.

"Maybe if you came along, she might be more amenable to the suggestion," he recommended.

"I have a lot of work to do around here, and it's actually my only free day."

Travis shot her a dry look. "I can't believe I'm talking to a woman who would prefer to do housework."

"As I said, it's my only real free day," Lee insisted.

"My mother doesn't bite, she just barks a lot," he assured her. "In fact, most people get along with her. Ah, saw it! A real smile! Not one just on the lips, but one that almost reached the eyes." He looked triumphant, as if he had just been awarded a medal.

Lee shook her head in exasperation. "You don't give up, do you?"

He shrugged. "I'm as stubborn as they come." He finished his coffee, stood up and walked over to the counter. After rinsing out the cup, he placed it in the sink and grabbed his hat on the way out.

"Since Nikki doesn't want to come with me, I'll head on out now. I'll be back later with the parts."

Lee hurried after him. She had worked so hard to put her life back into order, yet she felt helpless next to this human roller coaster.

"Wait!" She grasped the doorknob, watching him stride down the walkway.

"Too late, Lee," he called over his shoulder with a wave of the hand. "Since the day is so cold, you wouldn't mind making me a hot lunch, would you?"

She stood by the half-open door, Nikki peering around her as the Jeep took off.

"The man doesn't listen," Lee murmured, closing the door, shivering at the lingering cold air.

"He's big," Nikki whispered, clutching the hem of Lee's sweater. "Mom, he's not coming back, is he?"

"I'm afraid so, baby." She wrapped a hand around her daughter's cheek, feeling her shiver under her touch and knowing the action had nothing to do with the cold. She crouched, framing her face with both hands. "Nikki, Sheriff Hunter is not a bad man," she assured her. "He wants to help us, okay? He won't hurt you."

Her lips barely moved. "He's still big and dark."

Lee sighed. So many times she had wished she could break through Nikki's self-imposed reserve, but that had always proved fruitless. In the end, Lee had decided to allow nature to take its course.

"Why don't you get dressed? If you'd like, I could call Susie's grandmother and ask if she could come back here to play," Lee offered. "Would you like that?"

Nikki's eyes lighted up. "She can stay all afternoon?"

She nodded. "If it's all right with her grandmother and her father."

The child chewed her lower lip. "Do you think her dad will let her come?"

Lee nodded again. "I have an idea he won't mind at all."

Nikki smiled and ran off to her room, promising to dress in record time.

Lee straightened up, feeling very old. She remembered the many times her little girl had wanted to have a friend from her preschool over—and the many times Lloyd had loudly rejected it, saying he had enough noise at work. In his coffee and found it rich and strong, just the way he liked it. "Lee, out here neighbors help one another in times of trouble. Now I have a hunch that you're not used to our ways, and you're trying to use your pride as an argument. It won't work. Look, let me figure out the parts you need and get them. And if you're trying to come up with another argument, let me remind you about your daughter. What if there was an emergency in the middle of the night? We only have the one ambulance, and if it's already out on a call, you might not have a way to take her to the clinic."

Lee bowed her head, silently admitting defeat. Travis was right about her pride; she didn't want anyone's help. She couldn't allow herself to get close to anyone. But if something did happen to Nikki, and she couldn't get hold of anyone else, she would blame herself for the consequences. She reminded herself that she had no choice but to accept his help. She needed the work done; she couldn't deny that.

"All right," she agreed in a low voice, aware she didn't sound grateful, but had trouble doing so after being bullied in such a subtle manner. Her head snapped up, and she looked him squarely in the eye. "But I will pay for the parts, and I want to repay you for your time."

Travis nodded. He glanced down at his watch. "Fair enough. We don't have a parts store here in town, but the next town over does. I'll head over there when it opens. Until then I'll go back out to my place." He looked at Nikki, who was pushing the bowl and juice glass onto the counter. "Would you like to go back with me and see Susie?"

She spun around. For a brief second, happiness flared in her eyes, only to be instantly dimmed as she realized what his question implied. "No."

"No, thank you," Lee prompted gently.

Nikki hunched her shoulders. "No, thank you," she whispered, slipping away.

Travis looked startled by the little girl's abrupt refusal. "Funny, most kids think I'm a real pushover," he mused, smiling at Lee.

"She's very shy around adults," she explained. "And she hasn't been around men all that much."

Travis thought about the girl running with the other children at the party, and couldn't equate the laughing, happy girl with the fawnlike one in this house.

"Maybe if you came along, she might be more amenable to the suggestion," he recommended.

"I have a lot of work to do around here, and it's actually my only free day."

Travis shot her a dry look. "I can't believe I'm talking to a woman who would prefer to do housework."

"As I said, it's my only real free day," Lee insisted.

"My mother doesn't bite, she just barks a lot," he assured her. "In fact, most people get along with her. Ah, saw it! A real smile! Not one just on the lips, but one that almost reached the eyes." He looked triumphant, as if he had just been awarded a medal.

Lee shook her head in exasperation. "You don't give up, do you?"

He shrugged. "I'm as stubborn as they come." He finished his coffee, stood up and walked over to the counter. After rinsing out the cup, he placed it in the sink and grabbed his hat on the way out.

"Since Nikki doesn't want to come with me, I'll head on out now. I'll be back later with the parts."

Lee hurried after him. She had worked so hard to put her life back into order, yet she felt helpless next to this human roller coaster.

"Wait!" She grasped the doorknob, watching him stride down the walkway.

He thought it over. "Because she reminds me of a little lost kitten who's never had anyone look out for her."

Maude fixed him with a look of disbelief. "You hate cats."

"Correction, I'm allergic to cats."

Deftly she flipped the eggs over and used the spatula to place them on a plate, along with three slices of buttered toast. "Call it a mother butting in where she's not wanted, but I'm going to say my piece, anyway."

"What else is new?" he muttered, smiling.

Maude tapped him on the head. "Travis, she doesn't belong to this town. She's basically a drifter. One day she'll suddenly pick up and leave. I won't see you hurt."

He sighed wearily. "Mom, I don't intend to marry the woman. I'm going to just fix her car. As a civil servant I'm supposed to help out the residents. That's all I'm doing," he informed her. "By the way, is Susie up yet? I thought she might like to go back with me and play with Nikki. Just call it another good deed on my part." He smiled winningly.

Maude looked at him, unconvinced. She knew that Travis believed what he was saying, and if she didn't know her son as well as she did, she wouldn't have bothered speaking her mind, even though she knew he would refuse to listen to her.

"Maybe that's all you think you're doing, but you're going to be in for a big surprise before you know it."

Chapter Six

Lee threw herself into her housework with fervor, but that didn't stop her from peeking out through the curtains every so often to watch Travis leaning over the fender of her car and hear the sound of metal striking metal punctuated with muttered curses. Taking her courage in hand, she filled a mug with coffee and walked outside.

"Would this help?" she asked shyly, standing to one side.

He looked up. "Is there any whiskey in it?"

She shook her head.

"Don't take it away. Anything good and hot is more than welcome." He wiped his hands on a rag before accepting the mug and drinking deeply.

"You don't like to work on cars, do you?" Lee asked, holding out her hand for the mug when he finished.

"Nope," Travis said cheerfully.

"Yet you're working on mine."

"Yep." He picked up a wrench and surveyed the size.

"Why?"

He shrugged. "Because your car needs fixing, and while I'm not an expert, I can put a battery in where it belongs and hook it up correctly."

Lee still couldn't comprehend someone doing a favor without expecting some type of payment. Her father and

Lloyd had drummed that philosophy into her head long ago.

"You are a very kind man, Travis Hunter," she whispered, hurrying back into the house before she said too much and caused questions she couldn't answer.

Lee checked on the two girls, who were playing together in Nikki's room, planning an elaborate wedding for their Barbie and Ken dolls.

"Your dress is so pretty," Susie cooed, fingering the white gown Lee had slaved over one year for Nikki's Christmas gift.

"Mom made it," Nikki said proudly. "She made all the clothes." She looked up, beaming at her mother.

"And when I finished the last outfit, I vowed to never do it again," she replied dryly. "How do you two feel about some lunch?"

"Could we eat it in here?" Nikki pleaded. "We'll be real careful, I promise."

"All right. In fact, we'll set it up like a picnic," she suggested. "Who wants to help me fix the sandwiches?"

"Me!" the girls said in unison.

Lee's task took longer with two seven-year-olds helping, but she wouldn't have traded their assistance for all the experienced cooks in the world. She soon had them settled on a blanket that she placed on the bedroom floor, lunching on peanut butter and jelly sandwiches and milk, with the promise of angel food cake for dessert.

"Where are the girls?" Travis asked, when Lee called him in for his lunch.

"Having a picnic." She dished a hearty beef noodle soup into a large bowl and set it on the table.

He looked at her, then out the window, where rain clouds threatened ominously. "You're kidding."

Lee shook her head. "They have everything they need for the picnic except ants, and for all I know, they're pretending they have those. They're in Nikki's bedroom, pretending it's the Fourth of July."

A smile split his face. "Brave soul."

"They promised to clean up, and I intend to hold them to that." Lee poured him a cup of coffee.

Travis sat down at the table and watched her bustle nervously around the room. "Will you give us both a break and sit down?" His lips twisted when she perched on the edge of a chair. "Aren't you eating anything?"

"Not right now." Not when her stomach was rolling a mile a minute. Nikki was right; he was tall and dark and his strength was frightening. Yet he had never raised his voice to either of them or to his own daughter, so why couldn't she feel more comfortable around him?

Travis took a tentative sip of the hot soup. "This is very good."

Lee shrugged. "Part can, part spices. I'm afraid I have a habit of throwing spices and herbs into everything, whether it needs it or not."

"My mother does the same thing," he replied, picking up a warm muffin and slathering margarine onto it. "She doesn't feel anyone can spice up food the way she can, and she doesn't care who knows it. Did you learn about cooking from your mother?"

Her lashes swept downward, hiding the expression in her eyes. "No, I read a lot of cookbooks." She jumped up, hurriedly refilling his cup.

Travis watched her nervous movements, once again wondering why she acted so warily around him. He tried to tell himself it might be men in general. After all, she was a widow; he doubted that she dated very much. At least, that was what his intuition told him.

"I wish you would eat something," he urged. "I bet you've been on the go since you got up this morning, and probably didn't eat any breakfast, did you?"

Her reply was an undignified rumble in the depths of her stomach. She blushed. "I usually only drink coffee in the mornings."

"Not a very good example, when you're trying to tell your kid she should eat something from the four basic food groups."

"Nikki's idea of the four basic groups is anything chocolate, Cheetos, blueberry pie and root beer."

Travis made a face. "Talk about a royal upset stomach. Sounds like Susie's favorites. That's probably why they get along so well."

Lee jumped when the phone rang. She reached for the receiver and lifted it gingerly. "Hello?"

"Lee? This is Maude Hunter. Is my son still there?"

"Yes, he is. I'll get him for you."

"No, it's you I want to talk to." She chuckled. "Actually, I called to see if you would like to come to dinner tomorrow."

Lee felt tongue-tied. "Well—"

"No refusals, now," Maude went on. "We usually eat around two. If you'd like to come over earlier, that's fine also. We get home from church between twelve-thirty and one."

Lee gripped the receiver, staring at Travis with pleading eyes. He got up and took the phone out of her hands.

"Mom?" He rolled his eyes as he listened to her rambling. "Yes, I'm almost finished here. Yes, I'll pass on the message. Yes, you are overdoing it." He hung up and turned to Lee. "Trust me, you're better off accepting the dinner invitation. When my mother gets something into her head, she keeps on until she gets her way."

"You don't understand," she said, feeling more helpless than she had in a long time.

"Then why don't you tell me?" he suggested gently.

Lee snapped her mouth shut, afraid she'd say too much. "It's just that Nikki and I don't make friends easily."

"Are we going away again?" Nikki stood in the doorway, looking appalled at the idea. Susie stood behind her, looking just as upset. "Mom, you promised we could stay here. You said everything would be all right. I have a friend now!" She spun around and ran off.

"Susie, go with her," Travis said quietly, noticing Lee's white features. "Look, I'm almost done outside. I'll finish in record time and get out of your hair. And don't worry about tomorrow. I'll get you off the hook." He walked out the back door.

Lee collapsed into a chair, feeling as if her world could soon collapse around her.

"If I hadn't gone over there that night," she muttered. "If I had only fought back more when it counted. If only..." She blew out a gust of air and straightened. She grabbed the phone book, found the number she was looking for and dialed, before she lost her courage. "Mrs. Hunter? This is Lee Davis. Yes, tomorrow would be fine," she said swiftly. "Is there anything I can bring? No? All right, we'll be there before two, and thank you for asking us." She hung up and leaned against the counter, feeling as if she had just run the Boston Marathon. She couldn't help but wonder if she hadn't just lost what little sanity she still had left.

"WHY DIDN'T YOU tell me yesterday she was coming, instead of listening to me give you all those plausible excuses as to why she couldn't?" Travis demanded, watching his mother take a roast out of the oven and baste it.

"Because it was infinitely more interesting, listening to you give all those ridiculous reasons," she said serenely, pushing the pan back into the oven. "Now why don't you change out of your suit before you get something on it? I already told Susie to change her clothes and make sure her room was picked up.''

''Mom, I am not ten years old,'' he insisted between clenched teeth.

''Maybe not, but you certainly act it sometimes.'' Maude brought out a mixing bowl and ingredients for frosting.

He loosened the tie that seemed to be constricting his breathing. ''You only asked her over to find out about her.''

''Is that so wrong? You seem interested in her, so I would like to know more about her.'' She measured powdered sugar and poured it into the bowl along with softened margarine and milk. ''It's a mother's prerogative.''

Travis released the strangling collar button. ''I am not interested in the woman. And she's definitely not interested in me, so let it rest, all right?''

''Let me be the judge of that. Now will you please change your clothes?''

''Why should I be interested in a woman?'' he grumbled, stalking out of the kitchen. ''I have more than enough women around here to boss me around.''

''Put on that dark green shirt. It does nice things for your eyes,'' Maude called out.

ANY MISGIVINGS Lee had about having dinner at the Hunter household were dispelled by Nikki's excitement at the prospect of spending more time with her friend. For once Lee didn't have to order the girl to make her bed or put her dirty clothes into the hamper before they left.

Maude's casual greeting also helped relax Lee as she ushered them inside and suggested Susie take Nikki to her room.

''Can we go out and look at the kittens?'' Susie pleaded.

Maude shook her head. ''You wouldn't have time to thoroughly clean up before dinner.'' She turned to Lee.

"Travis is allergic to cats, but they keep the barn rodent-free, so he takes medication when he has to work in there. Why don't you come along to the kitchen while I put the finishing touches on dinner? Would you like some coffee or iced tea? I know this weather isn't exactly normal for cold drinks, but sometimes I get so tired of hot drinks just because it's chilly outside."

"Iced tea sounds fine," Lee replied, following her into the large kitchen, which was clearly one of the most used rooms in the house. "I agree with you. One time there was a blizzard outside, and I was inside making lemonade, just because it sounded good."

Before she knew it, she was sitting at the butcher-block table with a glass of iced tea before her and a bowl of beans to be snapped. Maude thought nothing of roping company into helping with dinner preparations.

"How do you like it in Dunson?" Maude asked as she frosted a white cake and sprinkled coconut on top.

"It's very nice, and I'm not saying it for lack of anything else to say."

The older woman nodded. "We like it. Of course, I grew up here and the population wasn't exactly booming then, but with all the surrounding towns and their slow but steady growth, most of us don't mind the solitude. We all pretty much stick together, probably because we're all we have."

"I think you can get used to anything, if you put your mind to it." Lee finished the beans and put the bowl to one side. "Now, what else would you like me to do?"

Maude chuckled. "Since you're such a willing helper, how about rinsing off the salad makings?" She opened the refrigerator door and withdrew the proper ingredients.

"All right." Lee pushed up her sweater sleeves past her elbows and turned on the faucet as she grasped a head of lettuce.

Maude glanced over, then looked again as something caught her attention. Feeling her gaze on her, Lee looked up, then lowered her eyes to the several small round puckered scars that marred the soft skin on the inside of her elbow.

"An odd place for a burn," Maude commented.

"Not if you're a smoker," Lee said, sounding too casual.

"I didn't realize you were a smoker."

"That's why I quit." Lee kept her head down as she rinsed the fresh vegetables.

Maude said nothing, but studied the small scars on Lee's arm a moment longer, before returning to her own task.

Lee quickly finished the vegetables and pushed down her sweater sleeves; without saying a word, she hunted through the drawers until she found a knife and began cutting them up and layering them in a glass bowl with deft efficiency.

"I should have you over more often," Maude complimented her, looking at the colorful salad. "Mine don't come out half as nice."

Lee blushed. "I've always liked working around the kitchen," she said enthusiastically, "but Nikki isn't eager to try anything that doesn't resemble hamburgers, hot dogs or spaghetti."

"That sounds just like Susie. I made teriyaki chicken one night, and my granddaughter acted as if I was trying to poison her," Maude said. "It seems I only get to try out any new recipes on the ladies' club."

Lee's gaze swept over the shelves filled with various cookbooks and was frankly envious.

"Go ahead and browse through them," Maude invited. "I can handle everything from here."

Lee needed no further urging, and ran her finger along the book spines until she came to one that looked interesting. She sat down at the table to leaf through its many pages.

"The way you're devouring that book, I'd say you must have a large collection yourself," Maude commented.

She thought of the library of cookbooks she had been forced to leave behind. "Not anymore," she murmured. "It's difficult to keep track of things when you move around a lot." Lee froze, hoping her slip of the tongue wasn't noticed.

If Maude heard her, she gave no indication. "Then please feel welcome to borrow any of them. I can only use one at a time, and the rest tend to gather dust."

"I'd like that, thank you," Lee said quietly, accepting the silent offer of friendship that she sensed went along with the offer. She laughed softly. "Perhaps I can find something that will tempt Nikki's taste buds."

Maude walked over to one of the shelves and selected a book, handing it to her. "This one should work."

Lee read the title and laughed. "Oh yes, I'm sure *365 Ways to Cook Hamburger* would be entirely to her liking. But I'm also tempted to study one of the county fair cookbooks."

"Oh yes, they are just wonderful. I have friends living around the country I trade books with. They send me theirs, and I send them the one from our fair. I think you'd enjoy this one." Maude handed her another book.

"What's this, you two swapping recipes already?" Travis teased, walking into the kitchen, bringing the crisp outdoors coupled with the earthy scent from the barn with him.

"No, I'm telling her what a horrible child you were. And after dinner I intend to bring out the photo album and show her all your baby pictures," Maude said serenely. "Especially the ones of you reclining on the bearskin rug."

Travis rolled his eyes. "I guess I'd better head for the family room and hide those albums, although why you would want to ruin her dinner with pictures of a bare-bottomed baby, I don't know."

Lee smiled. "I think it would be fascinating to see pictures of the sheriff in a less than professional setting."

"There's no problem there," Maude said with a laugh. "Now, Travis, you go in and get washed up, because dinner will be ready soon. And tell the girls to wash their hands, and to use soap this time."

Lee was grateful that Nikki ate her roast and mashed potatoes without any fuss. She decided that the fact that Susie ate heartily had something to do with it. As she ate, she watched the way grandmother and father listened to the two girls' chatter with amused smiles. No matter how outlandish Nikki's and Susie's comments were, they were never made to feel silly. It was such an enjoyable change from her other life. For one very brief, improbable moment, Lee wondered what it would be like if they were a real family.

The dishes may have been blue- and pink-flowered white stoneware instead of fine china, but it didn't detract from the good taste of the food. Neither did it matter that their napkins were paper instead of linen, nor that the table-cloth, an old, but she felt a treasured one, was on the kitchen table instead of on a formal dining table, in a room furnished with all the trappings of the wealth she had once been smothered by.

Lee knew of another very important difference: the company. She wasn't listening to her husband complain that she hadn't cooked the meat properly. Nor did she hear her father make a negative comment about the vegetables. And her mother wasn't there to look around the room with that narrow-eyed glance of hers, trying to find fault with something or other. Lee had never enjoyed any of those dinners; in fact, she'd usually left the table feeling a terrible burning in her stomach. It wasn't until just before the divorce that she'd discovered she was suffering from an ulcer.

"You look as if you're off in another world," Travis commented, noticing first her smile, then how a bleakness shadowed her eyes.

She shot him an apologetic glance. "I was so busy enjoying this food, I forgot about anything else."

"Then I hope you aren't going to mind if I recruit you to help with the dishes," Maude warned.

"After this meal, the exercise of washing dishes will be appreciated."

"What prompted you to choose Dunson to live in?" Maude asked, flashing a pointed look at the cauliflower on Susie's plate. The girl wrinkled her nose and picked up her fork, beginning on what was obviously her least favorite part of the meal.

For once, Lee decided to tell the complete truth. "Actually, I was only passing through, but the Help Wanted sign in Lorna's restaurant and her agreeing to hire me, then finding the house seemed to be a sign," she replied. "I can't really express it. There was just something about this town that said 'Stay.'"

Maude nodded. "I surely can understand that."

Lee applied herself to the meat, cutting it into tiny pieces. "The people are real here," she murmured.

Travis frowned, sensing more than had been said. But with two children with extremely big ears sitting at the table, he felt he couldn't pursue the subject.

"We get dessert, don't we?" he asked, deciding it was time to change the course of the conversation.

"When you clean your plate." Maude silently directed the girls to carry their dishes to the kitchen counter.

Travis grinned at Lee. "As you can see, my mother doesn't care how old you are. You still have to eat your vegetables if you want dessert."

"You won't be giving this woman any bad habits, if I have any say in it," Maude said tartly.

Nikki's head turned from one adult to the other, her tiny face reflecting her worry at what appeared to her to be the beginning of a quarrel.

"I ate all mine," she said in a quavery voice, gazing up at Maude with wide eyes.

Maude looked down at her and immediately realized the cause of her distress. "You certainly did, pet, and you shall have the first slice of cake," she promised with a broad smile. "In fact, would you like to help me serve it?"

Nikki looked at Lee, who smiled and nodded.

"Yes, please," she whispered, sliding off her chair.

Under Maude's direction, Nikki proudly carried slices of the white cake and portions of chocolate ice cream to each person. She kept a close eye on Travis as she slid his plate in front of him, then scurried off, not hearing his quiet thanks.

When they finished, Maude suggested that the girls watch a Disney videotape and that Travis join them while she and Lee did the dishes.

"I know I'm considered a tyrant," Maude told Lee as they rinsed off plates and loaded the dishwasher. "But I have to be, so no one ever finds out what a softie I really am."

"Meaning you're all bark and no bite."

"Oh, I'd bite if necessary. Especially where my family is concerned." With everything done, she dried her hands and squirted on a dollop of cream, rubbing them briskly. She turned to Lee, her dark eyes piercing as she asked in a matter-of-fact voice, "Why is your daughter so afraid of adults?"

Chapter Seven

Lee's mind raced madly for an answer that wouldn't prompt further questions. She knew she couldn't offer a flip answer because Maude was too astute to be put off.

She spoke slowly, her words chosen very carefully in an artful mixture of truth and lies. "Her grandparents were very stern people," she explained. "They were of the school that believed children must display proper table manners, no matter how young they are, and they were never to speak unless spoken to. And heaven help a child who spilled anything on their clothing or the tablecloth."

Maude looked shocked. "Even as a toddler?"

Lee nodded. "That was the way they believed a child should be raised, whether one of theirs or someone else's."

"What about your views and your husband's? Surely he didn't agree with them?"

She didn't want to tell the older woman that Lloyd had always agreed with her parents.

"My—husband had trouble relating to a little girl. Many men do," she said defensively, inwardly wincing as she recalled the loving and easy relationship Travis enjoyed with his daughter. "I just wanted Nikki to have a normal childhood, but it wasn't always easy to do."

"Some parents are too hard on their children," Maude acknowledged after a moment. "I think the best thing for

Nikki is to discover that all adults aren't like that. I want you to know that she's welcome here anytime."

Lee licked her lips, trying to figure out what to say without giving anything away. "That's very kind of you."

She chuckled. "Kindness has nothing to do with it. It's much easier to have two children underfoot than one. Besides, I'm sure there are times you wouldn't mind having an afternoon to yourself."

Lee smiled. "I have to admit the idea is tempting, but I couldn't allow you to do that."

"Of course you can. Besides, if I want an afternoon to myself, I'll just let you take Susie," Maude said shamelessly. "Believe me, there're times she's a real handful. She takes after her father more than her mother."

"What was her mother like?" Lee asked curiously, wondering what Maude thought of the woman Travis had married.

The older woman smiled. "Julie was one of the dearest and kindest women you would ever know. She never had an unkind word for anyone and always had a ready smile." Her own smile disappeared. "Sometimes I think she was too good for this world. It was a shame they never had more children."

Lee felt a lump in her throat as she listened to the description of what sounded like a perfect marriage. She felt she would never be allowed to experience something that special, and after what she had gone through in the past, wasn't sure she could ever trust a man enough to find out. Yet there was something about Travis that fascinated her.

"I just wish he would find someone before he turns old and cranky," Maude went on. "But I doubt he will."

"Because of love for his wife?" Lee probed, then fell silent, realizing she had no right to be so curious.

"More like because he doesn't want to take the time t court a woman," Maude rumbled. "Well, should we se what the trio is up to?"

They entered the den, finding Susie snuggled up next t her father on the couch, while Nikki lay sprawled on th carpet as they watched *Cinderella*. By the time the ani mated feature was over, both girls' eyes were drooping from fatigue.

"Time for someone to be in bed," Lee spoke up, kneel ing beside Nikki. "Come on, honey, time for us to be goin home."

"I'm not tired," she protested even as she yawned widel lifting her arms to her mother.

"You want me to take her?" Travis offered. "She's to heavy for you."

Nikki's eyes flew open. "I can walk," she said swiftl scrambling to her feet.

"The independence of a seven-year-old," Lee told Travi in an effort to soften Nikki's rejection. "Sometimes she act like my baby, and other times I wonder if she isn't rapidl approaching her thirtieth birthday. This was a very nic day. Thank you for inviting us."

Travis walked them out to the car, where Nikki quickl climbed inside. "And to think you weren't too sure yo wanted to come," he teased softly.

Lee shrugged. "People can be wrong, as you delight i pointing out."

Travis smiled down at her. "Perhaps next time m mother will be kind enough to allow me to sit in on some o the discussion."

"Perhaps," Maude interjected as she bore down o them, carrying what appeared to be several books. Sh pressed them into Lee's hands. "But I sincerely doubt it.'

Lee looked down, discovering several cookbooks "Thank you," she said softly.

The older woman's normally stern features softened. "No matter how independent some of us try to be, there might be a time we could use a fairy godmother."

"YOU'RE GOING to the carnival, aren't you, Lee?" Jake Hale, one of the neighboring ranchers, asked her as he dug into his apple pie à la mode. "You sure can't miss one of our biggest social events of the year." He grinned. "Hell, excuse my language, it's our only social event!" he guffawed.

"The way Nikki has been talking about it, I don't think I'll have any say in the matter," she replied, refilling his coffee cup. "It appears they even close the schools for two days."

"It's the first big event we have, once spring starts showing its head around here, so we don't like the kids to miss out on it," he explained. "Although I think the adults have more fun than the children." He winked at her.

"Hey, Jake, does your wife know you're flirting with beautiful women?" Travis slid onto the stool next to him.

"She doesn't mind as long as I don't touch," Jake replied with a grin. "How ya doin', Travis?"

"Fair enough." He smiled at Lee. "How about a bowl of Lorna's heartburn chili and a large glass of water to wash it down with?"

"I'll bring the antacid tablets with your meal," Lee said pertly, writing out his order and moving away.

"She's sure not the same woman who first came to work here," Jake commented when Lee was out of earshot. "She smiles a lot more and even jokes with us now."

"She's probably realized it's the only way to survive in this crazy place." Travis watched Lee's slim figure move behind the counter, stopping to inquire if the other customers needed something and taking away dirty dishes or

refilling coffee cups. He couldn't keep his eyes off her rea
end, encased in snug jeans.

A few moments later Lee set a steaming bowl in front o
him. "Lorna said to tell you she added extrastrength chi
powder, just for you."

Travis took a cautious bite and gasped, reaching for hi
glass of water. "No kidding," he wheezed. "Lorna, mu
dering an officer of the law is a felony," he called out.

"This from the man who's always sworn he has a cas
iron stomach," she responded with a laugh. "Don't worry
Lee can just leave a pitcher of water with you."

When Travis later paid his bill, he held on to his mone
as he offered it to Lee.

"You going to the dance?"

She stared down at his hands, a funny feeling curlin
deep in her stomach. "I don't think so. I'm sure by the
Nikki will be tired from the carnival, and she isn't o
enough to appreciate a dance."

"Then why don't you let her spend the night with Susi
and you could come with me?" he suggested matter-of
factly.

Lee's face snapped upward. "Are—" she swallowe
"—are you asking me to go to the dance with you?"

He smiled. "I thought I was. Of course, I am out o
practice, so I may not have done it right. Should I tr
again?"

Lee laughed nervously. She felt flattered that he'd aske
her. "I haven't danced in a long time," she said, thinkin
to warn him.

Travis's smile broadened. He was glad she hadn't give
him an outright rejection. "Then we'll be perfect togethe
because I have two left feet," he told her in a low, confic
ing tone. "We don't even have to stay the entire evening, i
you don't want to. Still, I think you'd have a lot of fun. Al
right?" He looked hopeful.

She nodded, summoning a faint smile. "All right."

"Fine, we can work out the details later. Look at it this way. You sure couldn't be with anyone safer than the town's sheriff."

Lee looked out the plate glass window, watching him stride down the sidewalk.

"You're right, I couldn't be safer," she murmured with a wry smile on her lips.

"Mom, look!" Nikki's head swiveled first one way, then another so quickly that Lee was certain it would snap off at any moment. She pulled on her mother's hand, obviously hoping to make her walk faster.

"Honey, calm down, we're going to be here all day," Lee said and laughed.

"But I don't want to miss anything," the child almost wailed, looking up at her mother with a pleading expression.

"I promise you we won't miss anything," she vowed. She understood the girl's excitement. After all, this was her first carnival. And now she herself felt more comfortable moving among the public. Thanks to working in Lorna's restaurant, she had already met most of the town's residents, and while she was extremely careful not to relax her guard, she wasn't about to deny her child a day of fun.

"Hi Lee," Jake greeted her, his footsteps dogged by his wife and five children. "I see Lorna let you have the day off."

"She told me it was for Nikki's sake," she explained. "And Sally said she could handle it on her own. She preferred letting her husband bring their kids here." Lee looked around the large lot dotted with colorful striped tents and the typical carnival rides. The air was permeated with the smells of popcorn, cotton candy and every other kind of junk food imaginable. "I can see why she didn't mind my coming."

"This is my first carnival," Nikki spoke up proudly.

Jake hunkered down until he was at eye level with the girl. Nikki tightened her hold on her mother's hand, but didn't back away from him. Obviously the kind-looking older man didn't frighten her, Lee thought. "Then, honey, it will be the most special carnival you will ever know," he informed her with a smile. He straightened up, groaning as all the children began talking at once, each having their own idea about what to do first. "Okay, I get the hint." He grinned at Lee. "Have fun."

"What first?" Lee asked when they were left alone. Feeling the morning chill, she zipped up her cream-colored heavy fleece jacket and tucked her hands into the deep kangaroo pockets.

Nikki screwed up her face, looking around. "I don't know," she admitted with a mournful sigh.

"Then let me make a suggestion. Try the clown faces," a jovial male voice intruded.

They both turned, to see Travis walking toward them with a giggling Susie tucked under his arm.

"It's easier to keep track of her this way," he told Lee, letting Susie down.

"What's a clown face?" Nikki was clearly screwing up her courage to ask him, although she still refused to look directly at him, even when Lee nudged her for her rudeness.

"People paint clown faces on us," Susie said excitedly.

"For once the kids have paint that washes off easily all over their faces," Travis assured Lee.

Nikki's mouth opened wide. "Can I have a clown face, Mommy, can I?" she pleaded, tugging on her hand. "Please?"

"May I."

"That's what I said!"

Lee hesitated. It appeared that this might be the beginning of the two families spending the day together. She could feel her muscles tighten and stomach burn at the idea. Yet she had already agreed to attend the dance with him, so why was she bothered about their being together today? Why should she worry, when there were all these people milling around? And deep down inside, she did want to spend the day with him. She tried telling herself it was because of Nikki that she wanted to do this; to give her a chance to learn that not all men were cruel. But she knew better.

She smiled down at her daughter. She would do anything to keep that expression of happiness on her face. "It appears you're going to end up with a funnier face than the one you normally wear."

Travis lowered his head and murmured into Lee's ear, "If it will make you feel better, you can have a clown face, too."

She shot him a wry look. "I think that's one treat I can live without."

Lee and Travis stood back, watching two gaily dressed young women apply a white base to the two girls' faces and then add bright orange circles on the cheeks and bright red lips. When finished, Susie had a blue tear under one eye and Nikki boasted a gold-painted star on her cheek.

"Think we can handle squiring around such colorful kids?" Travis asked Lee as they walked along.

"At least they'll be easy to find."

He stopped her with a hand on her shoulder and pointed with the other. "Think so?"

Everywhere they looked were children of various ages, boasting brightly painted clown faces.

"Then I'm glad I dressed Nikki in a bright color." Lee indicated the heavy cobalt-blue pullover sweater the girl wore with her jeans. "That way I'll have a bit of an edge." She glanced at his uniform shirt and faded jeans. "I gather you're here in an official capacity." She hoped the tension she felt wasn't reflected in her voice or body language.

"I'm combining business with pleasure," he explained. "This way someone's on duty here, although Cal will be over later in the day, along with someone else this evening, since the teenagers will be running all over by then. We don't allow beer on the grounds, but they tend to sneak it in, unless we keep a close eye on them. There will be more than one set of parents gotten out of bed tonight to pick up their kids at the station."

Her head was downcast. "You really care about the people around here, don't you?"

He nodded. "Yeah, I do. In fact, we all care about one another." He looked at her. "Obviously you're not used to that."

"No, I'm not. There's a lot of towns where the residents don't believe in that philosophy," she said softly.

"Maybe so, but here we all work together when need be, and we celebrate together."

"'One for all, all for one,'" Lee murmured.

"Is that so bad?" Travis asked.

"No, in fact it's a very nice feeling." Lee turned her head when Nikki tugged on her hand.

"Mom, look!" She pointed at a large merry-go-round in the center of the rides. "Can I go on it, please?"

"Pick out which horse you want to ride."

Nikki and Susie ran toward the carousel and after careful deliberation chose their mounts; Nikki, a white steed with silvery-blue reins and saddle and Susie, a prancing black horse with a bright red saddle. Lee and Travis stood behind the gate with the other parents as the merry-go-round began moving in time to the calliope music.

When finished there they walked over to another ride, where the girls rode bright black-and-yellow bumblebees in a circle around a hive.

"You know, this is the most uninhibited I've ever seen Nikki," Travis remarked.

Lee looked away. "I told you before, she's very shy around people she doesn't know."

"At least you don't try to keep her that way." He went on to explain. "I noticed how you'd give her a nudge anytime she didn't answer one of my questions. I don't want her to feel forced into something she doesn't want to do."

"She's always been very shy around adults, and I don't want her to continue seeing them as something frightening," she replied quietly, flexing her stiff fingers in her pockets.

They stood behind a split rail fence, watching the two girls bounce around inside a large enclosed tent filled with multicolored Ping-Pong balls.

While the girls enjoyed themselves, Travis was able to study Lee's face in great detail; he noticed the graceful sweep of her cheekbones, the curve of her lips touched with coral lipstick, the eyes highlighted with a taupe shadow and deep green eye pencil. The faint scent of a spicy floral fragrance drifted upward. Even with her mousy hair she had a delicacy about her that had caught more than one man's attention today. She was dressed in faded jeans and a heavy sweater, but still radiated a light that fascinated him. But he also saw even more in her. He kept asking himself what a classy lady like Lee was doing in his town, but couldn't come up with an answer. Then he worried that she might decide Dunson wasn't for her and leave before he could learn all about her. He took an extra step to the side until he stood right next to her.

After a messy lunch of hot dogs and French fries they wandered through the many craft booths featuring quilts, knitted goods and carved wooden toys.

"It's more like a fair," Lee told Travis after they stopped by a booth filled with homemade jams and jellies.

"Yeah, I guess it is." He smiled and nodded at a couple walking past them. He touched her shoulder and turned her slightly. "Look over there. That's our infamous Zeke and Wilma."

Lee looked in the direction he indicated and saw a tall, gangly bald man wearing patched jeans, a heavy plaid jacket and a Stetson. The woman walking with him was rawboned and stern looking. She bit her lower lip to keep from laughing.

"That's the Casanova of Dunson?"

He nodded. "That's him, all right. The last time he went roaming, she threatened him with her granddaddy's buffalo-skinning knife. He's lucky he's all in one piece."

A giggle escaped her lips. "Travis, he's so old."

"Well, the way Zeke puts it, being old doesn't mean nothing works," he observed with a chuckle. "To be honest, I think it's a game between Zeke and Wilma. She goes after him with that scattergun of hers, but she hasn't shot him yet. Of course, there is always the first time, so I don't like to get too comfortable where they're concerned."

Lee hurriedly stuck her hands into her pockets to hide their trembling. She looked away, fearing what might be on her face.

"Hey, Sheriff!" Cal walked up with a young blond woman hanging on to his arm. "This is even better than last year."

"I think we say that every year," he replied. "Hi, Mary Ellen. I guess you two have made up."

"Not exactly," she replied pertly. "But I'm considering giving Cal a second chance. Don't worry, I'll make sure he does his duty while he's here."

After the couple walked away, Lee looked down at Nikki, who was leaning against her mother.

"I think someone's had enough of the carnival," she commented, taking hold of her hand. "Time for us to be heading home."

"It's about time for us to think about leaving. We'll walk back with you," Travis suggested.

"Aren't we going to stay?" Susie begged. "Please Dad, I'm not tired at all."

"No." His voice was gentle but firm. "We've seen pretty much everything, and if you'd like we can come back for a little while tomorrow, but there's things to be done at home."

When they reached Lee's car, Travis placed his hand on the hood.

"How's it doing? Running all right?"

She nodded. "You may claim you don't know a lot about cars, but I haven't had any trouble with it." She unlocked the passenger door and opened it to allow Nikki to get inside. "Thank you for sharing your day with us," she said softly.

He smiled. "I think it's me who should be thanking you. Susie's already getting to the age where she doesn't like going out with her dad as much as she used to. I'll see you tomorrow night for the dance." He didn't notice Nikki's look of horror.

When they drove away Nikki turned to Lee. "Mom, are you going somewhere with Sheriff Hunter?"

"Yes, he's taking me to a dance," she explained. "And you get to spend the night with Susie. Doesn't that sound like fun?"

She frowned. "Why would you want to go with him?"

"Because he asked me and he's a nice man."

"Aren't you afraid of him?"

Lee sighed. She often wondered if she shouldn't have scraped up the money to take Nikki somewhere for professional counseling, to find out just how much she remembered of their past life. It was at times like this that she feared it was much more than Nikki let on.

"Nikki, Sheriff Hunter has never done anything to frighten me or to hurt you," she pointed out. "Has he?"

"No." The admission was reluctant.

"Has he ever shouted at you?"

"No."

"Or called you bad names?"

"No," Nikki muttered.

"Then there's no reason to be afraid of him, is there?" She wondered how many times she would have to remind her that not all men were bad.

"Will he be there when I'm at Susie's house?" Nikki asked after a long silence.

"I'm sure he will, since he lives there," Lee said reasonably. "But then, we're going out. Besides, you'll be able to play with the kittens in the barn, and Susie's grandmother is going to let you two make fudge tomorrow night. Now doesn't that sound like a lot of fun?" She groaned inwardly at the thought of the massive task ahead of the older woman and silently applauded her patience.

Nikki brightened at the thought. "And we get to stay up late?"

"That will be up to Mrs. Hunter."

She chewed her lower lip. "Well, maybe it won't be so bad."

Lee hid her smile. "Maybe it won't."

Chapter Eight

"As I live and breathe, the man has gotten a haircut, shaved and—" Maude moved closer to take a sniff "—put on cologne. You haven't looked and smelled this good since your senior prom."

Travis shot her a telling look. "All right, you looked almost as good at your wedding—at least, you would have, if you hadn't been so hung over from your bachelor party." She smiled serenely.

"Give me a break, Mom. I'm an adult, the law in this town and you still treat me as if I was still a kid with skinned knees and a black eye."

"That's because I'll always remember you that way." She smiled again, smoothing down his shirt collar over his jacket.

"Where are the girls?" Travis looked around. Maude had driven into town earlier to pick up some groceries and had offered to collect Nikki at the same time.

"In Susie's room, changing into their pajamas before we get down to the serious business of having dinner and making fudge. You just go on and have a nice time," she admonished her son, still smiling.

Travis stopped by the bedroom to say goodbye to Nikki and Susie and left the house, not wanting to be late in picking up Lee. While it might have been a long time since he had gone out on a date, he still remembered that a gentleman didn't keep a lady waiting.

The lump in Lee's throat grew to gigantic proportions when she heard the knock. She smoothed down the front of her lace-tiered skirt and walked slowly to the door. Her hand hovered over the knob before she finally grasped the cool metal and slowly turned it.

"Hello." She offered him a weak smile. "Ah, would you like to come in?" She stepped back.

Travis's eyes widened in amazement. Lee wore an off-white, Victorian-styled blouse with a band of lace for a collar and a peach and blue floral calf-length skirt with matching lace along the ruffled tiers. With her hair pinned on top of her head in a variation of a Gibson hairstyle, she looked as if she had stepped out of a cameo.

"You look lovely," he said huskily, suddenly wanting to take her into his arms, yet afraid of making any move that would send her into retreat.

She laughed nervously, just as strongly aware of him as he was of her. "Thank you. I'll be honest. I've been going crazy all afternoon, trying to figure out what to wear. I finally called Sally, and she told me pretty much anything went and not to worry." She looked at his white shirt and tan Western-cut jacket and slacks and was glad she had decided to give in to her feminine side.

Clearing her throat, Lee went to the hall closet. Stepping behind her, Travis took the coat from her and held it out, dropping it slightly so that she could slip her arms through the sleeves. He looked down at her nape, softly shadowed by wisps of curls, and inhaled the fragrance of her perfume. He swallowed, wondering if counting to ten would help him overcome those male urges again. He decided that even counting to a million wouldn't.

Once her coat was on, Lee stepped away. "Thank you," she whispered, feeling very shy.

"We're lucky tonight isn't too cold," he told her as they walked outside to his car, a well-cared-for Buick that had to be ten years old.

Lee looked at their mode of transportation. "This doesn't look like your Jeep."

"That's more my official vehicle and for work around the ranch. Not the kind of transportation for taking a lady to a dance." He opened the door with a theatrical flourish.

Lee slid inside and waited until Travis got in. "You don't sound like a rancher."

He looked amused. "Oh, what is a rancher supposed to sound like?"

She blushed, realizing her comment could be taken as an insult. "To be honest, I don't know. I guess someone who worries more about their cows and hay and whatever else they have on their ranches than what goes on in the outside world."

"Whereas I sound like someone who's had more than a grade school education." He still seemed to be more amused than affronted.

Lee looked down at the hands that lay clenched in her lap. "I made that sound very bad, didn't I? I'm sorry."

"Hey, no apology. It's understandable you would think that we're all country bumpkins. Admittedly, a good many of us come across that way. Actually I graduated from the University of Montana with a business degree to make my mother happy, but ranching had always been in my blood, so I came back here after my stint in the navy, instead of going to New York to take the town by storm, the way my mother hoped I would."

"What did you do in the navy?" Lee asked curiously.

"Shore patrol."

Her stomach tightened. "Which is why you're the sheriff."

He turned the car into a large dirt parking lot already al-most filled with cars and trucks. "It gave me a bit of an edge, since I had some law enforcement experience." He fitted the car neatly between two pickup trucks and switched off the engine.

"Yes, I guess it would," Lee replied, as they walked to-ward the large hall, through whose open doors the sounds of music were spilling outside.

They entered the hall, finding it lighted by hundreds of tiny twinkling lights over the dance floor, and smiling and greeting people they knew as they went.

"Lee, you look lovely. And here you were so worried earlier." Sally walked up, dragging her husband behind her. "Hi, Travis. You going to save me a dance later on?"

"If Will won't mind giving you up," he teased the florid-faced blond man with a stocky build who was standing be-hind Sally.

"Hell, the way she likes to dance, you can have her all evening," Will joked back, earning a good-natured pinch from his wife.

"Just for that, you can start making up for that crack right now." With a jaunty wave of the hand she dragged her husband toward the dance floor.

"Poor Will. He has two left feet and is tone-deaf, while Sally dances like Ginger Rogers and sings in the church choir," Travis explained.

Lee's lips twitched in a smile. "The perfect couple."

He looked toward the two people dancing on the fringe of the crowd. "Yeah, they are." Seeming to shake himself awake, he turned back to Lee. "Ready to take a chance? I promise not to step on your feet too often."

The band may have been distinctly amateur and the mu-sic more country and western than waltz, but Lee had little trouble learning the steps, and soon discovered Travis had lied about his dancing ability.

"Two left feet, my eye," she declared as they circled the dance floor. "You're a wonderful dancer."

He looked unrepentant. "I figured if I sounded pathetic enough, you'd feel sorry for me and come to the dance."

Lee looked up into his eyes, feeling herself drawn into the dark brown depths. Wildly she wondered if the room temperature had suddenly risen. With Travis's arms loosely draped around her waist she felt protected. She'd never thought she would feel that way in the presence of a man. As the evening progressed, a few men came by to ask if she'd care to try it with them. She couldn't help but notice that Travis didn't bother dancing with any of the other women, but merely stayed on the sidelines, his eyes never leaving her. Lee was certain that if anything happened, he would immediately be at her side. Now she felt more than protected; she almost felt cherished.

She decided that Travis was the perfect escort. When he thought she was looking a little tired, he made sure she had a glass of punch, and coaxed her to try the sugar cookies that lay prominently on a glass platter on the refreshment table.

"Mrs. Zimmerman makes the best sugar cookies I've ever had," he explained. "They're the soft chewy kind, instead of hard and crunchy. I used to stop by her house once a week for some." He smiled at the silver-haired woman presiding over the refreshments. "And she refuses to divulge her recipe to anyone."

Lee bit into a cookie and discovered it was just as excellent as Travis had assured her. "I don't blame her," she said to Travis. "These are wonderful," she told the woman, who beamed at her compliment. "I wouldn't want to give the recipe away, either."

"Oh, someday I will." Mrs. Zimmerman chuckled. "Actually I'll will it to the most deserving person, but they'll have to promise not to give it out to just anyone."

Lee smiled again as she took another cookie. "I think that sounds like a wonderful idea."

They selected a table off to one side that afforded a bit more privacy than the others, but that didn't stop people from wandering over.

Lee shifted uncomfortably after a few minutes of close scrutiny. After several more people had stopped by, she leaned across the table toward Travis.

"Is there a reason for all this attention?" she asked.

He grinned, looking a little uncomfortable himself. "I don't usually escort anyone to the dances."

Lee now felt even more self-conscious. "Are you telling me you haven't dated since your wife's death, and I'm the first?" Her voice squeaked on the last word.

Travis's face turned a light shade of red. "Not exactly. I just haven't seen anyone who lives around here."

She was amused to recognize that he felt as uncomfortable as she did. "Oh, I see."

"Good, then can we please get off the subject?" he growled, downing his punch as if it were something stronger.

Lee sipped her own punch to hide her smile.

"You look real pretty tonight, ma'am," Cal told her as they danced around the floor, his arm pumping hers up and down as if she were an oil well, and his boots narrowly missing her shoes a few times. "It sure surprised us when we saw Travis walking in with you. With a lady, I mean," he corrected himself, stumbling over his words.

"I already gathered he hadn't done this before." Lee stepped back quickly before her toes were well and truly smashed.

"No, ma'am, he pretty much stays away from these shindigs," Cal explained. "Though Maude never missed one."

"You let your mother miss tonight just to watch our children," she accused Travis when she was gratefully released into his care. "I learned that she's never missed one."

"She volunteered to look after the girls, so you'll have to take that up with her." Travis noticed the dimming of the lights. "Means it's midnight and the last dance. Shall we?"

She smiled back. "Why not?"

They slowly circled the floor to "Good Night Ladies," their steps in perfect rhythm.

Lee felt a strange tingling, both along her back where Travis's hand rested and on the hand he held in a warm clasp. She slowly lifted her head and found him gazing down at her with a strange look on his face, as if he had never seen her before. Unable to think of something to say to lighten the moment, she could only look into his eyes and wonder what he was thinking.

She's beautiful, Travis thought, stunned by the abrupt shift in his thinking about Lee. She has beautiful eyes, skin, nice figure, and a wonderful personality. Where has she been all this time? His arm unconsciously tightened around her.

Lee could feel the warmth change to an icy cold, but she refused to give in to old fears now. She found it difficult to breathe, yet inhaled deeply, breathing in the spicy scent of Travis's after-shave. When he held her close against his chest, his body heat chased away the cold. Her breasts swelled, the tips brushing against the soft fabric of her blouse and the hard planes of his chest. She closed her eyes, allowing the various sensations to wash over her as the music retreated into the fog that surrounded her in a world where only she and Travis existed. She couldn't remember the last time she'd felt this way, then realized it was because she never had. She tilted back her head, not caring if her thoughts were evident in her eyes. There was a strange tingling feeling running through her veins, and she felt more alive at that moment than she ever had before. As far as she was concerned, it was a night when fairy tales came true.

Travis easily read the unspoken message in Lee's eyes, certain his own said the same. How long before they could be alone? He knew just holding her wasn't nearly enough.

When the music ended, they drew apart, reluctant to return to the real world. Lee wanted to leave as quickly as possible, but the people stopping to chat made their progress to the door slow. So she forced stiff facial muscles to smile and spoke, although later she had no idea what she'd said.

When they finally reached Travis's car, Lee slid inside, unsure whether to feel relieved that she was out of the hall or worried that her new feelings might be wrong.

"I'm sure most men would suggest going out for a drink or something, but this town and the neighboring ones don't go in much for late-night entertainment," Travis said, shrugging and smiling faintly.

"That's all right. I'm awfully tired, anyway," Lee whispered, turning to look out the window. Why had she allowed her new feelings to flower so dramatically? She, who had always examined things so carefully, had ignored good sense and now didn't know what to do to rectify the situation. She felt a need to be alone so that she could examine her feelings toward Travis at greater length.

He frowned, wondering what had prompted the abrupt change in her manner, then put it down to what she had said. He let the motor run for a few minutes before turning on the heater, adjusting the vents to blow indirectly at Lee.

"Warm enough?" he asked, willing her to look at him. She nodded without turning around.

Travis jockeyed into the line leaving the parking lot and was soon on the road. "Lee, are you sure you're all right?"

"I guess I'm just more tired than I thought. I'm not used to doing all that dancing," she said huskily.

The silence in the car was deafening during the short ride. Travis pulled into Lee's driveway and got out, but before he could walk around to open her door, she was out of the car and walking toward the house.

"I want to thank you for a lovely evening," she said, speaking rapidly, her words blowing gusts of frost into the air as she unlocked the door.

"Just as long as you enjoyed yourself." Travis was still puzzled by the mixed signals he was receiving, and, for the first time in his usually uncomplicated life, wasn't sure what to do. He finally decided to let nature take its course. He inclined his head, lowering it slowly until his mouth rested lightly against hers in the gentlest of kisses.

Lee's heart almost stopped beating at the delicate touch. Her first thought was to push him away and run into the house, where she would be safe. Her next was to hold on to him as tightly as she could. Before she could give in to either idea, Travis moved back, a tiny smile on his lips.

"Thank you for going with me," he said softly. "You better get inside, before you turn into an icicle."

Her head bobbed jerkily, and she quickly opened the door and stepped inside. She leaned against the wall, listening to the sound of the car's engine accelerate, then fade away. Lee touched her tingling lips, unaware of her sad smile. She knew she couldn't afford to let things go too far. Any man in her life could prove dangerous, especially a lawman.

During his drive home, Travis couldn't stop thinking about Lee, the way she'd felt in his arms and especially the way her lips had felt against his. He knew he was grinning like some sappy school kid, but he didn't care. Not after the evening he'd just spent.

After he parked the car in the garage, he walked through the back door into the kitchen, where he found a covered plate of lopsided fudge squares and a carafe, which he knew would hold coffee. He poured himself a cup and took a piece of fudge, then walked into the den, where he found Maude watching the late show. She looked up and flipped the Mute switch on the television's remote control.

"I didn't expect you to be home so early," she greeted him. "How was your evening?"

"How were the girls?" He flopped into his easy chair, sipping the hot coffee.

"Fine, sound asleep. How was your evening?"

Travis nibbled on a corner of the fudge. "Not bad. Who did most of the beating?"

Maude stared at him long and hard. "They both did. Now if I have to ask you about your evening one more time, I won't be responsible for the consequences."

"She looked beautiful tonight." He had an idea he still had that idiotic smile on his face, but he didn't care. He was only speaking the truth.

"And?"

Travis glared at his mother. "Is there a reason why you need a blow-by-blow description of my date?"

Maude smiled serenely. "Yes, because you came home in a strange mood. And because you've always talked over your dates with me. Well, almost always. You never did tell me about that time you went on the hayride with DeeDee Truman." Her eyes danced when she noticed Travis's red face. "I thought so. She always had a reputation. Now, back to Lee. Did you kiss her?"

He rolled his eyes. "Am I not allowed to have any secrets?"

"No." Maude leaned forward. "Travis, you are my only son. Lee is the first woman you've taken out seriously since Julie's death. And that means a lot. You're a man of strong feelings, and I'd say she has done something to knock you for a loop."

He grimaced. "She did. And if you don't mind, I'd like to sort things out on my own."

"I wouldn't expect anything else. Just as long as you know I'm here for you." She paused, then pushed on. "About Nikki."

Travis looked over. "You mean there was a problem, after all?"

She shook her head. "No, she's an absolute darling. But she says so little of what they've done or where they've been before coming here. It's as if they have no past."

His eyes darkened with anger. "Mom, did you try to pump her? A seven-year-old child?"

"Of course not, but many children do talk about things they've done in the past. She doesn't. Nikki appears skittish about certain things. When they were ready for bed, she came up to me and asked if it would be possible to have a night-light. I would go so far as to say she is genuinely frightened of the dark."

He shrugged. "That's nothing unusual. A lot of kids are convinced there are monsters under their beds or in their closets."

"No, nothing like that. I just wish I could put my finger on it," she said with a sigh.

Travis finished the fudge and coffee and stood up. "I'm going to bed. Four-thirty will be here before I know it. I'm too old to hold down two jobs."

"Then tell them to hold the election for sheriff early," his mother suggested.

"Nope, another six months and I'll have more than enough to get a new bull."

"Then something else will come up. You're torn between helping the town and working for yourself," Maude chided. "You want to help too many people, Travis. Pretty soon there won't be enough of you left for anyone important."

He smiled. "For someone important, I'll make sure there's more than enough of me."

"Travis, someone's here to see you." Cal stood by his Jeep as Travis climbed out. His expression and tone of voice indicated that he wasn't impressed with their visitor. "He insisted on waiting for you in your office." He lifted his shoulders in apology. "I couldn't stop him."

Travis nodded, aware his deputy wasn't as authoritative as he could be. "That's okay, Cal. I'll see what he wants."

He strode into his office where he found a heavyset man sitting in the chair across from his own.

"I'm Sheriff Hunter," he said crisply, hanging his hat and sheepskin-lined jacket on the coatrack. "I understand you wanted to see me."

"Sure did, Sheriff." The man spoke with a heavy Southern drawl. He reached into his coat pocket and drew out a white business card, handing it to Travis.

He glanced down at the black engraved print. "J. D. Porter," he read. "Fine, you're a private investigator. What brings you up here from Houston?"

"Hell, this is just another backwater town for me." He dug into his coat's inner pocket and withdrew an envelope. "I've been trackin' a bloodthirsty broad and her child for nigh on to three years now. Thought you might be able to help me out." His smile could only be described as oily.

Travis never liked people who looked down on the residents of small towns. This man's manner put him right into that category.

"I still don't see any reason why you'd try here. Newcomers in this town are few and far between."

The man smirked. "After seeing what little there is, I can well understand why. Let's just say I'm followin' a hunch." He pulled a photograph out of the envelope. "This is about three years old, but it should give you some kind of idea what they look like. Wonder if you'd seen either one of them?" He handed the photograph to Travis.

He stared down at the picture and felt shock waves rock his body, although he was certain their impact didn't show on his face.

The little girl with the broad grin, bright eyes and dark blond curls was Nikki with her beautiful heart-shaped face. The woman standing beside her sent a giant-sized fist to his gut. The hair color was strawberry blonde instead of brown, but the sorrow in those eyes was recognizable. The man standing behind the woman had an arm around her waist in a possessive gesture. He was tall, blond with moviestar good looks and an arrogant manner. Travis didn't know the man and he already didn't like him. He knew he wasn't going to swear the woman and girl were Lee and Nikki, and he certainly wasn't going to say anything to this bulldog until he knew more about the story.

"Why're you looking for them?" he asked, adding just the right casual touch to his voice.

"Anne Sinclair almost killed her ex-husband and kidnapped their kid three years ago," Porter explained. "She was labeled an unfit mother during the divorce case and lost custody of the kid. Let me tell you, anyone who would shoot a guy for no reason at all and kidnap a kid has to be nuts. The father is worried that his daughter will get hurt. 'Course, for all we know, she could have dumped the kid somewhere and taken off with some guy. Sure wouldn't put it past her. Her reputation down there wasn't the best. Mr. Sinclair is offering a hefty reward for her return, and I'm sure anyone in this town could use the kind of money he's offering," he added craftily. "After all, she broke the law and deserves to be locked up."

And I just bet you'll get even more money for yourself, Travis thought grimly to himself. He leaned back in his chair, lacing his fingers behind his head. "What makes you think she got this far north?"

The man shrugged. "A hunch. My last lead was a motel about two hundred miles south of here, where they stayed last fall. 'Course, who knows what name she's using by now. It seems to change with every city, along with her hair and eye color. That's why it's been so damn hard for me to catch up with her. I figured it wouldn't hurt for me to check out some of these small towns. She might have thought it would be safer. I figured I'd check in here first, since you'd probably know if anyone new showed up within the last six months."

Travis worked hard at keeping his expression bland. His first impulse was to throw the odious man out on his fat butt, but he knew the creep would only kick up a fuss, not to mention do some searching on his own, both of which he didn't need. He didn't want that to happen until he'd heard Lee's side of the story, although how he was going to introduce this subject to her was something he didn't know. He recalled Lee's wariness around him and Nikki's fear. As the town's sheriff he had always worked hard to keep an open mind, and he was more than determined to do just that with this situation. He tossed the photograph onto the desk.

"You're right about us being so isolated out here. I'm usually one of the first to hear about any newcomers in this town. It's not as if we have any kind of industry around here that brings in people. Not to mention I'd hear about a good-looking woman like that." He nodded his head slightly in thought. "Yep, I'd guess you're the first stranger we've had in town in well over a year," he lied without a qualm.

Chapter Nine

Travis leaned back in his chair, still studying the damning photograph lying on his desk. He stared down at the woman and girl, picturing them in different clothing and coloring. His gut tightened at the vision.

"Well, Lee or Anne Sinclair, what have you got yourself into?" he muttered.

"Hey, Travis, what's going on with that guy?" Cal stuck his head around the door.

"Good question," he said grimly. "I want you to spread the word that I don't want anyone talking to that creep. He sees us as a bunch of dumb country hicks, so let him keep on thinking that. For once I'm glad we don't have a motel here. No matter what, he'll have to be gone by nightfall, since the nearest motel is sixty miles away. And if he tries to sleep in his car, I'll arrest him for vagrancy."

Cal looked down at the picture, and shock flashed across his pudgy features. "Say, isn't that—?"

Travis's head snapped up, the expression on his face demanding silence. "Just do as I say, Cal, and don't waste any time. And no personal points of view to anyone. Understand?"

The younger man nodded slowly. "Sure, anything you say." He backed out of the office and headed for the front door, determined to do the job his boss had given him.

Travis leaned forward, bracing his elbows on the desk and covering his face with his hands. He suddenly felt as if he had been thrust into a situation he wasn't sure how to handle, without everything blowing up in his face.

"If she's the one he's looking for, I'm hiding a fugitive from the law, and if she's not, I'm protecting her from scum," he groaned, fighting with his scruples. He shut his eyes, wanting nothing more than to forget the past twenty minutes. Then something occurred to him. He grabbed the phone and punched out a number. It was picked up on the first ring.

"Yeah?"

He breathed a sigh of relief that Lorna was the one to answer the phone. "It's Travis. Is Lee working today?"

She chuckled. "Of course she is. Why?"

He paused, knowing he was taking a step in a direction whence there would be no return. "Get her out of there. I don't care how you do it, just get her out right away. There's a private investigator nosing around town, and he's the kind who would sell his own grandmother if the money was right."

Lorna took no time to ask questions. "I'll send her over to the Hendersons for more eggs, and a few places after that. Don't worry, Travis. No one in this place will say anything about her, if they know what's good for them. Not if they want to eat here again!"

He grinned, relaxing for the first time that morning. "Ah, Lorna, if you weren't already taken, I'd marry you."

"Sure. That's why you're looking out for you know who. Now, let me get off the phone so I can get this taken care of."

Travis continued grinning as he hung up. "With Lorna looking out for Lee, no one will dare say anything about her, unless he wants a shotgun shoved up his nose."

"THAT MUST BE a joker's idea of a private investigator," Jake muttered to Lorna, watching J. D. Porter enter the restaurant. Lorna had already alerted the diners to the man nosing around, and it appeared she had done so just in time.

"Mornin'," the man greeted them with a smile, hefting his bulk onto a stool. "My, that pie sure looks good. Is that peach?"

"Yeah, it is." Lorna was unmoved by his praise.

"I sure would appreciate a piece and a cup of coffee," J.D. continued as he looked around the restaurant. He nodded and smiled at some of the other men sitting nearby. "I guess you all would pretty much know everyone in this sweet little town of yours."

"As I've lived here all my life, I 'spect I would," Jake replied. "Why?"

"Well, I'm looking for somebody." He pulled a photograph out of his jacket pocket, along with two twenty-dollar bills. "This lady tried to kill her husband and took their little girl. A dangerous woman, if I do say so myself. Maybe you've seen her pass through town or somethin'?"

Jake studied the photograph and ignored the money. "Can't say as I have."

"Take another look," Porter invited him. "That picture's a few years old, so the girl would be about seven now. The child's daddy just wants his baby back. He's real worried something might happen to her. He's offering a big reward."

"Let me see," Ernie, the town's plumber asked. He looked it over carefully and returned it—with a smudge of grease on one corner. "Nah, we'd sure remember someone like her. We don't have a whole lot of good-lookin' women come through here. 'Course, there was Lew Watson's new wife, but she's from Canada."

"Mister, you can shove that money under my nose, and I'd be only too happy to take it," declared Thaddeus Stone, owner of the hardware store, "but I still ain't seen the lady."

LEE BEGAN to wonder over the next few days if she had changed, or if the townspeople had. Everywhere she went, she felt as if people looked at her differently. Yet there was nothing to back up her suspicions. If anything, some folk were friendlier. Still, she was jumpy and wary of everyone, beginning to wonder if it wasn't time to move on once more.

"Young lady, you're in need of some of my spring tonic if you're going to do that to my salads," Lorna told her, staring at the salad covered with catsup instead of French dressing.

Lee looked at the concoction, her face a picture of dismay. "I don't know what happened. I was certain I was putting on dressing."

The older woman glanced toward Travis, who sat at the counter, waiting for his salad. Nothing in his expression gave his thoughts away.

He was proud of the fact that the townspeople had banded together to protect a woman they'd come so quickly to think of as one of their own, even if they weren't aware of the entire story. He was astute enough to know his own backing up of Lee had helped some, but it was mainly the fact she was a woman, alone, with a child that had brought out their protective instincts. He was relieved that the private investigator hadn't gone into great detail about Anne Sinclair when talking to the others. Evidently the man had preferred bringing up the idea of the reward. Little did he know that all people weren't money hungry.

"That sleaze bag you warned me about came in here just after the lunch crowd," Lorna murmured, leaning on the counter in front of Travis. "He flashed around a woman's picture and some twenty-dollar bills to jog people's memories." A smile flickered across her face. "Thaddeus told him he'd be more than happy to take one of the twenties, but he'd never seen the woman. From what I hear, anyone questioned said pretty much the same thing." Her dark eyes reflected worry. "She's sure in a lot of trouble, isn't she? He said she was wanted by the law, but he wouldn't say much else. Told us if we had any information to get in touch with him through his office."

"A lot of people are wanted by the law," Travis said laconically. "Such as Wilma on a regular basis."

"That girl wouldn't harm a fly, so whatever she did can't be as bad as he hinted." She straightened up and smiled as Lee approached them. "I see you found the French dressing."

Lee's face turned a bright red as she set the plate in front of Travis. "I guess my mind was elsewhere." She smiled weakly and hurried away.

Travis looked down at the salad and grimaced. "I didn't have the heart to tell her I ordered blue cheese. I hate French dressing."

When he paid the bill he smiled at Lee. "Mom wants you to come out for dinner again this Saturday," he said. "She has a nasty hen she wants an excuse to roast."

"Oh, no," Lee protested. After the past few days, she knew she couldn't bear the thought of spending any more time in the sheriff's house. "You've had us out there already."

"So? Mom likes to cook, and the more the merrier. The girls can ride in the big corral under adult supervision. You know how much Nikki loves horses."

She did. Nikki had been invited out several times after school, when one of the hands supervised the two girls in taking turns riding a docile mare around the main corral.

And each time she returned home, she was even more excited about her newfound riding ability. In fact, as each day passed, Lee saw more and more of the bright-faced little girl she had always hoped Nikki would become.

"You know I can't turn you down," she said with a sigh. "You should be ashamed of yourself, using my child like that."

His grin lighted up his dark eyes. "Hey, whatever works. Why don't you come early? Say about three or four."

Lee couldn't argue, because deep down she looked forward to going out to Travis's ranch. She told herself it was crazy, not to mention dangerous.

"Susie's grandma said I can call her Grandma," Nikki announced out of the blue during the drive to the Hunter ranch.

Lee looked surprised. "Did she?"

Nikki nodded. "And she's gonna let Susie and me make chocolate chip cookies."

"I thought we were going out there so you could ride," she reminded her daughter.

"Oh, we're gonna do that, too," Nikki said blithely, as if time had no meaning.

Lee shook her head, smiling at her daughter's expectation of doing everything at once.

The moment Lee parked along the side of the house, Susie was running toward them, chattering before Nikki had a chance to get out of the car.

"Hey, where's your manners?" Travis shouted, following more slowly.

"Hi, Mrs. Davis," Susie called out, dragging Nikki in the direction of the barn.

He shrugged. "I guess I should be glad she heard me." He closed the car door for Lee and looked her over from head to toe. "Good, you're wearing jeans. Can you ride?"

Lee was surprised by his question. "Some, but it's been a long time."

"It will come back to you." Without touching her, he steered her toward the same barn the girls had run to. "Casey, they all ready?" he asked, looking at a man in his twenties who was leading out two saddled horses.

"Yes sir. I saddled up Starlight for the lady." He nodded toward Lee.

Unthinking, she clutched Travis's sleeve. "I told you I haven't ridden in years," she whispered.

He looked down and smiled. "Starlight's the same as a rocking horse, except she doesn't stay in one place. Don't worry, I'll be right alongside you. You'll do just fine."

With some trepidation she allowed herself to be led to the horse and assisted into the saddle, as Travis gave her a leg up, then handed her the reins. "I'm not so sure this is a good idea." She looked down, discovering the ground was farther away than she'd thought. "Besides, I came here for dinner. I really should be inside helping Maude." She made a move to dismount, but Travis's hand on her thigh stopped her, his touch burning her through her jeans.

"She knows what we're doing." He moved away and swung into the saddle of a large bay gelding with the ease of a man who spent many hours on a horse. "We decided it was time you saw more than the house and the barn."

Lee swallowed as the horse began to walk slowly, following Travis. Soon enough her body adjusted to the rocking gait, and she began to relax enough to look at her surroundings, not to mention the man riding beside her. Sitting straight and tall in the saddle, Travis looked like an ad for the Old West. Since he was now riding a bit ahead of her, she could look her fill.

The hilly country was still brown from the harsh winter, but she could see tiny shoots of green dotted across the landscape. She sniffed the air and was convinced she could smell spring coming, even though she could feel the chilly air penetrate her heavy jacket. Travis pointed out the grazing cattle, mentioning special points of his plans for them.

She looked over at him, not surprised at his love for his land. She doubted he was the kind of man to do anything halfway and couldn't help but wonder if that extended to his lovemaking. She quickly shook off that thought and forced herself back to reality. "If you're so serious about your ranch, why are you working as sheriff?"

He pulled on the reins and waited until she halted next to him. "Because I need a new bull, and it was a fairly easy way to get the money. Oh, I know it sounds hokey and all that, but I truly believe in the judicial system." For a split second he could have sworn he saw bitterness in Lee's eyes at his words. "If I didn't have the ranch, I probably would have been a lawyer, but I knew I couldn't devote the right kind of time to both, and as far as I'm concerned, the land comes first. Since the town was willing to let me juggle both, and the arrangement isn't permanent, I saw no reason not to take the job on."

Lee wanted to tell him that the system doesn't always work for the right people, but thought better of it. That kind of statement could cause questions she couldn't afford to answer. Instead she chose a safer topic. "You're sheriff because you need a new bull? No offense, but that doesn't make a lot of sense."

Travis pulled his hat down over his eyes, looking out over land that had been in his family for years. "My bull is getting old, and a new one costs money I don't have. When our sheriff died, the town council came to me and asked if I'd be willing to take on his job for the rest of his term. I had experience in the military police, which was why they thought of me. The money was tempting, and I needed it. Admittedly, I had to hire an extra hand to help out at home, but I still have enough left over to put away toward my bull. By the end of the year I should have enough. End of story."

"Do you think you'll run for the position when elections come up?"

He shook his head. "Part of me wants to, but another part reminds me that I should be out here full-time. We have a pretty quiet town except for the occasional drunk. I think it's time to go back to the land." He turned toward her. "What about you? Think you'll stay?" He hoped his question sounded casual, although he waited tensely for her reply.

She forced herself to look him straight in the eye. "Who says what a person will do? Although Nikki's happy here, and that's what counts."

"What about you? Don't you count?" *Trust me,* his mind pleaded with her. *Tell me what that creep was talking about. Tell me why you ran away.*

Lee turned away. "My daughter is all I have, and I'll do anything in my power to keep her safe." Her voice hardened, as memories of the past intruded once again.

Not by a blink of an eye did Travis let his thoughts be shown, but his mind was furiously filing away her statement. Lee had just admitted that Nikki meant everything to her. Was that why she'd shot her ex-husband? Because she lost the custody case?

"Yeah, our kids tend to inspire our protective instincts, don't they?" He decided to subtly press the subject. "Susie got the measles last year, and I suffered through every red spot with her. Mom said she was glad I had gotten them when I was ten, because I'm one of the worst patients around."

Lee's lips curved slightly. "Men usually are."

"Was your husband a lousy patient when he was sick?" He cursed himself when he saw her face freeze.

"He didn't believe in getting sick." Her hands tightened on the reins. "It's getting late, isn't it? Shouldn't we be getting back?"

Knowing he wouldn't get anything else out of her, Travis nodded and guided his horse in the direction they had come from. The ride back to the barn was silent.

When Lee pushed herself out of the saddle, she felt Travis's hands on her waist as he guided her to the ground. She turned around slowly, aware of his hands still resting lightly on her hips. The air fairly vibrated around them as they gazed at each other, each of them trying to read answers to unspoken questions. The warmth of the barn, coupled with the earthy scent of horse and hay mingled in the air, only added to the tension their bodies felt. Lee's mount broke the spell when she turned her head and nudged her in the back. Grateful for the respite, she grasped the reins tightly.

"I'll unsaddle her for you." Travis's voice was rough with emotion, but Lee shook her head.

"I can handle it. As you said, it all comes back to you." She reached under the horse to loosen the cinch and pull off the saddle before leading the mare into the barn. The two of them worked in silent harmony as the horses were brushed down and stabled. When Lee began to leave the barn, Travis walked toward her until she was backed up against a post. She looked up, her eyes wide.

"You have the most expressive eyes, did you know that?" He spoke softly, his tone even. "I would have sworn you thought I was going to hurt you."

"You may be the town's sheriff and a loving father, but that's all I know about you," she whispered, feeling both the unyielding wood behind her and the body heat that was reaching out to her. His hands were braced on the post on either side of her, but he still hadn't touched her in any way.

She breathed deeply, but only the scent of horse, leather and man reached her nostrils.

"I'm housebroken, no nasty habits and I'm kind to children and animals."

Lee licked her lips, immediately catching Travis's attention. "Yes, but do you have references?" she murmured, entering into this flirtation game.

"Give me a couple minutes, and I'll write up all the references you'd ever want."

"What are you doing?" Her voice was raw.

Travis's gaze traveled over her, from the dark gold scarf her hair was tied back with to the open throat of the brown and gold plaid wool shirt under her unbuttoned jacket.

"I'm looking at a lovely woman that I wish I knew how to convince I'm not such a bad guy," he murmured, staring at her coral-glossed lips. He slowly lowered his head and lightly brushed his lips across hers. He could feel the tension in her body and sought to banish it.

"Do you know you taste like a rare spice?" he murmured against her tightly closed lips.

"No, I don't," she whispered. "That's the kind of line you read in a book."

"Maybe it is, maybe that's where I got it, but you still taste very special." Travis's tongue darted out to outline her lips, then he concentrated on taking teasing little nips at the corners of her lips and flicking his tongue along her bottom lip. "You know, I think I could stand here all day and just kiss you."

Her breath caught in her throat. "Just kiss me? No man wants just a kiss."

"I'm not just any man." He proved his point by still not trying to touch her anywhere else.

Lee was tempted to believe him, but past lessons had taught her too well. Still, Travis hadn't tried anything else. Not to mention the fact that he made her feel so warm inside. And all this from nothing more than a kiss. Each time his lips touched hers, she relaxed a little more. Very slowly she lifted her hand and rested it on his muscled forearm, feeling the skin tense under her touch. When she tipped her head slightly to one side, he began exploring her ear and along the side of her neck. She shivered at the pleasurable sensations that were skittering across her nerves, inhaling the warm, horsey scent of his skin and thinking it better than any expensive men's cologne.

"Why are you doing this?"

He smiled against her slightly parted lips. "I told you, because you taste like a rare spice."

"Why me?"

"Because you're a little prickly, you don't wear a lot of makeup and you don't chew gum." His tongue found an enticing corner of her lips. "Not to mention you make me crazy, every time I look at you. Is that a good enough reason? If not, I could probably come up with a few more."

"No, I think they're just fine, thank you." Lee's breathing grew labored. She couldn't remember the last time a man had given her so much attention without wanting something in return. In fact, she doubted it had ever happened. Her breathing grew still more labored with each touch, each caress of the lips. Her other hand found his waist, the body hard against her palm. This was the body of a man who worked hard for a living. The muscles were well earned, not the product of a health spa, the hands callused from the same kind of work that kept his body lean. She also didn't miss the fact that he was most definitely aroused, but it didn't frighten her as it would have before, because she instinctively knew he would never do anything to hurt her.

"You know, as much as I would like to stand here and kiss you for the rest of the day, I guess we should get inside before someone walks in here," he said quietly, easing away from her just a bit.

His words were more effective than a cold shower. What if Nikki had walked in and seen them so close together? Would it have brought forth dark memories the little girl had blocked out? She pushed him away and turned around to face the wall, breathing deeply to regain her equilibrium.

"Lee, I won't apologize for what I did." Travis spoke to her back. "In fact, given the chance, I would certainly do it again. I don't know what exactly put you off men, but I don't want to be one of that particular species."

"You're very sure of yourself, aren't you?" Her words were so soft that he barely heard them.

"No, not where you're concerned."

His simple words were enough to make her turn back. Lee stared at him long and hard, but found nothing but sincerity in his gaze. Without saying anything more, she walked out of the barn and up to the house, aware that he followed close behind. Deep in her heart she knew this was a turning point between them. She didn't want to call it a relationship, because it sounded too intimate, not to mention the fact that she couldn't afford to have such a thing happen. She opened the kitchen door and walked in , without bothering to knock, as if she had always done so.

"Dinner will be ready in about fifteen minutes," Maude informed them. "You have just enough time to wash up. Lee, why don't you use the bathroom across the hall from Susie's room? I laid fresh towels out for you."

"I need my purse." She looked around, as if expecting it to materialize in front of her.

"Nikki brought it in for you. I put it in the bathroom."

Lee nodded, her eyes still vaguely unfocused from the events in the barn. She walked out of the room without looking at Travis. Maude grasped his arm as he prepared to leave.

"I may be a woman who's been a widow for a lot of years, but I still know what a well-kissed woman looks like. She's fragile, Travis, handle her with care," she warned.

He smiled. "This from the woman who warned me away from her not all that long ago."

She released his arm. "And I'm still warning you."

Travis nodded, but said nothing more. He, more than anyone, knew one of the reasons why Lee acted skittishly. And he had a strong idea of what made her so wary around men. The idea wasn't a pleasant one, and he knew he was going to have to get her to trust him enough to tell him everything, before he could decide whether to contact the Houston authorities. He knew someone in that area he could talk to, and made a mental note to do just that, first thing Monday. Until then, he would just work on showing Lee that he wasn't like the man who'd so badly frightened her. He had a sick feeling that that person was her ex-husband.

Dinner was punctuated by chatter between Susie and Nikki as they talked about their ride in the main corral. Lee watched her daughter closely, but found nothing to worry about. The little girl talked freely, although she rarely looked at Travis unless he spoke to her directly, and then her answers were mumbled. Lee quietly suggested to her she speak up so she could be heard, but didn't push her in any other way. She knew that Nikki would have to come around on her own.

After dinner, Lee helped Maude with the dishes, while Travis watched a movie with the girls.

"I'd help you ladies, but someone should oversee the children. You know, to make sure they watch the proper programs," he explained, herding Susie and Nikki out of the kitchen.

"You just say that because you don't like to wash dishes and you want to watch the movie with us," Susie accused her father.

He leaned down, tickling her sides until she shrieked with laughter. "Nah, I just like to make little girls laugh themselves silly." He glanced up, noticing Nikki standing to one side, watching them with a solemn look on her face. He could have sworn he also saw longing in her eyes for a brief moment. "Come on, if nothing's good on TV, I'll take you two on in a hot Monopoly game."

"Just don't cheat this time," Susie said haughtily as they walked toward the den.

Lee chuckled. "Are they always like that? Or is it for our benefit?" Her laughter stuck in her throat as she realized what she had just said.

"Usually they're worse," Maude replied, rinsing off the plates and handing them to her. "Sometimes I think I have two children running around here. He can act the father role when need be, but he's also become her friend, and that's very important for a child." She speared Lee with a sharp glance. "It's a shame you weren't allowed that."

Lee grimaced, remembering the few things she had said the last time she and Maude had talked. "I've come to realize that some people aren't meant to be parents. Mine definitely weren't."

She nodded. "An excellent way of looking at it. Just be grateful you didn't turn out like them. So many children turn out to be like their parents, and the end result isn't always a positive one."

Lee knew that fear. She sometimes wondered if she hadn't gone overboard at times to insure she wouldn't become like her mother or father. Every night she prayed it wouldn't happen. So far she considered herself lucky it hadn't.

"Travis is a good man and a good father," Maude went on. "No real bad habits to speak of. At least none I know of. He's tried to quit smoking, but hasn't succeeded yet. He drinks rarely and hasn't gotten drunk since the day he was discharged from the navy. At least, he's always sober around me. He even washes behind his ears."

Lee smiled. She was getting used to Maude's habit of switching subjects in midstream and found it entertaining, because she never knew what the older woman was going to come up with next.

"It sounds as if you're trying to palm him off on some poor, unsuspecting soul." She closed the dishwasher door and leaned against the counter.

"I have an idea a man is the last thing you're looking for," Maude said shrewdly.

Lee busied herself with wiping off the counter with a damp rag. "My marriage wasn't a happy one," she murmured, absently digging at a tiny speck with her fingernail. "I'm not in the market for another one, and to be honest, I don't think Travis is, either."

"Not everyone who's been married before looks actively for a new partner," Maude pointed out. "That doesn't mean they should ignore anyone thrown their way."

Lee carefully rinsed the rag and draped it over the faucet before turning back to Maude. "I admit I don't know you very well, but I would say that you wouldn't see me as a viable partner for Travis."

Chapter Ten

"Mom, are we going away from here?" Nikki asked, watching Lee wipe up the milk she had accidentally spilled as she ate her breakfast.

"What brought that up?" she asked, pouring herself what she knew to be her third cup of coffee.

"Because you always act this way before we move." The young girl drew circles in her cereal with her spoon. "I don't want to leave." She lifted a spoonful of soggy cereal to her lips. "I feel safe here. I even have friends." Her tone was wistful, sending a shaft of pain through Lee's body.

"You've never said anything like this before," Lee said through stiff lips.

"Because you were always worrying and I didn't want you to. I never tell anyone about where we lived before or anything. I just let them talk. But we won't move from here, will we, Mom?" she pleaded. "I can't leave my friends. Plus, I'm working on something important in my art class and I can't leave till it's done." Her large eyes were eloquent with feeling. "And Susie's grandma is teaching me to cook."

Lee sat down in the chair before her legs gave out. She had believed that Nikki had few memories of those early years, because they were never brought up by either one of them. So Nikki's revelation was a big surprise. She had never before told her mother that she felt safe in any of the places where they had previously lived. But then, Lee hadn't felt very secure in them, either. Here she did. Then Travis had offered her friendship. That was what had kept her awake most of the night—fear that he would learn her secret and alert the Texas authorities. After all, he was the town's sheriff and obligated to turn her in. There was no reason for him to believe her side of the story. She looked at the hands lying in her lap, but that didn't stop their violent trembling.

"Sometimes people have to move for reasons beyond their control, Nikki," she said slowly. She leaned forward, her voice low with intensity. "You do realize that what we talk about here in the house cannot be repeated to anyone. Not even to Susie."

The child nodded unhappily, her voice a mere whisper. "I know. I never say anything to anyone, because I want us to live here forever. Can we?"

Lee breathed deeply several times. She hated to act like a heavy-handed mother but she had no choice. "Nikki, you're old enough to know that I can't make any promises."

"Yes, you can!" Nikki burst out. "You've made promises before."

Lee closed her eyes, feeling incredibly weary. "Don't do this. Please try to understand."

The girl's lower lip quivered. "All I want is a friend. Now we'll probably leave in the middle of the night and I'll never see Susie again. It's not fair. I hate you!" She slid off her chair and ran from the room.

"Nikki!" Lee hurried after her and found her sprawled across her bed, crying her eyes out. "Honey." She sat on the edge of the bed and pulled the tiny body into her arms. She felt helpless against a sorrow that had been stored up for so long.

Lee wrapped her arms tightly around her daughter. "Oh, Nikki, you've been robbed of so many things," she whispered. "You deserve so much that I can't give you."

"Don't worry anymore, Mom," she assured her with a wisdom beyond her young years. "We have each other, don't we?"

Lee's laughter was shaky with tears. "Yes, darling, we certainly do. What do you say that we cheer ourselves up with a movie? We could drive over to Cotton Creek for one and a hamburger afterward." She knew she was offering a bribe, but she'd do anything possible to cheer up her daughter.

"And a hot fudge sundae?" Nikki asked hopefully.

Lee burst out laughing. "I think that can be arranged."

For a little while longer the world was right again.

TRAVIS PUSHED HIMSELF through his morning chores like a madman. But no matter how hard he worked, visions of Lee's pale face and haunted eyes swam in front of him. Finally giving up, he swore long and hard before returning to the house. He was barely civil to his mother as he stalked through the kitchen to the small room he used as an office and slammed the door behind him. Rifling through the address book in his desk, he found the Texas number he wanted.

"Travis, old son," Hank Douglas greeted him with the booming voice he well remembered from their years together in the navy. "You finally getting smart and leaving that dead-end town? Or is this an invitation for another one of those infamous fishing trips of yours?"

He chuckled. "No on the former, and I'm not too sure on the latter. We didn't come back with any fish, although we had some pretty powerful hangovers and insect bites. Actually I'm calling for some information, and I figured you might have it, since you have all that fancy computer equipment as a state police officer. You know, we small-town sheriffs are lucky to have an electric typewriter.''

The other man laughed. ''Give me a break, Hunter. As for the information, it depends on whether it's something I can tell you about,'' he said cautiously.

''Ever hear of a P.I. named J. D. Porter?''

Hank sighed. ''Yeah, I've heard of him, all right. His fees are high, and he's been known to stretch the truth a bit, if it will help him, and he doesn't care who gets hurt in the process. Trust me, Travis, you don't want anything to do with him. He can be a mean bastard when crossed. Tell me, where'd you hear about him?''

He grimaced at the idea of telling the truth, but knew he owed his old friend that much. ''He was in my office a little over a week ago, looking for someone.''

''Anne Sinclair,'' Hank said instantly.

Travis's interest was piqued even more. ''How did you know?''

''I'd heard the Sinclair family had hired him, along with a few others, but rumor has it Porter's leads are warmer. Still, what was he doing in your neck of the woods? That's pretty far off the beaten track for anyone, even him.''

''Looking for Anne Sinclair, what else?'' Travis deliberately kept his voice casual.

''And you're calling to find out what the true story is. Well, I can tell you what the Sinclair family says, and what the police think is the truth.''

He straightened in his chair. ''Shoot.''

''I'll try to make it short and sweet. Basically, Anne Sinclair is the daughter of a well-known local banker with a volatile temper.'' Travis's harsh curse vibrated across the phone lines. ''Lloyd Sinclair, heir to a large manufacturing firm, married her but didn't give up his old girlfriends after the wedding. When drunk, he's an extremely abusive man. Anne was in the hospital several times, but that was kept under wraps, due to the Sinclair clout. No one knew exactly why she finally got up the courage to file for divorce and custody of their daughter, but it all hit the fan when she did. Lloyd dragged her name through the mud in order to gain full custody, and Anne was left with nothing.''

"What about her family? Weren't they around to support her through all this?'' Travis demanded, picturing the events in his mind and not liking what he saw.

"Are you kidding? They were both on Lloyd's side. Probably because the Sinclair money resides in the Williams bank,'' Hank said with a snort of disgust. "In my book, she got a lousy deal all the way down the line.''

"So she shot her ex-husband and kidnapped the kid.''

Hank sighed. "Yeah, and what really happened that night, no one knows. At least, not her side of the story. Lloyd claims she came by to ask for a reconciliation, and when he refused she went crazy, found his gun and shot him. He knows what to say to the right people, but I don't really trust the guy. One of his ex-girlfriends claimed he beat her up and had the bruises to prove it. Then when it came time to go to court, she suddenly backed down, saying she had made it all up. She left town soon after. The man is no good.''

Travis groped for a cigarette and lighted it before leaning back in his chair. The harsh tang of nicotine burning his lungs was more than welcome about then.

"You think she had just cause, don't you?'' he rasped.

"This stays between you and me,'' Hank warned. "But you bet I do. I have an idea Lloyd could have easily pushed her into it, maybe even batted her around a bit, before she got hold of the gun and let him have it. He ended up lucky. A few inches lower, and she would have shot him through the heart.''

Travis frowned, not liking the familiar way Hank seemed to talk about Anne. "You seem to know a lot about her." He wasn't aware that he sounded more accusatory than casual.

"I should. She was hot news around here for quite a while. You couldn't pick up a newspaper without seeing a news story about her." Hank was silent for a moment. "Travis, if you happen to have any information about her..."

"No, I was just curious about Porter and the story he was spreading around. You know me. I don't like anyone I don't know nosing around my town." Travis winced, realizing he came across like television's view of a Western small-town sheriff. "I figured it wouldn't hurt to check up on him."

"Then I'm surprised you didn't do it a week ago," Hank said shrewdly. "As for Anne, I mean it. If you know anything, give me a call. I'm one of the few who's willing to give her a fair shake. She's not helping herself by not coming back and getting this all cleared up. Of course, with the Sinclair family against her, I guess I can't really blame her."

Travis felt sick to his stomach. "I would think after three years a person could be in Mexico or Europe. Look, I'm getting the high sign from my foreman. Why don't I call you in a few weeks and we can talk about another fishing trip?"

"Sounds good to me." Hank appeared to recognize his friend's need for a change of subject. "Give me a call, no matter what. Okay?"

"Yeah."

Travis hung up and sat there staring at the phone for a long time, then slowly rose to his feet. Feeling like a very old man, he walked out to the kitchen, where he found Maude standing at the sink, cutting up vegetables for stew.

"You look as if you just lost your last friend." She watched him pour a cup of coffee and seat himself at the table.

"I only wish it was that easy," he said and sighed.

Maude put down her small knife and rinsed her hands under the faucet, wiping them on her apron. "Does it have something to do with Lee?"

He nodded. "What I'm going to tell you can go no farther than this room. I mean it, Mom."

"Done."

One thing Travis trusted about his mother was her closed mouth. She might like gossip, but she knew when to keep certain subjects to herself. He told her about the private investigator looking for Lee, and his own conversation with Hank.

"Oh, my Lord," Maude breathed, sinking into a chair. "That poor child."

"You're taking her side without even knowing why she did it—if she even is Anne Sinclair."

Maude shot him a sharp look. "Do you believe she is?"

Travis dug into his shirt pocket for the photograph he had kept with him since that day and handed it to her. She studied it carefully for several minutes, and turned it over to read the information written there before handing it back to him.

"The use of some hair color, colored contact lenses, different clothing and she could get away with it," she said. "But the facial features aren't as easily disguised. No wonder she wanted nothing to do with you. She figured you'd put her in jail if you found out who she was. So why didn't you, when you found all this out?"

"Because I have no valid proof she really is Anne Sinclair," he explained. "And if I happened to be wrong, I could be charged with false arrest. Although I'd rather see that happen than find out she really is Anne Sinclair."

Maude's expression said it all. She couldn't remember the last time her son had been wrong where his intuition was concerned. "What are you going to do?"

Travis shook his head, more frustrated with life than he had felt in a long time. "Wish I knew. Somehow I've got to get her to trust me enough to talk about her past. I don't think it's going to be easy."

"Then I suggest you start reading some current magazines," Maude told him. "There've been a lot of articles written about abused women and children."

Travis closed his eyes. Was that why Nikki was so afraid of men? "The thing is, if she really is Anne Sinclair and I have proof, I have to contact the authorities, otherwise I'm in just as much trouble for hiding a fugitive from the law. That's why I need to find out her side of the story before I can do anything. Still, if she had defended herself by shooting him, she should have just told the authorities."

Maude shot him a pitying look. "Travis, you still believe the system works for the wronged party every time. My darling son, it just doesn't. I sure wish you'd get rid of that blind spot of yours before you get badly hurt."

"I'm a lawman and I have to believe it, or I wouldn't be of any use to anyone, would I?"

She nodded, knowing that no matter what, her son would do what was right for the individual, although she feared personal feelings could be involved this time. "You're falling for her, aren't you? You certainly don't believe in doing anything the easy way, do you?"

He slammed his palm on the tabletop so hard that everything bounced, but Maude didn't flicker an eyelid.

"It's a good thing your daughter isn't here to see this horrible display of temper. It might give her ideas she doesn't need. As for Lee, I suggest you start taking her out more, get her to trust you. That's the only way she'll even think about talking about her past. But don't count on it working right away. By the way, you will be subtle, won't you?''

''Of course I will,'' he replied crossly.

''Then ask her out to dinner and a movie. You both survived the dance, didn't you?''

''Yes.'' He gritted his teeth, hating it when his mother treated him as if he were still ten years old, but Maude was blithely talking on.

''Watching two girls is as easy as watching one, so Nikki can stay here. She's a lot more relaxed here than she was the first time. In fact, why not start right now? Give Lee a call. Ask her out for next weekend.''

''Mom, as much as you tend to forget the fact, I am an adult and can make my own dates in my own time,'' he informed her. Still, he stood up and walked out of the kitchen.

''There's a phone here.'' Maude gestured to the one near the back door.

''I'm also adult enough to not require my mother's attendance while I call a lady for a date,'' he frostily informed her.

''Why can't family life be the way it used to be portrayed on TV?'' she murmured, returning to her cooking.

''WELL, LOOKIE HERE!'' Zeke howled with laughter when Travis entered the restaurant. ''Who're the flowers for, Travis? Lorna, the sheriff's come a-courtin','' he shouted toward the rear of the restaurant.

Travis knew his face was bright red as he marched through the dining room with the small bouquet of flowers in his hand. He suddenly wished he had thought of something else, but asking a woman out on a date in front of the gossipy townspeople was new to him.

''Can it, Zeke,'' he growled. ''Or I'll give Wilma back her shotgun.''

"Whoee, who smells so good?" another man chimed in, laughing loudly as he slapped his knee.

Lorna looked up, and a broad smile broke out on her face as she watched Travis seat himself at the counter.

"I guess I can't expect those are for me," Sally teased him as she poured him a cup of coffee.

For a moment Travis panicked. What if Lee wasn't there? He hadn't thought of that.

"Lee will be out in a second to take your order," Sally told him before moving away.

When Lee walked out, she didn't expect to see her newest customer holding a small bouquet of flowers in a delicate vase.

"These are for you," Travis muttered, holding out the vase.

She managed a brief smile as she accepted the offering. "Thank you," she murmured.

Travis grimaced, wishing he had kept trying to get her at home, so he knew he would have to do this while he still had the courage. Or, never hear the end of it from the others.

"I'll just have a burger and fries," he muttered, chickening out again.

She nodded. Lee sensed that he had wanted to say something more, but that something had held him back. "I'll get your burger." With a quizzical expression on her face she walked away to place his order.

"You're batting zero," Fred, a neighboring rancher, teased, as he passed Travis on his way out. "And here we old-timers thought you were one of the smooth ones."

He turned his head and managed to smile. Did everyone but the person involved know what he was clumsily trying to do? "Yeah, well, the movies make it look too easy, Fred."

"If I didn't have to get back home, I'd stay to see how it comes out. Still, I'll know by tonight." The older man clapped him on the shoulder as he left.

Travis took his time eating his hamburger, hoping that everyone would leave, but no luck. Instead, it appeared no one was in any hurry; they all asked for numerous refills on their coffee. By the time Lee left him with his bill, he knew he had to stumble ahead.

"Ah, Lee—" he grimaced "—I was wondering if you'd like to take in a movie this Friday night. My mom said she'd be more than happy to look after Nikki for you."

Lee knew it was dangerous for her to see Travis more than she should, but something deep inside nudged her. She told herself she was only agreeing because she couldn't bear to reject him in front of their avidly listening audience.

"That sounds very nice," she said softly. "I'd like that." Her lips quivered with laughter as she heard the sigh of relief he gave at her reply.

"I guess you could tell I'm out of practice," he whispered as he paid the bill.

"That's all right," she whispered back. "Think of the fodder we've given the town gossips. It will keep them busy for the rest of the afternoon."

LEE SHOULD have known that she couldn't stop with that evening at the dance—not when she was with such a caring man as Travis, who was the perfect escort anywhere they chose to go. After their first public appearance, the town followed the slowly budding romance with watchful eyes.

"Do you realize we've become the talk of the town?" Lee asked Travis one evening, as they walked out of the movie theater in a nearby town.

He grinned. "It's difficult not to."

"But doesn't it bother you?"

Travis shook his head. "Are you kidding? Mom's driving the townspeople crazy by not giving them any good gossip. Right about now I guess we're better than TV." He walked alongside her to his car and unlocked the door. "You want to stop for something to eat before heading back?"

"You certainly can't be hungry after all the popcorn you ate during the movie," she teased.

He smiled, just happy that he made her relax. "Popcorn isn't all that filling. So how about it?"

"Sure, why not?"

Travis found a fast-food restaurant open and they ordered hot dogs and French fries. By unspoken agreement they sat outside in the cool, spring night air.

"It's hard to believe school will be over soon," Lee said with a sigh. "I just wish I knew what I was going to do with Nikki while I work. I asked her if she wanted to take some summer school classes, and she acted as if I had asked her to walk across hot coals."

Travis chuckled. "Susie pretty much got the same suggestion, except it was after I saw her last report card. I admit math has never been my best subject, but I think I did better with the basics than she did."

"I hope Nikki's behaving for Maude." Lee dipped a fry into catsup and nibbled on it.

"The kids worship the ground she walks on, since she promises to allow them to mess up the kitchen, baking all sorts of cakes and cookies. I'm sure they had the time of their lives tonight. In fact, since it's getting so late, why don't you just let her spend the night? Most of the times when we get back, she's already asleep."

"No, I couldn't do that," Lee said swiftly.

"Eat up. You're too skinny." He was used to changing the subject now, in order to keep her from growing too wary of him—just as he kept questions to a minimum and only on a casual basis, in order not to frighten her off. His good-night kisses were kept light and almost impersonal, when all he wanted to do was crush her in his arms and protect her from the world. For his patience he'd gained a woman who smiled more, even when he told her his corniest jokes, and she didn't shy away from his touch when he held her hand in the movies.

"'You can never be too rich nor too thin,'" she quoted.

"Yeah, well, nobody would say that if they saw you. Why do you think Mom cooks all those big meals when you come over for dinner?" Travis swiped one of her fries and dipped it into catsup before offering it to her.

Lee laughed, the sound rich and full before her lips closed on it. When a slight tug from Travis's end caught her attention, she looked up. Her eyes, luminous in the outdoor lighting, caught his and held. For long moments they stared at each other.

Lee knew her body yearned to be closer to Travis, but common sense told her she couldn't take the chance. When a car drove by, stereo sound blasting out through the open windows, the mood was rudely destroyed. Lee's head jerked back, breaking their self-induced trance. She chewed slowly, watching Travis pop the rest of the fry into his own mouth. He acted as if nothing had just happened between them, but from the darkness in his eyes and his flushed features she knew better.

"It's getting late, and we have a long drive back." Lee's voice was raspy with the need she had long denied, but couldn't allow herself to give in to.

Travis gathered up the papers and handed Lee her half-finished cup of soda. She finished it there before tossing it into the trash can. They walked slowly back to the car, both lost in their own thoughts. Travis half turned in the seat, his arm draped across the back.

"If I really kiss you, will you promise not to be frightened of me?" he asked quietly.

Her lips parted slightly, the expression in her eyes giving away her inner feelings.

"I think I gave up feeling frightened of you a long time ago," she whispered, unknowingly admitting she'd once had such a fear. But the doubts reflected in her eyes couldn't be erased as easily.

Travis knew that if he wanted to win her trust, he would have to make each move slowly and carefully and let her set the pace. He brought her palm to his lips.

"Do you know sometimes you watch me as if you're memorizing everything about me?" His breath was warm against her skin. "Although I wouldn't mind if you were watching me because you think I'm the sexiest guy you've ever met."

"You're the kindest man I've ever met," Lee murmured, not realizing she had moved closer to him.

"I guess that's close to being sexy," he said ruefully.

"Even better."

Travis lowered his head and brushed his lips softly against hers several times, until he felt them relax under his touch. Even then he waited another minute before he tried to deepen the kiss. When his tongue slid along her lips, they hesitantly parted, just enough to allow him entrance. He felt a rush of heat in his veins, but quickly tamped it down before he moved too fast and frightened her. He continued tantalizing her with light touches.

"Travis," Lee breathed, tentatively sliding her arms around his waist and moving until their upper bodies lightly touched.

"Lee," he whispered, again and again dipping his tongue into the sweet cavern of her mouth.

Her answer was to take one of his hands and place it against her throat with a trust that almost unnerved him.

Travis's fingers splayed out, the heel of his palm resting in the valley between her breasts. He could feel her breathing deepen as his fingers moved lightly against the bare skin her open collar revealed. The rust wool sweater carried her body heat and her spicy floral fragrance. When he moved his hand to one side to cover her heaving breast, he felt the tension suddenly enter her body. He did nothing more than keep his hand resting lightly on her breast, making no sudden moves as he compared her to a small wild animal who didn't need taming as much as she needed to know she wouldn't be hurt.

Lee wanted to smile with joy at the idea that such a simple caress could leave her wishing for so much more. She wanted to throw herself into Travis's arms and bury her face against his neck, inhaling the clean fragrance of his skin and absorbing his inner strength. She had been alone with her secrets for so long that the need for someone to share them with grew every time she was with him. She buried her face against his neck, feeling the slightly rough skin against her lips.

"I feel safe with you," she whispered. "You don't know how much that means to me."

He chuckled. "Maybe about as much as this means to me." When his mouth lowered to hers this time, he didn't hold back. He wanted her to know how much he desired her, and for the moment it was the only way he could tell her.

Lee's hands dug into his scalp, her fingers combing through the thick strands, allowing his hair to curl around them. She tipped her head to one side when his mouth found her ear and sighed when his tongue darted inside the shell-like orifice. When his hand kneaded her breast, plucking at her nipple until it stood up straight, she felt as if she were melting.

"You're making me think of things not suitable for the mother of a seven-year-old child," she whispered on a sigh.

"That's all right. I'm thinking the same thoughts and I'm a father," he murmured, before kissing her harder and even deeper. "Lee, you're going to have to help me here. If we don't stop soon, we may get involved in some heavy-duty necking in the front seat, and that hasn't been my style for about twenty years."

A soft giggle escaped her lips. "It could be embarrassing for us, couldn't it?"

She drew back first, but Travis wasn't about to allow her to withdraw too far. When he slid back behind the steering wheel, he pulled Lee over to sit close beside him.

"Just because I can't kiss you and drive at the same time doesn't mean you can't sit next to me." He switched on the engine and waited a moment before putting it into gear. He turned on the radio and checked the channels until he found one playing golden oldies. To the sounds of the Beach Boys, he gunned the engine and pulled out of the parking lot.

Lee felt freer than she had in a long time as she and Travis talked and laughed during the forty-minute drive back to his ranch. She saw him as more than the town's law officer now; she saw him as a man she was strongly attracted to. She drove all memories of her past out of her mind as she allowed her thoughts to wander to happier ideas—what life with Travis could be like. Again giving in to impulse, she leaned over and planted a kiss on the corner of his mouth.

"What was that for?" he asked, surprised and pleased by her action.

"Just because you're you," she said happily. "And because you make me feel like a new person."

"Be careful, or I'll drive on past my place to yours, where we can discuss this at greater length," he warned playfully.

"Knowing you, there wouldn't be much talking done." Now she even felt free to tease. "So no driving by. Nikki will be expecting me, no matter how late we are." Her attention was diverted when she noticed streaks of white light race across the dark sky. Her body stiffened. Thunder and lightning always reminded her of the night that had changed her life so drastically. She feared for Nikki, who usually suffered from nightmares in weather such as this. She prayed that this time would be different.

"Hmm, looks like we're in for a big storm," Travis commented, unaware of her sudden withdrawal. When the lightning flashed again, Lee jumped. "You okay? It's just lightning. It can't harm you, as long as you don't stand under a tree." He tried to treat the subject lightly, hoping to help her to relax.

"I guess I'm worried about Nikki." She was glad she didn't have to lie about that. "She's never liked thunder storms."

"Maude's with her," he assured her.

But that didn't comfort Lee at all.

Travis had barely stopped the car in front of the house when Maude, a harried expression on her face, stepped out onto the porch. Lee felt a cold shiver race across her spine as she got out of the car and heard a child's screams echo from the house.

"I don't know what happened." The older woman looked helpless. "She fell asleep on Susie's other bed, then she woke up screaming a little while ago, and won't allow me near her."

Lee barely heard the words. She was racing inside the house and down the hall, where she found her daughter cowering in a corner of the room, while a frightened looking Susie sat up in bed watching her friend. The little girl looked up when her father and grandmother appeared in the doorway.

"We both woke up because of the thunder," Susie burst out, looking ready to cry, as well. "She wouldn't stop crying, and I didn't know what to do." She looked miserable because she couldn't help her friend.

But Lee knew what to do. Past experience had taught her that. She sat on the floor, holding her daughter in her lap as the little girl clung to her with a death grip, begging her not to leave her.

Chapter Eleven

By the time Lee had Nikki calmed down and back in bed under the warm covers, she felt so exhausted that she could barely walk out to the den. There she found Travis seated in his favorite easy chair, drinking what appeared to be whiskey from a squat, heavy glass. She was stunned when she looked at the clock and saw that more than two hours had passed since she had first entered the house. Maude, seated on the couch where she was mending a pair of Susie's jeans, put her work aside and stood up.

"I put a robe and clean towels in the bathroom. I want you to take a long, hot bath," she ordered, walking over to Lee and putting an arm around her. She held up her hand when Lee opened her mouth. "No arguments. That little girl is exhausted, and so are you. You can sleep in the guest room." She guided Lee out of the room and down the hall. A few moments later Maude returned to the den. "Are you going to wait up for her?"

Travis nodded, still concentrating on his glass.

"Then I'll say good-night," Maude said quietly. "Just remember, it's been as rough a night for her as it was for Nikki."

"I will."

Lee opted for a hot shower instead of a bath, for fear she'd fall asleep if she relaxed in a tub. After pulling on the fleece robe Maude had left out for her, she looked down the hall, noting that the den light was still on. Her first thought was to escape to the guest room, because she didn't know if she could talk to anyone, especially Travis, but something prodded her toward the den. She found him still seated, the one light burning next to his chair. The rest of the room was in darkness, except for periodic flashes of lightning. Lee stiffened at first as memories threatened to overwhelm her. Steeling herself, she walked into the room. Travis looked up.

"Would you like a drink?"

"No, thank you," she murmured, continuing across the room to the large window.

"It happened on a night just like this," she murmured, not even knowing if she was talking to herself or to the man watching her so closely. She rubbed her hands up and down her arms to combat the chill that had stolen into her bones, despite the hot shower. She stood there, staring out the rain-lashed window.

"What did?" His voice was so quiet that it barely reached her ears.

"The night I shot my ex-husband."

Travis sat very still. "You told me you're a widow," he said in a quiet voice.

"No, but I wish I was."

"Well, if you shot him, you must have had a good reason to do it. You don't seem the type to do something just for the hell of it." He kept his voice low, every sense on alert as he sat in the chair watching her. She stood in front of the dark glass, staring at the white-hot flashes of light in the sky as if they had induced a hypnotic trance.

"True, I'm the type to avoid altercations. But I learned that night that when you realize you're going to be killed, you tend to do everything possible to protect yourself," she explained, her voice holding no emotion whatsoever. "After what I had been through, death would have been a blessing, except that there was Nikki. I knew I couldn't let her go through that same kind of hell. Lloyd had hit her. She was so tiny then, so gentle and sweet. She couldn't have survived it. I had to take her away.'' She reached up, running her hands through the tangled waves of her still-damp hair.

"Did your husband beat you, Lee?''

She laughed, but there was no mirth in the sound. "Let me explain. My real name is Anne Sinclair. My ex-husband is Lloyd Sinclair of Sinclair Manufacturing, Houston, Texas. When I first met him, I was convinced I had met Prince Charming. I received red roses every day, he flew me to New York for dinner and a play one evening. He treated me as if I was someone very special. And when he proposed, I wanted out of my home life so badly that I didn't stop to think. I just said yes and unknowingly went from one living hell to another. You see, my father is a bank president with a very nasty habit. When he had problems at work, he brought them home and took them out on my mother and me with his fists. Not a pretty story, is it? Although nowadays it doesn't seem to be all that uncommon.''

Travis swallowed the nausea rising in his throat. He wanted nothing more than to jump up and hold her in his arms. He wanted to banish all the evil, but he knew he had to sit there until Lee had said all she wanted to say.

"Didn't your mother ever try to fight back or leave him?''

She shook her head, feeling the past begin to smother her, but she fought it. "No. You see, she felt it was all my fault. She used to enjoy telling me she hadn't wanted children, and if she could have gotten rid of me, she would have. So she didn't care what my father did to me, as long as he left her alone.''

Travis paused to light a cigarette, disconcerted to find his hands shaking as he lifted the lighter. "Did he ever try anything other than hitting you?"

Lee laughed bitterly. "No, Clinton Williams just liked to beat his daughter until she cried for mercy. I guess I should be grateful for that."

He drew the acrid smoke deep into his lungs. "Did he mind your getting married?"

She continued looking out into the night as if she could find all the answers there. She stood still as a statue, her figure an ethereal reflection in the glass. Her mind was numb, as were her emotions. She knew that if she allowed herself to feel the least bit of emotion, she would break down in a way she had never allowed herself. "Since the Sinclair fortune was in his bank, he didn't mind one bit. His advice to me was not to screw it up, or he'd make me pay for it."

"But?"

"But no one told me that Lloyd was an abusive alcoholic," she replied softly, her lips twisted. "Do you understand that term? Of course, you would, wouldn't you? I'm sure most law enforcement officers have dealt with a few in their time."

"Someone who can't hold their liquor and turns mean when they drink," Travis replied woodenly.

She nodded. "That was Lloyd. I first learned the meaning of the term on my wedding night. Quite an auspicious beginning, wouldn't you say? My new husband had too much champagne during the reception, and by the time we got to our hotel, he was going on about how he was going to show me the kind of wife he wanted." She rested her forehead against the cool glass, perversely seeking to chill still more of her already cold body.

Travis's breath hissed between his teeth. He closed his eyes to the visions running through his head. If Lloyd Sinclair had stood there before him, he knew he would have killed the man with his bare hands.

"To his way of thinking, I wasn't the perfect wife," she continued. "I seemed to be always doing something wrong, whether it was dinner being served five minutes late, or his favorite shirt didn't come back from the laundry in time for a certain occasion." Her voice dropped to a pain-filled whisper. "The only time he didn't hit me was when I was pregnant. Probably because his father wanted a grandchild so badly and was the only person Lloyd feared. After all, he could have cared less if he had a family. When I first told him I was pregnant, he told me all he wanted from me was someone to entertain his clients and be in his bed. Nothing else mattered." She held on to one of the draperies as if it were a lifeline, something to keep her in the present, even as the past threatened to drag her back into that black pit. Her hand tightened, then released the heavy fabric.

Travis groped for his pack of cigarettes and lighted another, breathing in deeply. "And then Nikki was born."

Her smile returned to her voice. "Oh yes, my Nikki. Her real name is Nicola Marie Sinclair. She was such a beautiful baby. I'm sure I'm prejudiced, but she was always so happy and never cried. Lloyd liked that, since he didn't like his sleep disturbed." Her voice lost its joy when she mentioned his name again. "Her two grandfathers weren't happy that I didn't give them a grandson. They conveniently forgot that it's the man's genes that provide the sex of the child. In their eyes I could do no right." A tear appeared at the corner of one eye. "Yet that didn't stop them from trying to spoil her. As for Lloyd, I was to hand her over to a nanny and be his hostess again. The only blessing was that he had a mistress, one of many in the course of our marriage, and pretty much left me alone, except for his tries to get me pregnant again. His father still demanded a grandson, to be groomed for the family business, and Lloyd was determined to give him one, no matter how I felt about the subject.''

"How did you find out about the other women?" Travis asked, watching her tiny figure standing so straight and tall as she continued with the story that she must have known could send her to prison for many years.

"His current one came to see me. She was convinced if I gave Lloyd a divorce he would marry her. When I told him about her visit, and that if he wanted a divorce, I wouldn't stand in his way, he grew angry, as if it was all my fault. The battle was short and not very sweet, and the girlfriend was never heard of again. A year later I knew I couldn't take any more of his cruelty, so I filed for divorce." She stroked the folds of the drapery absently, apparently using it again as that desperately needed lifeline. "Naturally, Lloyd acted like the wronged husband. He even went so far as to warn me I would lose Nikki, and that my reputation would be shredded beyond repair if I continued with the proceedings."

Travis lighted yet another cigarette, even though he hadn't finished with the one he had. "Why didn't you just get out then?" he asked in a hoarse voice. "You could have filed for your divorce from another state. The law was on your side, Lee, not his."

She shrugged. "When you're convinced you're the wronged party and will see justice served, you're not afraid of anything or anyone. I should have known better, when I had so much trouble finding an attorney who would even consider my case. In the end I had a young man fresh out of an Eastern law school, who had no idea of the Sinclairs' power. Their attorneys chewed him up into little pieces and spat him out. I even told both sets of parents everything Lloyd had done to me over the years, to make them understand why I was divorcing him. My father said that I probably deserved it, that I always was a headstrong child and needed a firm hand.'' She almost choked on the words. ''And Joshua Sinclair said that Lloyd might be a little hotheaded at times, but he knew his son loved me.'' Now she sounded bitter. ''They dared to call the beastly way I was treated love! Well, I learned my lesson quickly. Lloyd fought for custody and won, after he brought in scores of men stating I'd had affairs with them and used drugs. I was branded an unfit mother and he gained full custody. I wasn't even allowed visiting privileges.'' She held up her head, breathing deeply to calm herself.

''Lee, what about the night you shot him? What happened then?'' He forced himself to keep his voice even, because his intuition told him that every word he'd heard so far was the truth. ''Can you talk about it?''

She cleared her throat. ''Lloyd called me that night. There was a terrible thunderstorm, and Nikki was having trouble going to sleep. He demanded I come over and calm her down. I went, because I hoped to talk to him about working out an alternate custody arrangement. I knew he didn't want her. He just wanted to use her as a tool to hurt me. I found liquor bottles all over the house and a woman in the living room. Nikki was in the bedroom, screaming the way she was tonight. I calmed her down and got her back to sleep, but I also noticed a bruise on her cheek and I knew that he had hit her. I wasn't about to put up with that. The woman was gone when I sought out Lloyd and found him in his study. I tried to talk to him about Nikki, but his answer was always the same. No. Unfortunately I made a big mistake. I lost my temper and told him exactly what I thought of him. He grew even angrier and started hitting me. Nikki woke up and ran into the room, pulling on him and demanding he leave me alone. He hit her again, and I screamed for her to go back to her bedroom. Luckily she obeyed me.'' She closed her eyes, clearly reliving those last few minutes of her old life. Her body tensed, as if those blows were again being directed at her.

"Lee, you don't have to go on with this," Travis interjected swiftly. He felt he had to warn her about what she was doing. "You don't realize—"

She held up her hand. "Yes, I do." Her voice was strong with conviction. "What I'm telling you will lock me away for the rest of my life and send Nikki back to hell. I always knew I couldn't run forever, and I guess this is as good a place as any to end it. But first I want someone to hear my side of the story, because otherwise it won't have a chance to be told."

Travis swallowed a lump in his throat. "What happened next?"

Lee shook her head, for the first time looking bleak. "I'm not exactly sure what happened. I do remember I was bent backward over his desk with his hands around my throat, choking me. I groped in his top desk drawer, looking for a letter opener, anything to use as a weapon. I only meant to use it to get him away from me. I guess I found the gun and it went off. The next thing I knew, I was standing over him with the weapon in my hand. At first I thought I had killed him, until I saw that he was still breathing. After that I didn't stop to think. I just grabbed Nikki and put her in the car, then called 911, saying I'd heard shots. Although I'm certain if the positions had been reversed, he would have let me die." Her body trembled violently.

"Why didn't you wait for the police and tell them what happened? It was a clear-cut case of self-defense," Travis pointed out, leaning forward in the chair, his arms resting on his thighs. "You and Nikki had the bruises to prove he abused you."

She laughed bitterly. "Maybe I had that kind of proof, but Joshua Sinclair had the connections, and he never forgave me for daring to divorce his son. He would have made sure I was locked up for the rest of my life, and Nikki would have been poisoned against me, or turned into a battered child without any hope of a normal life. I couldn't allow that to happen. So we've been on the run for more than three years. There're private detectives after us, I'm sure, because the Sinclair family wouldn't allow me to get away with what I did, and because they want Nikki back.'' Slowly she turned, the pain and suffering she had gone through evident in her eyes. ''I wouldn't have had a chance, Travis.''

''You don't know that, because you didn't give anyone a chance to help you,'' he argued.

''I know the family. I also know I'll eventually be caught, and then I'll fight for the truth to be known. I'll lose, but I won't go down quietly.'' Slowly she walked toward him, her head still held high. ''I'm a fugitive from the law, and as the town sheriff, I understand you will have to lock me up. All I ask is that you do everything possible to help Nikki. She remembers so little from those early years, and it's only been recently that she's begun to be the happy child I want her to be. Please find a way to protect her.''

Travis reached out and pulled her into his lap, wrapping his arms around her.

Lee was so weak from her confession that she didn't bother to struggle. She curled up against his warmth and slipped her arms around his neck, burrowing her face against the slightly rough skin. When warm droplets hit her cheek she tilted back her head. She brushed her fingers across his cheek and turned them around—to find them wet.

''You're crying,'' she murmured.

''Men don't cry,'' he said huskily.

''But you are.'' She stared into his eyes, eyes gleaming with moisture. ''You do believe me, don't you?''

"You told me a story that can put you away for many years, but all you care about is the welfare of your child," Travis said in a raw voice. "You've been led to believe your very existence is all your fault, yet you turned into one of the warmest, most loving women I have ever met. You're a very special lady." He wrapped one hand around her nape and brought her face against his chest.

For the longest time they sat in the chair, forgetting about cramping limbs and the storm overhead. All that mattered was Lee's ability to finally trust someone, and that Travis not only believed her, but called her special.

"Travis?" Lee's voice sounded sleepy. Her confession had sapped her strength.

"What?" He knew he should carry her into the guest room and let her sleep in a comfortable bed.

"I don't want you to do anything that will get you into trouble. I understand that I'll have to go to jail now, until you can contact the proper authorities."

He smiled in spite of himself. "Are you that determined to be put behind bars?"

"No, but I did shoot him and kidnap Nikki. Those offenses don't exactly merit a slap on the wrist."

He ran a hand over her hair, tangling his fingers in the silky strands. "Why don't you just relax and let me handle this, okay? I promise no harm is going to come to you."

She breathed deeply and exhaled. "Okay."

Travis stood up and with her still cradled in his arms, carried her into the guest room and laid her on the bed. After he draped the covers over her, he sat down on the edge of the bed, pulled off his boots and settled down on the other side, drawing Lee back into his arms. As if they had lain together many times, she automatically curled against him, laying her head on his shoulder.

The last words she heard before falling into a deep sleep were, "Don't worry, Anne, I'm on your side."

IT WAS THE SMELL of freshly brewed coffee that tempte Lee out of her warm bed and into a quick shower.

"They're right. Confession is good for the soul," sh murmured as she brushed the tangles from her hair, awar she felt freer than she had in a long time. Yet for just moment she couldn't help but wonder if she had made a big mistake in confiding in Travis. Her stomach burned wit fear and it took her several minutes to calm her racin pulse. Before she dared dwell on it anymore, she quickl left the bathroom.

Maude was sitting at the kitchen table drinking coffe when Lee entered the room. The older woman smiled an gestured toward the coffee maker. "It's freshly made." Sh rose to her feet. "How about some breakfast?"

Lee felt the way Alice did when she fell down the hole "I—didn't Travis tell you?" she asked, a note of despera tion in her voice.

Maude pulled out two pans and soon had eggs frying i one and sausage in another. "Yes, he told me everything.

Lee felt a chill trickle down her spine as she realized tha the house sounded suspiciously silent. "Where's Nikki? Her question ended on a frightened squeak. Was she to los her daughter so quickly?

"She and Susie are out with one of the hands. Don worry, she's perfectly safe," Travis's mother assured he When the food was ready, Maude set the plate in front o her. "Now I want to see you eat every bite. You're muc too thin."

"That's what Travis says," Lee murmured.

Maude sat down again and pulled her coffee cup in fron of her. "Lee, or shall I say, Anne, I want you to know tha I understand why you did what you did. It shows a grea deal of unselfish love that you looked out more for you daughter than yourself. I just hope you're prepared for battle to keep Nikki and prove you were an innocent vi tim. I've always believed in being blunt. You're not going to have an easy time ahead of you. My son tends to believe that justice will protect the right and convict the wrong. It's one of his failings, but I have to love him for wanting to see life that way. I only wish it were true. Still, you're going to have to be strong. Are you ready for that?"

"I've always been prepared," Lee said firmly.

Maude eyed her keenly. "Yes, I'm sure you are," she said, then added briskly, "Eat your food, before it gets cold. We have some things to think over. And from now on I'm calling you Anne. It's time you reverted to your real self. What about that hair of yours? Surely that can't be your real color?" She didn't want to tell Anne that she had seen a picture of her, until Travis broke the news about the investigator.

Anne grimaced. "It's a temporary rinse that washes out after so many shampoos."

"And what about your eye color?"

"Extended wear contact lenses."

Maude handed her a napkin. "We may as well begin now."

Anne bent over, using her fingers to stretch her eyes wide open, and brown discs dropped onto the napkin. Maude picked up the paper and tossed it into the trash.

"You won't need those any longer."

"But I have to work in town," Anne protested, seeing her disguise so carelessly discarded. "Everyone will know I'm not who they think I am."

Maude put her fingers under her chin and lifted her face, looking into vibrant green eyes. "My dear, you can't understand everything just now, but you will. Now, eat up, because after you finish your breakfast, we're going to wash that horrible color out of your hair. Let's see if we can find the real you, shall we?"

With Maude's enthusiastic assistance and half a bottle of shampoo, the brown hair color finally trickled down the drain. Anne was ordered to walk down to the barn to see Travis. She felt naked, walking out into the open with her strawberry-blond hair brushed back from her face in a casual style and her eyes their natural color.

When she reached the barn, she stood in the doorway until she heard sounds from the rear. Taking a deep breath to bolster her courage, she stepped carefully through the strewn hay until she found Travis in the rear stall, grooming the bay gelding he usually rode.

"Travis." She bit her lip, unsure how to approach him.

He looked up, smiled, then froze when he saw the woman standing before him. The clothing was the same as that she'd worn last night, but the face appeared different, the skin more translucent. Then he realized she must have worn a darker makeup base to go with the darker hair color. Her eyes were now a gemlike green, her thick hair the color of a rich sunset with red and blond strands blended in profusion. What he had seen in the photograph was a mere shadow compared to the real thing. She had a face he couldn't easily forget.

"I always knew you were pretty, but now you are so beautiful that you make my eyes ache," he said quietly.

She hesitated for a moment before moving closer to him. Travis reached out and drew her into a warm embrace.

"You should hate me," she mumbled against his shirt front.

"Why?" He kissed the top of her hair.

"Because I'm a liar, a fugitive, so many other things can't begin to count."

Travis rubbed his cheek against the top of her head. "You can say all you want, and I'll just come up with positive points. Did you eat anything?"

She smiled. "Do you honestly think Maude would allow me to leave the house without eating? She was also the one who made me take out the contact lenses and wash the color out of my hair. I swear my scalp is raw from all the shampooings she made me endure. She's a very strong-minded lady."

He chuckled. "Tell me about it." He nuzzled her ear and murmured, "Hold on to your hat, lady, because I intend to give you a kiss that says a heil of a lot more than good-morning."

Anne lifted her face as Travis sought out her mouth. His tongue darted between her parted lips, showing a passion she hadn't received from him before. Under his touch, she felt freer than she ever had in her life. Her hands roamed up and down his back, feeling the fabric that was damp from his exertions. The warm smells of horse, leather and man filled her nostrils, and she couldn't imagine anything smelling better.

"I don't feel like the same person anymore," she murmured against his mouth.

He grasped her around the waist and pulled her off her feet. "That's because you aren't," he pointed out. "You're no longer the Anne Sinclair from three years ago, nor are you Lee Davis, but you are the best of both women. Anne, I would never hurt you. You know that, don't you?" he insisted.

She smiled. "You've certainly been persistent enough to prove that to me."

Travis released her just a little, so that she slid down his body. "I'm going to do everything I can to help you through this."

"You're trusting me too much," she protested. "You don't know what they're saying about me. How can you believe me so easily?"

"For one very good reason." He brushed a stray lock of hair from her face. "A private investigator was in my office a while back, looking for Anne and Nicola Sinclair, and had a picture."

"You never said anything," she breathed, stunned by his casual announcement.

He rubbed her back between her shoulder blades. "Why should I? There was no guarantee that Lee Davis was Anne Sinclair."

"I'm surprised he didn't talk to anyone else," Anne mused.

"He did."

She was stunned by his revelation. "What?"

He grinned, clearly pleased with himself. "I told the people they weren't to give out any information, and they went along with it. Lorna sent you out on errands, so you weren't in the restaurant, in case he came around, which he did."

"And no one said anything." Anne couldn't believe it. "These people don't even know me."

He smiled. "Yes, they do. They knew enough about you to protect you. I know it sounds corny, but we do protect our own here. And you're one of us, Anne."

She hugged Travis so tightly that she was positive she almost cracked his ribs. "I wish I knew what to say. Nikki once asked me if we could always stay in Dunson, because she felt safe here. Now I truly understand how she felt."

He gently pushed her back a step so he could look down into her face. "You trusted me enough to tell me about your past. Do you trust me enough to help you with your present and future?"

Anne looked into his eyes and saw that Travis really believed that everything would be all right. She sadly wondered how a man so worldly in some ways could be so naive in others.

"Oh, Travis, I only wish it could be that easy," she said with a sigh.

He opened his mouth, prepared to argue with her, but was thwarted before he could say anything.

"Break clean, you two," Maude's voice called out. "The girls are coming in, and I don't want them to get more of an education than they need at this tender age."

Travis cursed under his breath. He held Anne close to him as he worked to regain his equilibrium.

"My mother has an incredible sense of timing." He dug his fingers gently into her scalp and tilted back her head. "Think you're ready to start facing people as yourself?"

"It appears I have no choice."

"I'm not trying to push you into anything you don't want to do," he insisted. "But you can't hide forever, Anne. You'll have to face them sooner or later."

"You may be right, but I also have my daughter to consider. And if it means running again to keep her safe, I will." Her face was stony with resolve, but Travis refused to allow her to even think of such a thing.

His fingertip brushed across her lower lip. "All running away will get you is another searcher, and where they've failed, I won't."

Chapter Twelve

"Mornin' Anne. You're lookin' pretty chipper today," Zeke greeted her as he accepted the cup of coffee she put in front of him.

"The sun's shining, my daughter is getting excellent grades in school, and I found a penny on the sidewalk this morning, so I'm not doing too badly," she replied pertly. "How about you? You behaving yourself?"

"Wilma won't let me do anything else but," he grumbled good-naturedly. "Why don't you give me some of Lorna's beef stew and dumplings?"

Anne nodded. "Right away." As she moved away to drop off the order, she silently marveled at the way the townspeople had so easily accepted the truth about her. From the first day she had walked into the restaurant, everyone had called her by her true name and acted as if she had always been a strawberry blonde! It was as if Lee Davis had never existed. It hadn't been until she sat down and talked with Lorna that she learned just how closemouthed Dunson's residents could be. She was informed that no P.I. was going to get any information out of anyone there. Since then she had lived each day to its fullest, blossoming under Travis's tender regard and the townspeople's easy acceptance of her.

"Hey, Anne." Cal ambled inside and seated himself at the counter.

"Hi, Cal. Where's Mary Ellen? Couldn't she take her lunch hour with you today?" Anne had gotten used to seeing the two come in most days for lunch in the past few weeks.

He flushed and ducked his head. "She's—eating at home today," he muttered.

Her smile dimmed. "Cal, take it from someone who's been there. She isn't worth it. You just go out there and find someone who will really appreciate you, and not only pay attention to you when there isn't anyone else around. Show her she isn't the only girl in town."

He brightened, beginning to look hopeful. "You think so?"

"I know so," Anne said firmly. "You've got a lot going for you." She leaned down to confide, "In fact, didn't I see Carrie Nash looking your way last weekend at the church social? Why, I bet if you asked her out to a movie or something, she'd agree."

Cal considered her words. "I guess I couldn't lose anything by asking."

"And, Cal, if Mary Ellen sees you with other girls and tries to get you back, start thinking about the way she's kept you dangling for so long," Anne advised. "Ask yourself if she's really worth it."

He grinned broadly. "You know, you're right. I've let her lead me around by the nose for quite a while now. In fact, I'm not even going to stop by the bakery tomorrow. And I'll call Carrie when I get back to the station. Thanks."

"No problem. So, what would you like to eat?"

"To be honest, I'd like to see Mary Ellen eat a very large portion of crow."

"I HEARD you're playing Dear Abby now," Travis teased Anne as they relaxed with their after-dinner coffee. Maude had agreed to baby-sit while they went out for dinner at a steak house in a neighboring town.

"So Cal did it," she said happily. "Good for him."

He nodded. "He called Carrie Nash up and talked to her for a solid half hour before asking her out to a movie. I'm sure word will get out pretty fast that this time Cal dropped Mary Ellen, instead of the other way around."

She frowned. "Isn't Cal going a little far?"

"Cal? That was Myrna's idea. She's never been too fond of Mary Ellen. She feels the kid's too full of herself." He chuckled. "I have an idea this is going to get pretty interesting."

"As long as Cal can hold out against Mary Ellen, if she starts coming around again."

"He'll definitely hold out. Everyone knows Carrie's had a crush on him since high school and never thought she'd have a chance. Now that she does, I'm sure she's going to do everything possible to hold on to him," Travis explained.

"Everyone knew about Carrie's crush?" Anne shook her head, laughing softly. "Tell me, are there any secrets in a small town?"

His dark eyes warmed her from across the table. "A few, but usually there aren't any all that well kept."

She knew exactly the few he talked about. When Travis laid a hand on the table, palm up, Anne reached out to cover it with one of her own, feeling his fingers close over hers.

"Tell me about the past three years," Travis said softly, rubbing his fingertips along the back of her hand. He felt safe in discussing it, since the tables around them were empty, and he sensed this might be the time to get her to talk about it more.

Anne trembled, whether from his touch or his question she wasn't sure.

"There's not much to tell," she murmured, feeling the old burning in her stomach that she thought had gone away forever.

He smiled, sensing her distress, but knowing he had to push. He knew he couldn't help unless he had the complete background. "Then the story won't be a long one, will it?"

She sighed. She was more than well aware of how stubborn Travis could be, and this appeared to be a time she couldn't evade the subject. "I won't bother giving you the names of towns we've been in, because I've forgotten most of them. As for jobs, they were basically minimum wage or less, because they were the only ones I could get without references. Most of the time I was a waitress, but I also worked in bakeries and stocked supplies in a hardware store. You name it, I did it. I was fired from my first two jobs as a waitress because I was so incompetent, but I finally got the hang of it and I think I turned out pretty well." She smiled wanly. "At least Lorna thinks so."

But Travis wasn't smiling. He leaned over to tamp out the cigarette he had been smoking, then grasped her hand between both of his. He needed to hold on to her and could only hope she felt the same way. "And that's how the two of you have gotten by all this time?"

She shook her head. "Not entirely. In the beginning, I once hid in a women's shelter for about a week, when one of Lloyd's detectives was too close on my heels. The people there didn't ask any questions, because most of them had been in the same boat. Actually it helped, knowing I wasn't alone. I also learned one very important thing."

"What was that?" He stared at her hair; she had pulled it up into a loose twist on top of her head, with several tendrils hanging down by her ears and caressing her nape. He badly needed to concentrate on something other than the bleakness in her normally bright eyes.

"Because my parents were abusers it didn't mean I had to be one, too," she murmured, lifting her head. "You don't know how frightened I used to be that one day I would lose my temper for no reason at all and strike out at Nikki. I once saw a program that mentioned the high percentage of abused children who turned into abusers themselves. I frightened myself so badly that I almost shipped Nikki back, but a counselor there assured me that didn't mean I would turn into one, especially if I had gone through everything I had without ever physically hurting Nikki."

"Did you tell her everything about your past?" He ached from listening to what she'd gone through and wishing he could have been there to help her.

Anne shook her head. "She knew I left my ex-husband and probably suspected I had kidnapped Nikki, but she never questioned me. Do you know there are actually underground railroads for women like me? People who actually help us stay safe. Can you believe it?"

"But you didn't make use of them." It was more a statement than a question.

"No, I was given a couple of phone numbers, but I felt the need to do it on my own. Although there were some days when I just wanted to crawl into a corner and hide, because I had no idea what I was going to do." Her voice dropped to a bare whisper.

Travis's features tightened at the thought of what she must have gone through. "Just tell me something. How did you get Nikki into school without arousing any suspicion, when she had no papers?"

"I have a fake birth certificate for her. Actually, one of the women in the shelter helped me obtain it. I don't know how she did it and I guess I didn't want to. It cost me my diamond and sapphire ring, but it was worth it, because I wasn't about to let her go without an education because of me. I did worry about what would happen when she reached high school. I guess I hoped and prayed that by then my days of running would be over, and she would be settled somewhere." She hated to tell him all this, since so much of it was considered illegal. She also disliked talking about the past, because she sometimes felt as if it held on to her with a grip guaranteed to never release her. There were nights when Anne walked the floors of the silent house, wondering if she wouldn't be better running away, but each time the dark thought came to mind, so did Travis's promise. And she knew he spoke the truth; no matter what happened, he would find her. "As of now I only have a couple of pieces of jewelry left, which I can only use in an extreme emergency."

Travis couldn't help but notice the tension in her body and traces of fear that still skittered across her eyes. He wanted to see it gone forever and would do anything in his power to do just that. His next words were meant to relax her. "Obviously, your car wasn't an extreme emergency."

Anne grimaced at his gentle teasing. "It was beginning to turn into one, until a certain mechanic turned up."

Travis looked around and realized they were one of the last diners present. He quickly took care of the check and walked Anne outside to his car. They remained quiet during the drive back to her house. When he pulled into her driveway, he cut the engine and turned in the seat to face her.

"Your days of running are over," he insisted harshly. "They're over in more ways than one, if I have anything to say about it. You're not alone any longer."

Hearing the intensity in his voice Anne looked up, finding herself caught in his liquid brown gaze. Very slowly her head tipped to one side and her eyes drooped shut as his mouth brushed across hers, then hardened when he sensed her receptivity. Travis leaned back against the driver's door and pulled her close, his hand cradling her breast in a loving hold as his thumb rubbed the peaking nipple. She moaned softly, a sound more of desire than fear.

"Am I frightening you?" he murmured, trailing nibbling kisses along her jaw.

"No," she breathed, convinced she saw stars behind her closed eyelids.

"I enjoy kissing you because you taste so good." His tongue traced the delicate arch of her eyebrow, then returned to her mouth.

This time she more than welcomed its evocative thrust, as they snuggled together for what seemed like hours, although it could have only been minutes. To Anne, feeling Travis's arms around her and returning his kisses gave her more pleasure than she had ever known before. From the back of her mind came the whisper of a word for the way Travis made her feel, but she ignored it. As she shifted her body, she felt his arousal and shied away.

Travis groaned inwardly, but sensing her withdrawal, gritted his teeth and ordered his body to behave. With great reluctance, he straightened up, keeping her in a loose embrace. He knew the best way to temper the situation, though he couldn't help wondering if this was the proper time to bring up his idea. Then he decided he would just have to take a chance.

"Anne, we have to plan some strategy."

She immediately knew what he meant. Her body tensed in his arms and she began to pull away, but he tightened his embrace so that she couldn't easily escape. But that didn't stop her from turning her face away, while her rigid posture told him she didn't want to listen to anything he had to say.

"Yes, I'm sure the reward money Lloyd is offering for my capture would more than buy that new bull you need so badly, wouldn't it?" She allowed her bitterness full rein. "Better yet, bypass that detective. I can give you Lloyd's number. Just be sure he has the money with him when you turn me in. He likes to play dirty pool."

"What do you think you're saying?" he shouted, grasping her by the arms and shaking her roughly. When he saw her eyes widen, he cursed and pulled her back against him. "Damn, I didn't mean to frighten you," he groaned. "I care for you too much to want to hurt you."

"That's what caring is all about, isn't it?" Tears laced her words. "Hurt and pain. You lost your wife early in your marriage, and I'm certain she wasn't ready to die. I lost my dignity. Is it really worth all that kind of agony?"

"Anne, you're making me crazy." He sighed, refusing to loosen his hold on her, no matter how much she struggled. "No, love doesn't always mean pain. Yes, I loved Julie and yes, it hurt when she died, because her death was a senseless one. But that was a long time ago, and I've gone on with my life. I've had to, because looking back didn't give me anything, and because I knew she would have wanted me to. Just as I would have wanted her to continue, if I had been the first one to go."

"And because of her you haven't remarried."

"That isn't the reason and you know it," he declared.

In the darkness her eyes burned like two glittering gemtones. "I have no future, Travis," she told him in a hard voice, her posture as distant as if she were a thousand miles away. "I shot my ex-husband, kidnapped my child and took her over several state lines. The time will come when I'm caught and it will be all over. No matter how many times I tell myself everything will work out all right, deep down I know differently. And so do you."

"So you get a good lawyer," he persisted, refusing to allow her to think so negatively.

Anne again shook her head, her expression sullen; Travis didn't know the Sinclair family the way she did. "A good lawyer would not take the case because of the power my ex-husband's family has in Texas. Not to mention the fact that I don't have the money to hire a top-notch lawyer."

"I have money put away," Travis insisted. "You'll have your chance."

"No, that's meant for your bull, and I wouldn't take it, even if it wasn't." Her eyes still burned with her resolve. "Travis, please, don't say any more. I'll pick Nikki up tomorrow after breakfast." She twisted away and grasped the door handle, opening it and getting out before Travis could stop her.

"Anne!" He quickly scrambled out of the car to catch up with her, but she had already slipped inside the house. His first instinct was to pound on the door until she let him in. Instead, he knocked and spoke her name softly.

"Please, Travis, no more." She sounded weary. "All we do is argue about this subject."

He closed his eyes and rested his forehead against the cold wood. "What if I told you that the last thing I want to do with you is argue? That I want to make love with you?" But there was only silence on the other side. He waited a few more minutes, sensing Anne was still standing just inside, but when he heard nothing, he finally placed his palms against the door for a moment, then walked away, his head down.

Anne stood by the window, watching Travis leave. For a moment she was tempted to walk outside and stop him, but she couldn't. The past still held on to her with a firm hand.

Travis was in no mood to go home. He drove out of town on back roads until he came to a dead end, stopped and got out. Standing by the open door, he spun around, slam

ning the top of the car with his fist. While the impact left
a burning sensation across his hand, it didn't help.

"What in the hell does it take for her to understand how
much she means to me?" he rasped. "Why won't she believe that I only want the best for her? I want a chance to
learn if she is the one."

Deep down he felt she was. He stood in the cold night air,
reliving every moment they had spent together. The more
he stood there and thought about Anne, the more convinced he became that he had to talk to her again. And he
wasn't about to wait until morning.

ANNE COULDN'T SLEEP. Every nerve in her body was quiv-
ering, and she knew why. All she and Travis had done this
evening was skirt the real issue. If they were to see each
other any longer, they would have to consider the next step.
And by every gesture, every word, she'd basically told him
he wasn't ready. Or was she?

"I really haven't given him much of a chance," she told
herself, rolling over onto her side and punching her pillow
for what was probably the hundredth time. She sighed.
"Except I don't want him to be in any trouble because of
me." She rolled over onto her back, staring up at the ceiling. She'd begun counting sheep when she heard pebbles
being thrown at her window. She slipped out of bed and
drew on her robe as she walked over to the window. She
wasn't surprised to find Travis on the other side.

"What do you think you're doing?" she whispered furiously, pushing up the window. She wrapped her robe
tighter around her to guard against the night's chill.

"I thought this was a romantic way to get your attention." He grasped the windowsill and pulled himself up and
inside.

Travis straightened, feeling a nasty strain in his back as
he turned around to close the window. "I'm too old for this

stuff." He stood still, a few inches from her. "I'll be hon
est with you, Anne. I didn't come here to talk, so if yo
want me to leave, say so, and I'll go." He waited for he
decision, while his gaze bored into hers with an intensity sh
hadn't felt before.

Her breath caught in her throat. "You certainly don
beat about the bush, do you?"

He made a face. "I admit I'm not always the most tac
ful man around, but I can promise you that I will never d
anything to harm you."

She smiled. "I know that. But I still ran away from yo
because that's all I'm used to doing. I've always run b
fore, because I had no choice. Now I do have an option."

"And?" His voice was harsh with need as he stared at he
face, dimly lighted by the street lamp that shone throug
the curtains.

Anne opened her robe, allowing it to slip off her shou
ders and pool around her feet. "I'll be honest with yo
Travis. The fear is still there, deep down, because I don
know how to get rid of it by myself. Perhaps that's where
need you."

He froze as he realized the import of her words. "Mayb
we need each other." He moved slowly toward her, his han
outstretched until it touched her shoulder, bare except f
a narrow ribbon strap. "How do you expect something li
this to keep you warm on cold nights?" he muttered, gi
gerly touching her skin and finding it slightly cool an
smooth.

She smiled. "That's why I have an electric blanket."

Travis's heart slammed against his chest at her smil
"Oh, Anne, if you refuse me now, I'll probably go i
sane."

Slowly she lifted her arms and linked them around h
neck. "I don't want you insane. I want you the way yo
are."

He hesitated no longer. He hauled her into his arms and held on to her tightly before using his finger to lift her face to his for a long and hungry kiss. For a moment Anne froze under the impact of his strength, but Travis's gentle insistence refused to allow her to draw away.

"Let me show you, Anne," he murmured, stroking her upper lip with the tip of his tongue as his hands first framed her face, then slid slowly down her throat and across her shoulders. When they reached her hips, they tightened tightly and moved around to lift her against himself. A tiny sound left her lips as she was swung up into his arms and carried over to the bed. He leaned over her prone figure, digging one knee into the mattress as he looked down at the woman who had occupied his thoughts for so long.

Anne lifted one hand, running it tentatively along his leg. She watched him move away and raise his arms to pull his sweater over his head, then dispense with his slacks. The silvery light slashed across his bare chest, tipping the dark hair moon-white. Leaving on his briefs, he crossed the room to stretch out on the bed next to her, drawing the covers over both of them.

With Travis's arm around her shoulders, Anne slid over and lay down next to him, her head comfortably nestled on his shoulder.

"There's no rush," he murmured. "We're just going to take this slow and easy. I want you to feel entirely comfortable with me before we go any farther. So why don't you just get used to me, the feel of me?" He buried his face in the tangled waves of her hair. "You set the pace, Anne."

Unable to believe he was allowing her so much freedom, she hesitantly touched his shoulder with her fingertips; even though the air was cold, his skin was warm. She traced the muscular structure, memorizing the texture, the path of an angular scar along the back of one shoulder, which she

learned had been the result of a fall into barbed wire whe
he was ten. She immediately kissed it better.

Anne allowed her lips to retrace the scar. "It would be s
much easier if our scars were always on the outside," sh
murmured, returning to her tactile exploration.

She learned that his nipples were as responsive as he
own. She circled the brown nub with her nail again an
again, fascinated by the way it bloomed under her touc
She raked her fingers through the crisp dark brown ha
that arrowed down to his waist. She paused and just looke
at Travis. With the way the light streamed across the be
she felt as if they were in a world of their own making.

Anne slowly pushed down the covers to the end of th
bed and looked at the rest of him. She laughed, soundin
a little anxious at the sight of his evident arousal and hai
roughened thighs. "You're nothing like Lloyd."

He smiled. "I hope that's good."

"Oh yes," she breathed. "It certainly is," but then sh
appeared a little nervous.

Travis took her hand, lacing his fingers through hers an
placing their entwined hands on his abdomen. "There
nothing to be afraid of," he assured her. "I told you b
fore, you'll set the pace. We won't do anything you don
want to."

She slowly released the three buttons in the front of h
nightgown and reached down for the hem, pulling it ov
her head and tossing it away. She sat there still as a stone a
Travis's gaze roamed over her naked form.

"Am I that bad?" She feared the worst as he remaine
silent.

"No, you're the most beautiful woman I've ever seen,
he whispered.

Travis smiled at her formality. His hands warmed h
skin as they skimmed over her breasts, finding the swolle
nipples that hardened under his touch. Not content just

ouch them, he lowered his head and took one nipple into
his mouth. He couldn't imagine anything tasting sweeter.
His hands moved down to the slender curve of her belly and
beyond. She moved restively under his touch, rotating her
hips toward him, silently asking for more. But he wasn't
finished. He turned her over, dropping a string of kisses
across her back and down her spine while his hands molded
her slender hips.

Turning her once more onto her back, he began to nib-
ble her lower lip, drawing it into his mouth. "Are you
sure?" he murmured.

"Yes!" she gasped, then laughed again, the sound rich
with expression and happiness this time. She wrapped her
hands around his neck, pulling his face down to hers. Their
mouths melded in loving hunger.

"Oh, Anne," he rasped, insinuating one leg between
hers. "There have been so many nights I've lain awake,
dreaming of you being here like this. So many nights when
I've wanted to show you what making love would be like
for us." His palm covered her breast in a possessive action. "Can you handle it?"

Her eyes glowed like two gems in the darkness. "Yes."

He groaned deep in his throat, as his mouth trailed
moistly across the shadowed valley between her breasts.
"Your trust in me means so much. I love you."

She shuddered under his touch, desiring more. Her hands
wandered down his back to his flexing buttock muscles,
caressing the rounded flesh. She discovered that touching
him was something she didn't want to stop doing for a long
time.

Anne arched up as Travis caressed her moist flesh with
his fingertips, making sure she was prepared for him. It
wasn't until then that he moved away to dig something out
of his pants pocket. "You are so beautiful," he whispered,
moving back over her, joining them together in a smooth,

fluid thrust. He remained still for several moments, so th
she could adjust to him, even though the tight friction o
her body against his own almost drove him out of contro
When he felt her relax, he began moving slowly, keeping h
hands on her hips to encourage her to equal participatio
Silently he urged her to give to him as much as he was gi
ing to her. He gritted his teeth, determined to present An
with the kind of lovemaking every woman deserved, t
kind she'd probably never known.

She kept her eyes wide open, staring at Travis's featur
because she didn't want to miss one moment of what th
were sharing. She had no idea her face was glowing, h
mouth stretched in a wide smile. When his movements gre
stronger, she rose to meet him, unwilling to be left behin
And when his face tightened, she felt her own release b
ginning to build. Soft cries escaped her lips, and as t
world exploded around her, she could hear Travis say h
name in a husky whisper.

Fully spent, Anne lay in his arms, her hand resting on h
damp chest, her fingers idly combing the soft hairs. Th
remained quiet for a long time, reflecting on what had ju
happened, both unable to believe that their loving cou
have been so explosive, or that they could still want eac
other again so soon.

"I wish you had been the first." Her voice was a har
and abrupt intrusion into their self-made world.

He smiled, understanding what caused her sorrow. "B
I was," he corrected. "Because I sincerely doubt you ha
ever before made love in a man's arms the way you did wi
me tonight."

"Travis!" Anne hid her head in embarrassment, ev
though she knew he couldn't see her in the dark.

"Well, did you?" He already knew her answer, but th
didn't stop him from asking her.

"You know I didn't." Her voice was muffled against his bare shoulder. "So you don't have to act so pleased about it."

"But I do, because we shared something so special." He sounded pleased with himself. "The only thing I'm going to hate is having to drag myself out of your very lovely bed to sneak back into my house."

"Um, yes. Maude would have some embarrassing questions for you." Anne yawned, feeling more relaxed than she had in a long time. She rolled over onto her side and nestled against him. "Travis, what will happen to us when the real world intrudes?" she asked in a low voice.

He knew she meant much more than Maude. "For now we'll take things day by day. And you're not to worry yourself, because I'm going to be beside you every step. You're not alone anymore, Anne Sinclair."

She smiled. "You know, that has a nice ring to it."

"Anne Sinclair?"

"No, that I'm not alone anymore."

Chapter Thirteen

"Congratulations! You got in just in time to change your clothes and get out to the south pasture to help the men."

Travis cursed softly as he stumbled over his feet. He straightened and turned around. "Aren't you up a little late?" He tried for a semblance of dignity, but didn't quite make it.

Maude turned on a nearby lamp and faced him with an unreadable expression in her eyes. "As you're a *responsible* adult, I won't ask where you've been until four o'clock in the morning, but as your mother I will speak my piece." When Travis opened his mouth to argue, she held up her hand, indicating she wanted silence. "That woman is very fragile right now. She's held in a very important secret for several years. Don't get into something that can seriously harm everyone concerned, and I'm including two little girls in that group. Now, speaking as a woman and one who's gotten to know Anne fairly well, I can tell you that if she feels emotions she can't afford to handle, she'll run."

"I already told her if she does, I'll find her," he replied in a gritty voice.

Maude's smile was sad. "Oh, my darling, if a person doesn't want to be found badly enough, they won't be."

Feeling the terror he had kept inside for so long, Travis dropped into a chair.

"The lawman in me says she has to go back and get all of this straightened out," he groaned. "The man in me wants to keep her here, where she can have her new life, and where we can learn if it's just more than a strong physical attraction."

"If it was just a physical attraction, you wouldn't have made love to her tonight," Maude stated baldly. "That's just the kind of man you are. Now, think like the lawman and not like a man in love, and do some checking. Find out what you can on Lloyd Sinclair, so you're not just relying on her story. I'm only playing the devil's advocate here because someone has to. Then start making some decisions."

"I offered her money for an attorney, but she won't take it," Travis replied wearily, half hating his mother for being so logical and loving her for it at the same time.

Maude looked up, beseeching higher powers; how could she have had a son who was so half-witted at times? "Of course she wouldn't! The woman has pride."

"She's going to need an attorney," he insisted.

"And she'll have one. Just go ahead and find one without her knowing it." She walked over and laid a hand on his shoulder. "I have some money put away. Add that to it. If these Sinclairs are half as powerful as she's intimated, we're going to need somebody with guts. Go take a shower while I fix you a large pot of coffee and some breakfast. Things may not look any better, but you won't feel as cranky as you probably do now."

Travis nodded and stood up. Before leaving he hugged his mother tightly. "One thing I hate about you, Mom," he murmured. "You're always so damn right."

"MOM, YOU'RE LATE." Nikki looked up at Anne with accusing eyes as the woman stepped out of the car. "You said you'd pick me up before lunch."

"I'm sorry, honey, I'm afraid I overslept." She smiled and drew her daughter against her for a hug. "Although I doubt you could have missed me all that much."

The little girl still looked suspicious. "You never oversleep."

Anne looked away, afraid the sudden color in her cheeks would give her away. Nikki was right; she was always up before the alarm clock went off. But after Travis had again made beautiful love to her before he had to leave, she'd felt so replete that she could only drift into a deep sleep. When she awoke only a bare hour ago, she'd felt more rested than she had in a long time.

"Even with my being late, were you able to have a good day?" Her voice was husky with the memories of a night filled with whispered endearments and tender caresses.

Nikki pulled away. "Yeah," she replied sullenly.

Lost though she was, Anne didn't miss the tone. "Nikki, sometimes things happen we can't control. Now, let's go inside, shall we?"

"Hello there! We'd 'bout given you up for lost," Maude greeted her. Her sharp eyes didn't miss the betraying flush in Anne's cheeks or the way Nikki hung back. "How about some coffee?"

Anne grasped the lifeline thrown to her with gratitude. "That sounds wonderful. I'm sorry I'm so late."

"No problem. Sometimes it's nice to be able to sleep late. Besides, Nikki here was able to keep Susie out of my hair while I cleaned out the refrigerator." She smiled at the girl. "They just finished their lunch, in fact. Have you eaten? I have plenty of tuna salad left." She nodded at the look on Anne's face as she took matters into her own hands. "Nikki, why don't you find Susie for me while I fix your mother a sandwich?"

Once Anne was seated with her meal and Maude sat across from her, the older woman eyed her keenly.

"You'll have to tell Nikki the whole story."

Anne choked on her sandwich and had to suffer a few hearty claps on the back. "Everything?" she wheezed.

"I'm not talking about last night. I'm talking about why you're running and what can happen. She's not a baby any longer and she's a very intelligent girl. She knows you and Travis have been dating and she doesn't like it, because she fears a man is going to take you away or hurt you again. She remembers more than you think she does, Anne. It's just that she's blocked it off, because she feels safer that way. Tell her," Maude ordered gently.

Anne shut her eyes tightly. "She doesn't remember anything. She was barely a baby then."

"Then why the nightmares? And why does she shy away from Travis?" Maude used each word like a knife, clearly determined to make Anne see the truth.

"She was barely four," she whispered. "And she never spoke of those times, so I thought it better not to bring them up. I'd hoped she had forgotten. But you're right. She just kept it hidden because I had. It was easier to ignore it than to bring it out into the open." She bit her lower lip. "I have to make arrangements to go back."

Maude nodded. "Have you told Travis?"

Anne shook her head. Suddenly her appetite was gone and she pushed her sandwich away. "Besides, you're right. I have to talk to Nikki, and I should do that before I say anything to him. I've kept my head in the sand long enough. Travis basically told me I can't continue running, and he's right, too. I will go to jail." Her voice began to fail her and she rubbed her hands together as if she were suddenly very cold. She coughed, clearing her throat, which was rapidly clogging with tears. "But I won't go without having a chance to air my story, even if no one will believe me." She jumped to her feet and grabbed her purse. "I'm sorry, I..." She shook her head as words failed her. Maude followed more slowly as Anne ran out of the house toward the barn. "Nikki!" she called out. "Come on, we're going."

The girl appeared in the doorway. "Now?"

"Yes, now." Her voice was sharp with agitation.

"I have to get my clothes."

"Then get them."

Nikki wasted no time in grabbing her pink duffel bag and climbing into the car. Without looking to right or left, Anne slid behind the steering wheel and started up the engine, driving away with a squeal of tires.

"Why's Nikki's mom so mad?" Susie came up to stand beside her grandmother.

"She's not, sweetie. She's just got a lot of things on her mind," Maude said softly.

Anne didn't say anything during the drive back to the house. Once Nikki had deposited her duffel bag on her bed, Anne asked her to come into the living room.

"Nikki, I have a lot of things to talk to you about," she said quietly. "Some you may not understand, and if you don't, just say so, and I'll try to explain it better for you. All right?"

Puzzled by her mother's serious tone, the child merely nodded.

Anne took a deep breath, knowing there was no other way than to plunge right in. "We have never talked very much about your father." She noticed the way Nikki stiffened at the word, but forced herself to continue. "Nikki, I had to leave Texas because I shot your father. If I hadn't gone away, I would have been put in jail. I took you with me because I loved you too much to leave you behind."

Nikki jumped up, screaming. "No! You didn't do anything bad, because he was a bad man." She leaned over her stunned mother, her fists clenched at her sides. "And he made you go away. All he did was yell at me and tell me to be quiet and leave me alone at night. And he—he broke the china tea set you gave me for my birthday. I hated him!''

"Oh, my God!" Anne whispered, shocked to the core by what she'd heard. "Nikki, why didn't you ever tell me any of this?" She reached out and grabbed her by the shoulders. "Why?"

Tears shone in her daughter's deep green eyes. "Because he said if I ever told you, a black monster would get me."

Anne breathed deeply through her nose to keep the darkness from overtaking her. She had feared her ex-husband for many years, but now a stronger emotion took over. The hate that was beginning to consume her canceled out the fear.

"No one will take you away from me, honey. No one," she stated emphatically, hauling Nikki into her arms and holding on to her tightly. "I was prepared to go back and take whatever they dished out, but now I'm going back to fight."

Nikki tilted up her head. "Mom, you can't go back there. I understand what you told me. You shot him and took me away. They'll put you in jail for that. And they'll make me stay with him, won't they?"

Anne's face hardened. "They can try, but not without a fight."

"Then we'll leave here, won't we? And I won't see Susie anymore."

Another subject she had to clear up. "Nikki, we also have to talk about the way you act toward Sheriff Hunter."

"I'm polite to him," the girl said stiffly.

"Let me tell you something to think about. Sheriff Hunter learned quite a while ago what I did and that I'm wanted by the police, but he didn't call them. In fact, he wants to help me."

Nikki didn't look convinced. "Are you two going to get married?"

Anne's stomach curled at the idea. While Travis was the kind of man any woman could dream about, she couldn't think about any kind of commitment right now. She had too many other things to worry about.

"No, we aren't."

"But he likes you. He takes you places."

"You and I have our lives to get straightened out before we can think about adding to our family," Anne replied, thrusting Travis from her mind. Right now, she had to concentrate on her daughter. "But I would like you to give him a chance. Think of it this way. If he was a bad man, I don't think Susie would love him so much, would she?"

The girl frowned with thought. "No, I guess not," she said slowly, as she edged out of her mother's lap and sat beside her on the couch.

"Nikki, I tend to forget that you're a big girl now and should be treated as such. I hope I'll do better in the future," Anne told her. "First of all, I think we should talk more about what you remember from years ago."

And for the next two hours, Anne learned that, once released, a little girl's memories were stronger than expected. Afterward, her resolve to go back and fight was even firmer. Deep down, she feared she would lose, but vowed that she would go down fighting.

Travis showed up that evening as Nikki was getting ready for bed.

"Can we talk?" he asked Anne, searching her face for answers to the questions filling his mind.

She nodded, stepping back so he could enter. As he passed her, he could smell the light lemony fragrance of her hair and the scent of her cologne, both of which brought back visions of the night before.

Nikki stood in the hallway, looking a bit uncertain.

"Hello, Sheriff Hunter," she said quietly, raising her head to look at him directly.

He smiled warmly. "Hi, Nikki. I had some of the brownies you and Susie made last night. Don't tell my mother, but they're better than hers," he added in a conspiratorial whisper.

A smile flashed across her lips. "Good night," she murmured, turning around and running back to her room.

Travis looked at Anne, silently asking the reason for the change.

"It's a beginning," she said. "I basically told her that if Susie loved you, you can't be all bad. Would you like some coffee?"

He shook his head. "It has been difficult to wait all day to see you, but after what Mom told me, I knew you'd want some time to yourself."

Anne collapsed into a chair. "Nikki and I had a long talk today. It appears she remembered more about that time than I ever dreamed she did." She quickly filled him in.

When she finished, Travis swore under his breath. "How could a man terrorize his own daughter?"

"If you knew Lloyd, you wouldn't ask that." She sighed. "I have to go back there and demand to be heard. And I am so scared about it that I can't think straight." She looked down at the hands clenched in her lap.

"I want to help."

Anne exhaled deeply and slowly shook her head. "No, Travis, I don't want you involved in this. After all, you are a lawman and should have turned me in the moment you knew the truth. They could charge you with being an accessory."

"Anne, you've been going it alone too long. Let someone help," he insisted, leaning forward, his hands loosely clasped between his knees. "Let me help."

A heartbeat went by before she spoke. "I can't make any promises."

"I'm not asking for any, but it wouldn't hurt for us to take things a day at a time and see what happens, would it?"

She grimaced. "You learned your logic from your mother, didn't you?" She pressed her fingers against her forehead, rotating them slowly. "No matter what I say, you're not going to listen to me, are you?"

"Nope."

"And you're going to stick your nose in where it might not be wanted."

"Yep."

"You're going to be just as stubborn as you were in the beginning."

"Yep."

Anne chuckled at Travis's cheerful tone. "I give up, Sheriff. Besides, it might be a good idea to have your input on how to handle this."

"Even to letting me find a lawyer for you?"

"Do I have any choice?"

"No."

"I thought so." She sighed in capitulation, then whispered, "I can't make love with you again, Travis. I can't afford to think about anything else but what will be coming up."

He stood and walked over to stand in front of her, hunkering down and grasping her hands, gently rubbing them between his own.

"I wasn't looking for a one-night stand, Anne," he said quietly. "I feel we have something, but I also know you have a lot on your mind now. All I ask is that you don't shut me out. That you give me a chance."

She edged her hands away from his and cupped his face, feeling the skin slightly rough from his evening beard. "Oh,

Travis, however did you manage to stay single so long?'' Her voice trembled with emotion.

He covered one of her hands. ''Probably because there wasn't a woman around to catch my interest.'' He leaned forward and kissed her softly, his lips a breath apart. When her mouth softened under his, he kissed her again, but pulled away before it could deepen too far. ''And that's my cue to leave, before I lose all gentlemanly restraint.'' He squeezed her hands lightly, then got to his feet. ''I have some contacts in Texas, so I'm going to make a few calls. I'm not going to use your name,'' he hastened to assure her when he saw her panic. ''But some groundwork has to be laid before you go back.''

''I don't know if I'll be able to go in to work tomorrow, acting as if nothing has happened.''

He smiled. ''Sure you will. You've done well so far. The rest should be a snap.'' He leaned down and kissed her again.

This time, Anne placed her hands on his shoulders, needing his warmth. A moan bubbled up in her throat to rest on his lips as she pressed herself closer. All the words she had spoken earlier came back to mock her, but she ignored them. As before, Travis drew away first.

''Honey, I can't always be the strong one,'' he breathed. ''Get a good night's sleep. I'll see you tomorrow. Just do me one favor. Have Lorna go easy on the chili powder.'' He opened the door and left swiftly.

TRAVIS WASTED no time in making his first call. The moment he stepped inside the station, he took care of any minor problems and shut himself up in his office. He sat at his desk for a long time before pulling out his personal address book. He was relieved that his call went through right away, before he lost his nerve.

''Hank Douglas.'' The drawl boomed in his ear.

"Hank, Travis," he identified himself.

"Is this one business or pleasure?" The man's tone of voice didn't surprise Travis.

"I'll leave that up to you. I want the name of a hard-nosed lawyer in your area who isn't afraid of anyone," Travis said baldly.

Hank swore under his breath. "What's this about?"

Travis leaned back in his chair, propping his booted feet on the desk and lighting a cigarette. "Hey, I'm just asking a favor from a good friend who I know I can count on."

"Does this have anything to do with our previous conversation?" the other man asked tautly, clearly being careful not to mention names over the phone.

"I'm just asking a favor, no more. Everyone needs a lawyer at least once in their lives," Travis said casually.

Hank groaned. "Old buddy, you're asking for something I can't do. I need some answers."

Travis shook another cigarette out of his pack and lighted it, forgetting there was already one burning in the ashtray. "All I'm asking you for is a name."

"Why me?"

"Because you're the only one I can trust," he said crisply.

Hank's sigh was audible over the wires. "All right, I'll get you a name, but you're going to have to be up-front with me when I get back to you. Don't leave me in the dark, for both our sakes."

Travis's voice hardened. "As a lawman my job is to protect the people who need and deserve it."

Hank didn't sound convinced. "How soon do you want a name?"

"Yesterday."

"After I get you somebody, are you planning on coming down here, too?"

"Might be," he drawled, unwilling to give away any more information than he absolutely had to. "It depends on what I find out."

The other man's voice was still taut with tension. "When?"

"When the time is right. Not before."

Hank exhaled, sounding more frustrated by the moment. "All right. I'll get you a name, and you let me know your flight information the minute you have it. Otherwise, old buddy, I won't be able to protect you. I hope you realize what you're doing, because I have a very nasty feeling that no matter how good a lawyer I can get you, this situation is still going to blow up in your face." He hung up without another word.

Travis slowly replaced the receiver. "There's no turning back now," he whispered, already wondering if he had done the right thing—or if he might have signed Anne's death sentence, after all.

"How COULD YOU do this to me? Damn you, by playing the role of the all-righteous lawman, you've thrown me to the wolves!" Anne exclaimed, pacing back and forth. Travis had told her at lunch that he'd come by late that evening, because he had something to discuss with her. Unfortunately, she'd had no idea how serious it was until then.

He looked at her pale features and kicked himself again for his impulsive gesture. "Anne, I had to. You had no way to contact anyone without someone leaking the information, and I knew I could trust this man."

"How?"

"He's with the state police."

She threw up her hands. "Oh, with the state police. Wonderful. You're so sure he won't tell a soul? He'll probably just catch the next plane up here and take me back in handcuffs!'' She stared at him, wild-eyed. "Thank you very much!"

"You know very well we can't put this off," he said tersely. "You talked about going back there, which isn't a good idea until you can have some protection. I'm not letting you set foot inside that state until we have a reputable attorney to represent you. I can get that person for you."

Her lips twisted. "You're not? Travis, I know all about extradition. If they find out where I am, they can come up here and just get me if they want to. We both know it."

He ran his hands through his hair. "I didn't mention your name, or even why I was asking for a lawyer."

She walked away, then spun around. Her features were taut with tension. "Come off it, Travis. The man is not stupid. He probably guessed, the minute you said something. He was the same man you spoke to before, when you asked about me after that private investigator was here. He had to figure it out."

"So what if he guessed." He breathed hard, in an attempt to keep his voice low so they couldn't be overheard. "Hank is a friend and a good man. He isn't going to say anything. He doesn't feel you got a fair deal before, and I know he'll do what he can for us."

She too breathed hard and fast, in a vain attempt to calm down. "Well, I'm glad you feel so confident about that, because it's my life you're playing with. Was it so difficult to wait a few days until we could discuss this? Or is the pull of being a sheriff so strong that you just couldn't resist calling in the big guns?" she asked in a hard voice.

Anne grew even angrier as Travis's lips started to form a smile. When his shoulders began shaking with restrained laughter, she seriously thought about punching him in the stomach.

"I'm glad you think this is so amusing," she said through her teeth, flexing her hands at her sides. "Because I certainly don't." She gasped when he picked her up and spun her around in a circle. "Travis! What do you think you're doing? Have you lost your mind?"

"You don't see it, do you?" he asked, slowing down. "In case you don't realize it, you just lost your temper with me."

She looked at him as if he didn't make any sense. "So?"

He shook his head, clucking at her denseness. "This from the woman who's eluded so many people over the years. You just lost your temper with me—a man," he said slowly, enunciating every word.

Anne's eyes widened as his meaning sank in. "I wasn't even thinking about what I was saying," she breathed, then burst out laughing. "I yelled at you. I really yelled at you."

Travis nodded. "You sure did." He hugged her so tightly that she protested about the safety of her ribs. "You yelled at me without even worrying about retaliation. Honey, I'm proud of you."

Anne still couldn't believe what she had done. "I usually gave in because it was easier, if not safer."

He kissed her long and hard. "You know what? I like it when you rip into me," he murmured against her mouth before stealing another kiss.

She buried her face against his shirtfront. "Oh, Travis, what am I going to do with you?" she moaned.

"Mom?"

They turned to find Nikki standing uncertainly in the doorway, her bare feet peeking out from under her nightgown.

"I heard yelling." She looked at Travis with eyes dark with caution and just a touch of fear.

"That you did," Travis said easily, tightening his hold on Anne when she tried to move away from him. "Your mom was letting me have it, for doing some things without asking her permission first."

Nikki tipped her head to one side. "Mom was yelling at *you*?"

He nodded. "Sure was. I'm glad you came out to rescue me."

"And you're not mad at her?"

"No reason for me to be. I did wrong, and she let me know it."

Nikki now looked at them as if they had both lost their minds. "I'm glad you're not fighting." She turned away to return to her room.

"Good night, Nikki," Travis called after her. "Thanks again for the rescue."

"I think some old memories were surfacing for her," Anne murmured.

"Probably, but with some work we can give her some new ones that will make her laugh."

Her lips tilted upward. "Another one of your promises, Sheriff Hunter?"

"The kind you can take to the bank."

Chapter Fourteen

"How do we know he's a good attorney?" Anne demanded, looking at the handwritten slip of paper Travis had given her when he came by the restaurant for lunch. He had deliberately taken an end stool and waited until the area was almost deserted before giving it to her.

"Hank believes in the guy and says nothing fazes him," he replied.

She shot him a knowing look. "How did you feel when you spoke to him?"

Travis looked properly injured. "Hey, I wouldn't do that," he protested.

"Of course not. What did he say?" She smiled. Try as she might, she couldn't get angry with Travis.

He looked chastened. "I just wanted to make sure he was the right person for you."

"Travis, you can be very pushy at times," she said softly, leaning across the counter.

He smiled into her eyes. "It's a crime you ever covered up such beautiful eyes and hair."

"After what I've done, those would only be considered misdemeanors," Anne said wryly.

"You smell good, too."

"You're changing the subject."

"Pushy people tend to do that."

She shot him a telling look that warned he should watch himself. "What did the nice man say?"

He lowered his voice. "He feels you should get back to Texas as soon as possible. Since it involves the Sinclairs, he feels he can get a quick court date for you."

Anne felt the old burning sensation return to her stomach. "It's going to happen, isn't it?"

He nodded. "Are you ready for it?"

"No, but when the time comes, I promise I will be."

TIME FLEW for Anne as she prepared herself for the coming ordeal. Travis had already purchased two plane tickets, reminding her he wasn't about to allow her to go alone. So much of her life had been a dark turmoil until he came along, offering her a peace that couldn't be duplicated.

"Why can't I go with you?" Nikki asked repeatedly. She hung on to Anne more and more since her mother had talked to her about her plans.

Anne sighed inwardly. "We've already discussed this at great length, honey. I want you to stay here with Mrs. Hunter and Susie."

"But Sheriff Hunter is going with you," the child argued.

"There's a reason for that."

Her mouth quivered dangerously. "They're going to put you in jail, aren't they? And if I go with you I'll be put there too, because I told you!"

Anne grabbed hold of her and held on tightly. "No, that isn't why," she soothed. "I just feel you'd be a lot happier here, where you can play with Susie." And be safe, she thought to herself. From the beginning, she had told Travis she wouldn't take Nikki with her, and she was grateful he hadn't argued with that. She wanted her daughter to experience as much happiness and laughter as was possible

Until then, she spent every possible moment with Nikki, since Lorna had given her the time off.

"We'll be praying for you, honey," the older woman had informed her. "Don't you worry at all. You'll be back here in no time." She slipped an envelope into Anne's hand. "Just a little something from everyone around here. And no arguments. We want to help."

When Anne opened the envelope and saw the carefully aligned bills she felt like crying. Instead, she smiled and hugged the woman.

"I never knew what friends really were until I came here," she whispered.

THE NIGHT BEFORE Anne was to leave she was exhausted, but couldn't sleep. She left her bed and crept into Nikki's room, where the girl lay curled in her bed. Anne carefully lifted the covers and crawled in next to her.

"Shh, baby," she whispered when Nikki mumbled. "It's just Mommy." She held her in her arms, holding back the tears as she cradled her daughter against her breast. Anne remained there for the balance of the night, unable to sleep as she imprinted the image of her daughter on her mind. A one tear appeared at the corner of one eye and trickled down her cheek to lodge at the edge of her lips, but she was determined that any sorrow she had at parting with Nikki would be kept inside when they arrived at Travis's in the morning.

BREAKFAST was a quiet affair at the Hunter household when Anne and Nikki arrived.

"I told Cal if anything comes up he feels he can't handle, to call Ron Johnson over in Cotton Creek," Travis told Maude as he concentrated on his bacon and eggs. "I also have Wilma's promise that she won't go after Zeke while

I'm gone. I'd appreciate it if you'd give her a call every so often to keep tabs on her.''

"If she knows that's why I'm calling, she'll never for give any of us,'' Maude said dryly, eyeing Anne picking at her food. "That's not the way to put meat on your bones dear.''

Anne managed a weak smile. "I'm not a very good flyer, so eating beforehand is never a good idea for me.'' The fact that her nerves were already frayed was left unspoken but well understood.

"Please try and eat a little,'' Travis coaxed. "For me.''

She nibbled on a strip of bacon, then set it down when Travis's attention was captured by Susie. But Maude no ticed and gestured toward the eggs.

All too soon it was time to drive to the small airport nearby for the commuter flight that would connect them to Helena. Standing out on the dusty airfield, Anne hugged Maude and Susie, then embraced Nikki tightly. The little girl never said a word, simply holding on to Anne and kissing her on the cheek. Then Nikki walked slowly over to Travis, who was hunkered down, talking softly to Susie.

Nikki stood very still and stared just over his shoulder waiting until he turned toward her. "Would you hug me the way you hug Mom and Susie?'' Her voice was so low that he had to strain his ears to hear her.

He held out his arms. "If you want me to.''

Her steps were tiny and unsure, but soon she stood much closer to him. Still Travis waited for her to make the final decision.

Anne stood back, tears in her eyes as she watched her daughter. Nikki laid a hand on his shoulder, but moved no closer. Travis made no move to enfold her in his arms, but the smile on his face was warm and loving.

"If you ever have to yell at me, it will be because I de serve it, won't it?'' Nikki asked softly.

He wasn't going to lie. "Yes."

She chewed on her lower lip. "You'll bring my mom back, won't you?" She took her hand away and stepped back.

He smiled. "You can count on it."

Before long the flight was called and Travis helped Anne board the small plane. They looked out the tiny porthole at figures that steadily grew smaller as the plane took off. She blinked rapidly to hold back the tears and didn't refuse the handkerchief he held in front of her.

"I wasn't kidding," she murmured, wiping her eyes carefully so as not to smudge her makeup. "I'm a very bad flyer."

Travis smiled. "Then I'll keep the airsick bag handy for you."

"Travis." She gripped his hand in a bone-crushing hold. "What if they demand I return Nikki right away? What will I do? I don't want her there during all this turmoil."

He smiled and carefully freed his hand. "Don't worry about it."

"Easy for you to say!"

He kissed the tip of her nose. "It's all taken care of. Just relax."

The rest of the flight was a blur for Anne. Since their plane was late getting into Helena, they had to run to catch their connecting flight to Houston.

By the time the jet landed there, Anne's stomach had grown a million butterflies, and airsickness was only a by-product. She tugged at Travis's hand, silently signaling that she wanted to be the last to depart. He smiled and settled back, waiting for the other passengers to pass by them.

"This is a very bad idea," she whispered, following him down the tunnel at last.

"Don't worry, Hank is meeting us," he assured her. "And we're seeing the attorney in the morning." He scanned the people milling around but didn't see his friend. A strange prickling sensation skittered across the back of his neck, and all defenses immediately shot up. He grabbed her arm in a grip that was tighter than usual. "Anne." He kept his voice low. "Smile. I want you to appear calm, not nervous." Her eyes shot up. "Just do as I say." Keeping smiles plastered on their faces, they walked across the terminal.

"Anne Williams Sinclair?" Two dark-suited men suddenly flanked them. One of them flashed a gold shield and a sheet of paper that Travis immediately snatched from him. "We have a warrant for your arrest." In a droning voice the stranger began reading her her rights.

"Travis." She looked up at him, shock and fear written on her face, as she was led a few steps away.

"Wait a minute," Travis began angrily, stepping forward, then flinching when flashbulbs seared his eyes. "What the hell is going on here?"

"Mrs. Sinclair is wanted for the kidnapping of her daughter and the shooting of her ex-husband," the other officer explained. "Who are you?"

"Sheriff Travis Hunter, Dunson, Montana."

"Then if you come down to the station tomorrow, we can arrange for you to get the reward money."

"We're to meet a Henry Douglas," he stated, glaring at a photographer who had got in too close. "Get out of my face, unless you want to lose yours," he growled.

"Travis!" Hank ran up, looking confused at the sight of the circus of photographers—and of a stunned Anne, who was being handcuffed. "Wait a minute here." He took one of the officers to one side and began speaking rapidly and gesturing.

"Travis!" Anne was looking more ill with each passing minute.

"Look, she isn't going anywhere," Travis told the man.

"You kidding? She's been on the run for three years. We're not taking any chances."

"Mrs. Sinclair, what have you done during this time?" one reporter shouted.

Anne said nothing, and began crying wildly as she was separated from Travis, who was vainly trying to keep the press away from her.

"Who are you exactly? Are you the latest of Mrs. Sinclair's conquests? Do you have any idea that she almost killed her ex-husband?" one reporter asked, pushing a microphone under Travis's nose.

"Travis!" Anne screamed when the detectives began pulling her away. A furious Hank stood on the sidelines, holding back his friend with a strong grip.

Travis turned on him with murder in his eyes. "You had to call them, didn't you? She was scared enough coming down here, without you turning it into a three-ring circus. I ought to take you apart and really give those news vultures something to film."

"I had nothing to do with this," Hank retorted. "I don't know how they found out, but I intend to."

"Just great. And, while you're doing that, she's turning into a basket case." Travis towered over his onetime friend. "Dammit, she's scared to death and she has good reason to be. I'm surprised they didn't put her in chains!"

Hank dug into his pockets and pulled out some change, heading for a nearby bank of pay phones. "I'm going to call Dave and have him get down there to bail her out."

Travis was on his heels. "Where are they taking her?"

"Oh no, you're not going anywhere near there. One riot is enough. You go down there and you're going to act like the masked avenger, which is the last thing she needs right now. Dave can handle it. I'm getting you to a hotel, where I expect you to stay until this is all straightened out." When his call was connected, he spoke swiftly and concisely. After he hung up, he turned back to Travis. "Dave is leaving now. Come on, let's get a drink and then we'll head for the hotel."

"Make that a double," Travis said grimly, still seeing Anne's tearstained face as she pleaded with him to help her. "Damn, I promised I'd keep her safe. I sure didn't do a very good job of it. She was right. She would have been better off in Dunson."

"No, she wouldn't, because someone would have caught up with her sooner or later." Hank led the way into a dimly lighted bar and found a corner table.

When a waitress approached them, Hank ordered two whiskeys. The two men didn't speak again until their drinks were placed in front of them.

"Am I reading something into it, or do you and Anne have something special between you?" Hank asked, fingering his glass.

"We were just beginning to find out," Travis muttered, tossing back his drink.

Hank's brows arched. "So that's the way it is, is it?"

"Yep," Travis said grimly, gesturing to the waitress for another drink and taking a pack of cigarettes and lighter out of his shirt pocket. "Now why don't you tell me what you know so far?" He made a frustrated gesture. "Damn, how could they just cart her off like an animal?"

"Calm down," his friend ordered in a low voice. "You're not going to be able to accomplish anything if you fly off the handle. And Anne is going to need your strength, if the two of you are as close as you claim you are." He held up his hands in defense. "All right, stupid comment. Just call it a casualty of a crummy day." He slid one of Travis's cigarettes out of the pack and lighted it. "Do you know where the daughter is?"

Travis eyed his friend blandly, now prepared to view him as the enemy until shown otherwise. "Am I supposed to?"

Hank sighed. "Travis, don't make this any harder than it has to be."

Travis's gaze was bone chilling as he leaned back in his chair and stared at the other man. "I'm not the one who allowed storm troopers to spirit away a frightened woman. All I have to say is, your friend better be as good as you claim he is."

"Dave and I had worked together for ten years when he decided to get out of police work and practice law. There's no one else I would trust, and he admitted he would like nothing better than to go up against the Sinclairs. They're not used to losing, and Dave only likes to win, so it should be interesting."

Travis leaned across the table. "Look here. Anne's life is at stake for all we know," he declared. "I'm not going to allow some grandstanding attorney to build up his reputation on her bones."

Hank's gaze hardened. "Don't push it, old buddy. I can understand where you're coming from, so I won't discuss your hiding a fugitive from the law or the consequences if anyone decides to dig into your part." He pulled out his wallet and dropped several bills onto the table before standing up. "Come on, let's get your luggage and get you to the hotel. And I mean it, Travis. You stay put and let Dave and me handle this. Because if you land in jail, I won't bother bailing you out."

Travis fumed as they stood by the luggage carousel, snagging his garment bag and Anne's worn tan leather suitcase.

"This is it?" Hank looked at the two pieces with disbelief.

"Yep," Travis drawled, swinging the garment bag over his shoulder.

Hank swore under his breath as they walked out of the terminal. Soon enough they were at his car and the luggage was stowed in the trunk.

"How long before we get to the hotel?" Travis looked around the booming city with distaste. After his years of living in a small country town he felt more and more like a hick who didn't belong. He wanted to snatch Anne up and go back. As far as he was concerned, it didn't take much to hate the noise, the heavy traffic and people hurrying.

"About an hour." Hank cut across the congested lanes with the ease of one who had done it for a long time. He glanced at his friend who lounged in the passenger seat, his elbow resting on the open window as he stared out. "What has she said about her time with Sinclair?"

His throat muscles convulsed. "Who's asking?"

Hank knew what he meant. "I'm asking as your friend, nothing else."

Travis sighed. "She's told me enough." His expression was filled with bleak pain.

"And the daughter?"

"She's safe," he replied, tight-lipped.

"I didn't hear that," Hank reminded him in a crisp tone. "And to keep her safe, I'm not going to ask any more questions."

The silence between them was heavy during the balance of the drive. When they reached the hotel, the check-in procedure was quickly completed and Hank and Travis rode the elevator up to the assigned room.

"I reserved two adjoining rooms as you requested. And they're both under an assumed name." Hank followed Travis into the room. He paused. "Look, as much as I like seeing you again . . ."

"You're right. You shouldn't even be seen with us." Travis could taste the bitterness of the past couple of hours. He dropped his bag onto the king-size bed and walked over to unlock the door leading into the next room, so that he could carry Anne's bag in there. He looked around, as if checking to make sure everything was all right, then returned to Hank. "This is very nice. Thank you."

The tension in Hank's features lightened. "I just don't want to screw things up for you. Tell me something. Do you have any idea how tough this is going to be for you, once the press gets wind of who you are? They're going to hound the two of you like crazy."

Travis stood his ground. "That's why I'm here. So Anne won't have to go through this alone."

Hank smiled. "Then old buddy, I have a lot of respect for you, because to be honest, I don't know if I could go through what you have ahead of you." He glanced at his watch. "Sorry I have to run out like this, but I've got some appointments I couldn't cancel. Dave will bring Anne back here. I told the front desk to screen your calls, just in case."

Travis held out his hand. "Thanks."

He took it. "Don't thank me just yet."

The afternoon dragged unmercifully. Travis paced the room until he was positive that the soles of his boots had worn thin. He smoked until his lungs burned, and ordered coffee from room service, drinking it until he felt as if he were floating. He refused to leave the room in case there was a call, and he didn't want to use the phone for the same reason. By the time the phone rang, the room was dark, because he hadn't bothered to turn on any lights. He snatched up the receiver almost before the first ring had finished.

"Yeah?" He spoke abruptly.

"Travis, what is going on down there?" Maude's voice was low-pitched and urgent.

He sighed. "More than you can guess."

"The news showed Anne getting arrested at the airport." Travis closed his eyes and swore pungently under his breath. "I was doing the dishes and had no idea the girls were watching it, until Susie called out to me that Anne was on TV and Nikki was crying. The poor baby was hysterical, and it took me a long time to calm her down and get her to bed."

Travis rubbed his eyes, burning with fatigue, with his fingertips. "Is she all right?"

"Yes, she and Susie are both asleep in my bed," his mother replied. "Was it as bad as it looked?"

"Worse."

"Is Anne all right?"

"I don't know," he burst out, feeling the frustration from the past hours build up. "Hank ordered me not to go to the police station, and the hotshot attorney he recommended is supposed to be bailing her out, but I haven't heard a word from him. If I don't hear anything pretty soon, I'm going to go out there myself."

"No, let a professional handle this," she ordered. "You sound as if you've been living on coffee and cigarettes. And you know what a monster that turns you into. Call down and order up a meal. Give Anne my love." With that she rang off.

Travis ordered a steak dinner but only picked at it, instead drinking even more coffee, which only left his nerves jangling. He lay on the bed, smoking and staring at the ceiling, thinking about Anne's ex-husband.

"Somehow this has to be linked to you, Sinclair," he muttered, drawing on his cigarette. "It just has to be."

The knock sounded loud and foreign in the silent room. Travis climbed off the bed and ran to the door.

Anne stood in front of him with a tall, lanky man in his early to mid-forties.

"Dave Harrison, Sheriff," he introduced himself with a weary smile. "I'm sorry. I had no idea it would take this long."

But Travis's attention was centered on the woman he loved. Her hair, which had been combed into a neat French braid that morning, was now loose and hanging around her face, and her clothes were wrinkled, with smudges of dirt on them. But it was her expression and manner that tore at his soul. She looked as if she had just visited hell.

Chapter Fifteen

Travis stood back and gestured for them to enter, even as he pushed his shirttail back into his pants. He walked around, switching on a couple of lights.

"She's had it pretty bad," Dave murmured, watching Anne walk woodenly across the room and stare out the window.

"What took so long?"

Dave inclined his head toward Anne. "Does she have a separate room?"

Travis nodded. He moved toward Anne, lifting his hands, then froze when she flinched.

"Honey, I put your stuff in your room over there." He pointed toward the open door. "Maybe you'd like to freshen up?"

"Yes." Her voice was devoid of feeling. "I would." She entered the other room and closed the door behind her.

Travis turned on the other man the moment they were alone. "What happened?"

Dave sighed. "It's called musical chairs with a prisoner. They shifted her around, obviously hoping I would get fed up and leave her there. Then I had to get a bail set, which wasn't easy. Let me warn you now, the Sinclairs are going to make it hell for you. Good thing I'm stubborn. Once they realized I wasn't going to give up, things went pretty swiftly. What happened to Anne was basically emotional. I gather they put her into a holding tank with some pretty rough ladies, so if I were you, I'd handle her gently tonight. Now I want to see her tomorrow, so we can get the ball rolling. Say around one?" He handed Travis his business card.

Travis nodded. "I'll have her there."

Dave hesitated. "This fight is going to be dirty. I'll be honest, it doesn't look good for her, so anything she can tell me will be appreciated. I don't like people who feel they can get away with anything, just because of their family name and social position, so I'm more than willing to go through with this. I just want to know, are you? Because once we start, there's no turning back."

There was no hesitation. "Since I intend to marry the lady, I hope we can get this over as soon as possible, but no matter how long it takes, I'll be here."

Dave smiled. "You've got guts, Sheriff. Hank said you did. Good thing, because you're going to need them." After that, he left.

Travis quickly called downstairs, asking for a light meal to be sent up, then walked into the other room. He noticed that the bathroom light was on and the shower running. He paused in the doorway and saw a sight that tore at his insides. Anne stood under the hot spray, crying so hard that her body was convulsed. More than anything Travis wanted to go to her and give her comfort, but sensed this wasn't the time. He quietly backed away and returned to his room to wait for her there.

When Anne finally appeared, she was clad in a robe, with her hair up in a towel, and her eyes were red and swollen.

"I ordered you something to eat." Travis gestured toward the table that had been set up.

She grimaced. "I'm not sure I'm hungry."

"At least try." He noticed that she edged around him as she settled into the chair. "Please."

Anne looked at the fluffy omelet and cut off a small piece with her fork. "I kept washing myself over and over, and I still feel dirty," she said in a small voice that trembled.

Travis reached for her free hand and hung on, even as she tried to pull back. "They're the dirty ones for what they tried to do," he told her.

She nibbled on her food and before she knew it, half the omelet was gone, along with a slice of buttered toast and a large glass of juice.

"I figured I drank enough coffee for the two of us," Travis explained.

She nodded. "Travis, I would rather die than go back there. You're not treated like a person, but some dirty thing that shouldn't be allowed out in public. They even tried to tell me that you only brought me back for the reward, and no one was going to bail me out or help me."

Travis cursed long and hard. "Now you know differently."

Anne glanced at the clock and uttered a sigh of dismay. "I should have called Nikki by now. She must be worried sick."

"I talked to her," he lied. "They're all doing fine. I told her you were with an old friend."

Anne looked at him as if she didn't believe him, but wasn't about to dispute his statement. "I had no idea how long I was there," she murmured. "Time has no meaning." Her lids drooped with exhaustion.

"You need sleep," Travis decided, assisting her out of the chair. "Can you dry your hair by yourself, or do you need help?"

"Myself," she mumbled, heading back to her room. Ten minutes later she appeared again in the open doorway. "I understand the reason for the two rooms, but please don't let me be alone tonight.''

Travis pulled back the already rumpled covers on his bed and smashed the pillows a few times before walking over to her. "I don't want to be alone, either."

Anne quickly crossed the room and got under the covers, watching Travis walk around the room, turning off lights and shucking his clothing before he climbed in next to her. With one arm curled around her shoulders he leaned over and switched off the bedside lamp.

"What did you do while you waited for me?" She rolled onto her side to face him.

"Counted the flowers and leaves on the wallpaper, each separately of course, smoked and drank coffee until I was climbing the ceiling, and watched HBO. I think we should invite Sigourney Weaver down. After what she did to those aliens, this would be a snap for her."

Anne showed the first smile of the day. "Sounds fascinating."

"Most of all, I missed you."

"You know how to make a woman feel good." She buried her face in the hollow between his neck and shoulder.

He rubbed his knuckles over her cheek, finding the skin silky-soft to the touch. "At least you got over your airsickness."

She wrinkled her nose. "Not the way you think. I got sick in the car. All over the detective who looked like Sidney Greenstreet."

Travis chuckled. "Serves him right."

"He didn't think so." She rubbed her cheek against the hair tickling her nose and sighed. "Travis, I want you to go back home tomorrow. This is going to turn into a circus, and I don't want you to be a part of it."

"Too late. I'm already in for the duration. Besides, I can't take the chance of you falling for your attorney, can

I?'' he teased her. ''You're supposed to love me, and I don't want you to get confused.''

''You don't have to worry. He's not my type.'' Anne sighed again. ''I think Lloyd or his father somehow found out I was on that flight, and alerted the police and probably the media, too. It would be just like them.''

His arms tightened around her. As much as he wanted to make love to her, he knew he couldn't after the traumatic day she'd just had.

''Go to sleep,'' he ordered huskily, fiercely determined to protect her even more after what had happened.

She yawned. ''Thank you.''

''For what?''

''For being here.''

''I'LL BE HONEST with you, Anne, this is going to be a tough fight,'' Dave said bluntly, as the three sat on a couch in his office. ''The Sinclair family wants you behind bars, and they don't care how they do it.'' There was no apology in his tone for his candid speech. ''And after all this time we're going to have trouble proving self-defense. So I'm going to need some information, anything you can remember. Dates you were injured, times you spent in the hospital, names of people who saw you. Anything I can work with.''

She nodded. ''I understand.'' Drawing a deep breath, Anne dug deep into her memory and began reciting bits and pieces, as if she were speaking about someone else.

For the next two hours Travis stood at the window looking out over the skyscrapers, trying not to listen to Anne's softly spoken words but unable to tune them out. When she finished, it took him a few moments to realize there was only silence in the room. He turned and found her gone.

Dave smiled knowingly at Travis's glare. "Don't worry. I haven't spirited her anywhere. She's just down the hall in the ladies' room."

Travis looked at the tape recorder. "What do you think?"

The attorney grimaced. "It's still her word against his, but I'm hoping to find a few more people to back up what she's said."

"Hiring investigators," Travis guessed.

Dave nodded.

"I want to help."

"Not a good idea."

"I know how to take notes and question people without applying thumbscrews," Travis argued.

"But you don't know the area and you don't know the people," Dave pointed out. "I know of several reputable investigators who can get the job done. I also want to do some digging into Lloyd Sinclair's background. Judging from what Anne said, it's not exactly spotless, although his father sure worked hard to make it look that way."

"What do you know about them?" Travis leaned against the windowsill, his hands jammed into his pockets.

"Just what the society pages tell us, and more than a few juicy rumors." Dave poured himself another cup of coffee. "The papers make Joshua and Sylvia Sinclair sound like saints. The rumors tell us that the Sinclair fortune was founded by an ordinary horse thief, who shot and killed more than his share of Texas Rangers, then conveniently found a couple of sacks of gold and decided to go legitimate." He glanced through the file folder before him.

"Sounds like the perfect all-American dynasty," Travis commented dryly.

Dave grinned. "Close enough. Joshua Sinclair will do anything for new contracts, and questions were raised when he branched out into the construction business—basically because of his methods of obtaining contracts. But nothing could be proven. Lloyd believes in living hard." He tossed a newspaper photograph of an older man toward Travis. "Some say old Joshua has half the judges in his pocket. I don't think I want to even know about the other half. Most of Lloyd's girlfriends aren't accepted at the family manor, due to their dubious occupations, and the old boy has been harassing his son to get married again and have some more grandchildren. The old man's never forgiven Anne for snatching his only one, even if she was a girl."

"He probably figures Nikki could marry someone worthwhile," Travis growled.

Dave winked. "Bingo."

Travis ground his teeth. "Sounds like something out of a soap opera."

"I agree," Dave said. "I'm going to tell Anne about it of course, but I've contacted her family."

"I can imagine that went over very well, considering how they feel about her."

"Like a lead balloon," the other man agreed. "The father said as far as he's concerned, his daughter is dead, after disgracing him the way she had, and her mother refused to talk to me or anyone from my office. In fact, I was referred to their attorney. It appears they want a piece of their granddaughter and would be willing to fight the Sinclair family for her. I gather she's safe with your family?"

He smiled coldly. "She's being well taken care of."

"Travis, I'm on your side," Dave reminded him. "It isn't going to take them long to serve Anne with a court order for her to return the child. I'm surprised it hasn't happened yet."

Anne had returned to the office in time to hear his words.

"No," she said coldly. "I will not give her up."

"I told you not to worry about it." Travis reached into his shirt pocket and tossed a long white envelope across the desk. "If they want to make a fuss, you can give them this."

Dave drew out a neatly typed sheet of paper and read it quickly. "Very nice," he complimented. "It's all couched in medical terms. Basically, Nicola Sinclair is under quarantine until further notice. Therefore she cannot be moved."

Travis looked at Anne and saw that she finally realized why he'd never worried about Nikki being easily taken away from her. He flashed her a broad grin. "Exactly."

BY THE TIME they left the attorney's office, Anne and Travis were exhausted. Dave had one of his clerks drive them back to the hotel and suggested they get as much rest as possible, because he had an idea things would escalate, once the Sinclairs decided to get the ball rolling.

Little did Anne know how fast things would happen.

When she wasn't having her brain picked about her years with Lloyd, she was trying to rest in anticipation of the upcoming trial and avoid the press. Any calls home were made from pay phones, because Travis refused to trust the hotel. After the press discovered where they were staying, they had no privacy. In the end, Dave offered them the use of a house on the city's outskirts.

"I'll be honest. The two of you cohabiting isn't a good sign," he told them when he drove them out to the house for the first time.

Anne was the one to reply first. "I am no longer a married woman, and I'm certain Lloyd hasn't been celibate during all this time."

"Yes, but you know how it goes. It's always the woman who suffers."

"I'll sleep in a separate bedroom if it will make people feel better, but I won't let Anne stay alone," Travis informed him. "She's been alone for three years because of him. No more."

Dave sighed. "Okay, but be prepared for the mud to be slung. So don't read any newspapers. And I may as well tell you now, the court date has been set for next Monday."

Anne gasped. "That soon?"

"I have an idea we got one so quickly because of the Sinclair name. They want this cleared up as soon as possible, while it's fresh in the public mind," he replied.

"But you haven't been able to lay all the groundwork you wanted to," she protested.

The attorney grinned. "That's what they're hoping for. Don't worry, I have a few tricks up my sleeve, too." He parked in the driveway of a sprawling, one-story house, led them up the walkway and unlocked the front door. "Rosa does the cooking and cleaning and lives in. She's also very reliable and doesn't gossip. The phone number is unlisted." He preceded them into the living room and turned on several lights.

Anne looked around at the Southwestern decor and ran her hand across the back of an apricot-colored sofa. "This is all very lovely, but I can't understand who you would know who would be willing to loan us this place."

"My wife. She owned this house when we got married. We usually rent it to business executives who are in the city more than a couple of weeks and want a place a bit more personal. It came available a few days ago, so I decided you two could make better use of it." He walked over to the pale blue draperies, drew them open and flipped a light switch.

"Pool and Jacuzzi," he explained. "Great for relieving tension. Rosa's quarters are off the kitchen, so she's available if you need her. This is her night off, but she'll be here to fix breakfast for you in the morning.''

"We might not want to leave after all this," Travis commented, looking at the wide-screen stereo television set.

"Trust me. When the time comes, you'll be out of here like a shot." Dave tossed him a key ring. "I'll be off now, but I'll see you tomorrow around eleven." He headed for the front door.

Travis followed him. "Dave, I want to thank you."

He smiled. "Wait to thank me after I've nailed them to the wall." He waved at Anne and left, after showing Travis how to activate the burglar alarm.

Travis returned to Anne, who was standing at the patio window, looking out at the softly lighted swimming pool.

"Sure a far cry from my place," he murmured, sliding his arms around her waist and pulling her toward him.

She tipped her head back and to one side, to allow his lips access to her ear. "Yes, but luxury isn't all it's cracked up to be. I like your place much better. Let's go for a swim," she said suddenly. "Dave said there're extra suits in the bedroom."

She disappeared into the master bedroom and returned in ten minutes, wearing a bright green maillot. She opened the sliding door and pushed it back, along with the screen, then glanced over her shoulder. "Are you coming?"

He grinned, relieved to see her more relaxed than she had been the past few days. "Yes, ma'am."

By the time Travis walked outside, Anne was swimming laps.

He dived into the deep end and swam over to where she was now treading water near the diving board. He grasped the coping as their bodies drifted together, then apart in the warm water.

"Anne, I'm proud of you," he said seriously. "The last few days haven't exactly been easy, and you've handled everything beautifully. Even the reporters."

She smiled. "You frightened most of them away—at least the ones you didn't insult. If your mother heard you, she'd wash your mouth out with soap."

"Nah, she'd be in there slinging mud back with the best of them." He paused. "Anne, I love you."

Her breath caught in her throat. "I'm a woman with a dubious past, who's considered violent."

His lips twitched. "If you're trying to talk me out of it, you're failing miserably."

Anne gripped his shoulders. "Oh, Travis, maybe that's what I've been feeling for you for so long. It's just that I'm afraid. I want to love you. I mean it, but..." Her voice faded. The trial hung over them like a dark cloud.

"Come on," Travis suggested. "I'll race you." When they reached the steps, they settled on the top step, leaning back to look up at the sky. "Remind me to think about building a pool in the backyard," he commented.

"After you buy the bull," she reminded him with a sad smile, as she thought about the money that was being used for her defense.

He grazed her chin with his fingertips. "After I buy the bull." He lay back and looked up at the stars. "They're brighter at home."

"No smog there." She sat up, wringing the water out of her hair.

"You know, you look pretty sexy in that suit," he told her. "Not at all like the mother of a seven-year-old girl," he teased.

Anne looked him over in the navy briefs that showed off his muscled body so well. "You're not so bad yourself. Of course—" she paused, tapping her chin with her forefinger in thought "—you really should watch yourself. After all, you have reached the big four-oh, and if you aren't careful, it could be all downhill from there.'' She squealed with laughter when he started tickling her. She escaped, only to be playfully tackled on the grass. For the moment the worries of the case were forgotten.

As he lowered his head to catch her lips, he murmured huskily, ''Then I guess I'll just have to prove to you this forty-year-old man has plenty of mileage left in him, won't I?''

She looked at him with darkened eyes. ''Travis, I...''

He smiled, guessing her unspoken thoughts. ''No, sweetheart, I'm just going to kiss us into a frenzy. Anything else can wait until the proper moment.''

Anne looped her arms around his neck. ''Did I ever tell you how special you are?''

''Yes, but I wouldn't mind hearing it again.''

Chapter Sixteen

The jury has found Mrs. Sinclair guilty of murder. Does the prisoner have anything to say in her defense?

This is all wrong! I didn't kill him! You can't do this!

There can only be one suitable punishment....

When Anne woke up that morning with those words ringing in her ears, she already dreaded the rest of the day. She was grateful for Travis's calm strength as they entered the courthouse amid a crowd of reporters and hurried down the hallway to their assigned courtroom.

"I'll be right back," she murmured to Travis and Dave. In the ladies' room she stared long and hard at her reflection, seeing the result of sleepless nights. By concentrating hard she was able to steady her shaking hand just long enough to freshen her lipstick before leaving.

"You look well, Anne, although not your usual stylish self." Lloyd Sinclair's cold blue eyes flicked over her simple olive skirt and pale green camp shirt with disdain. "My, my, it must be love that puts that look in your eyes." His smile was deadly, as was the expression he flashed toward Travis, who stood with his back to them, unaware of the confrontation. "Funny, I never would have figured you for the rough-and-tumble type. You didn't seem to like it when I wanted a little variety."

Her eyes reflected icy shards. "Probably because you enjoyed breaking bones too much."

His body stiffened. "So you're into cowboys now. Does he know *all* about you?"

She held her head high, determined not to back down.

His gaze hardened. "You're going to lose, Anne, and you're going to jail until you're a very old woman, if I have anything to say about it. I wonder if your cowboy will be around for you then. And I'm going to have Nikki. Just remember that."

"Anne." Travis's hand rested possessively on her shoulder. "I don't think your lawyer would appreciate you talking to us, Sinclair."

The other man straightened his raw silk jacket. "Funny, I always thought Anne had more taste than to wind up with someone who probably cleans out his own barn. It just goes to show that you never know someone, even if you've been married to them."

"At least I don't go around beating up women."

Lloyd's features tightened. "Be careful, or you'll go down with her." He walked away.

"Don't." Anne held on to Travis's arm, feeling the muscles tense under her touch. "He'd love to provoke you into fighting him, so he can come out looking even better. He's not worth it."

He looked down and smiled at her. "I'm just glad you know that."

They walked back down the crowded hallway, Travis a more than effective shield, keeping all but the most persistent away from Anne.

When Anne saw her parents across the hall, she stiffened but no expression crossed her features. The disgust on their faces was evidence enough that they wanted nothing to do with her, so she was surprised when they walked toward her.

"This ridiculous trick of some small-town doctor, putting Nikki under medical quarantine for an unknown ailment, isn't going to work. You may as well give us her now, Anne," her mother commanded. "Lloyd has promised us custody once she's returned."

Anne turned and stared deep into her father's cold eyes. "And will you hit her if one of your big loans defaults?" she asked with deceptive softness. "Or are you into breaking bones like Lloyd? Frankly, I'll be surprised if he gives Nikki up. She's too big a bargaining tool with his father."

The man's fists clenched at his sides. "You—"

"Don't," Travis advised with a deadly quiet. "Because if you dare to touch her again, I won't be held accountable for my actions."

Her mother shot them both a venomous look, then the couple moved swiftly away.

"I wonder what they promised Lloyd in hopes of getting Nikki," Anne mused, feeling freer than she had in a long time, because she had finally confronted her parents.

"Probably a new toaster and a gold-plated savings book," he muttered, leading her back to Dave, who stood talking to one of his assistants.

"Good news," the attorney greeted them before guiding them into a side room. "And bad news."

Anne sighed. "Give me the bad news first."

"The records for your two hospital stays read that you were in for gynecological problems," he announced.

She closed her eyes. "I cannot believe they've gone so far as to change them. How can they do that?"

"The Sinclairs will do anything to protect themselves," Dave explained.

Anne chewed on her lower lip, unaware that she was nibbling off the lipstick she had just reapplied. "Dave, tell me the truth. Do you believe everything I've told you, even though I don't have a shred of proof to back up my words?"

"Yes," he replied without hesitation.

She had to know more. "Why?"

He grinned. "If you were guilty you would have killed him, left Nikki and taken off for Europe or South America. And only someone incredibly stupid would come back."

Anne heaved a sigh of relief, taking comfort in Travis's fingers, which were laced tightly through hers. "Now what about the good news?"

"I found the nurse who took care of you when you were hospitalized for the broken ribs," he said proudly. "She's willing to testify."

Anne looked more hopeful than she had in days. "That's wonderful! How did this come about?"

Dave shook his head. "She read about it in the papers. And decided to come forward, because she never liked the way you were treated by your husband and family during your hospitalization. She'll be one of our first witnesses."

But Anne was still feeling nervous. "After the prosecution finishes with me, I may not have to worry about anything other than what to wear to my funeral."

"I wouldn't worry," Dave assured her.

But Anne wasn't as confident as she sat next to her lawyer, listening to people talk about her alleged temper tantrums, abrupt changes in mood and the way she refused social invitations; there was even a doctor, testifying she'd been treated for drugs.

Dave was genial as he questioned each witness, sometimes adroitly turning the negative statements in their favor, at other times unable to shake the person's story.

"Mrs. James, did you ever see my client take drugs?" he asked one woman, whom Anne had once thought of as a good friend.

She shrugged. "No, but everyone knew she did."

"I'm not talking about anyone else. I'm asking if *you* did," Dave pressed, still smiling. "Were you present during any of the times my client supposedly took drugs?"

She frowned. "Well, no, but—"

"Thank you. I have no other questions."

"Now, Mr. Carter, you say you and Mrs. Sinclair were lovers for several months." Dave's manner wasn't as friendly with this man, but he still assumed a "good ole boy" attitude.

The man sat back, leering in Anne's direction. "Yeah, we sure were."

"Then you know Mrs. Sinclair very well."

"I'd sure say so." He chuckled, grinning at the laughter running through the courtroom.

Dave nodded "Then you're more than familiar with her birthmark."

He shifted uncomfortably in the chair. "Well, uh—"

Dave leaned on the railing, lowering his voice a fraction. "That cute little star shape on her left hip?"

"What about it?"

He pressed. "You know it?"

"Sure, I do," Carter blustered. "I told you, I know all about her. Couldn't miss something like that, could I?" He winked knowingly at the people in the courtroom.

Dave smiled and stepped back. "Your Honor, I have a doctor's report here that states Mrs. Sinclair has no identifying birthmarks and never has had one. Obviously you didn't know the lady as well as you thought you did. No further questions."

Jed Carter stared at Lloyd, but the other man didn't look up as he walked past.

Lloyd's testimony was still the most damaging. Sitting in the witness stand looking movie-star handsome in a pale blue, Italian-cut suit, he presented the image of a man who had been badly hurt.

"Anne was my life, but when she began to change, I knew our marriage couldn't last. Her many lovers and the way she treated our daughter were just the last straw.

"I had to fight for custody. I didn't want to drag out her dirty linen, but how could I allow her to raise our child?

"That last night I had no idea why she came over. She began screaming obscenities at me, saying if we couldn't be together she'd rather have me dead. I didn't realize she had my gun until it was too late. I'm just glad Nikki was safe in her room. For all I know, she might have tried to hurt her, too. She appeared so unbalanced. I miss my daughter and I want her home with me. Why she refuses to give her up, I don't know, because I doubt she loves her."

A wave of sympathetic murmurs ran through the crowded room.

"If I didn't know better, *I'd* even demand I be lynched," Anne murmured, reaching behind her for Travis's hand.

Dave patted her shoulder and stood up.

"Mr. Sinclair, you say that you asked for the divorce because of your wife's infidelities," he began.

"That's right."

"Then why was Mrs. Sinclair the one to file?"

Lloyd's expression didn't change. "I allowed her to file to save face."

Dave nodded. "Tell me, do you ever lose your temper?"

He shrugged, looking at ease. "Everyone does at one time or another."

"Did you ever lose your temper with your ex-wife to such an extent that you struck her?"

Lloyd's gaze didn't waver. "Never."

"What about the times she was hospitalized for broken bones?"

"The only time she broke a bone was when she broke her wrist falling down the stairs, and she wasn't hospitalized for that," he explained, looking so sincere that Anne felt ill.

"But your house has no stairs," Dave pointed out with maddening logic.

"There are two steps leading to the house and a cement walkway. That's where she fell, because she was drunk when we came home from a party."

Anne moaned softly, scarcely feeling Travis's comforting squeeze of her hand.

Dave nodded. "Do you drink?"

"Socially."

The prosecuting attorney spoke up. "Your Honor, I don't know what Counselor is trying to prove here."

"If you'll give me a moment, it will become clear," Dave responded.

At the judge's nod, Dave continued.

"Ever get drunk?"

Lloyd shrugged, his manner relaxed, his eyes sharp. "As a teenager, like so many did."

"What about as an adult? Ever get drunk enough to hit your wife hard enough to send her to the hospital?"

"Objection!"

"Of course not!"

"Drunk enough almost to kill her, so that she had no choice but to strike out in self-defense and run for fear of her life?"

"Objection! Defense is badgering the witness."

Dave never stopped smiling as he stepped away. "I withdraw the questions."

When Lloyd stepped down, he walked past Anne but gave her a look that could have killed. She just stared at him.

No one was surprised when Travis was called to the stand, since he had already been served with a subpoena.

He sat there looking very relaxed and comfortable, fully prepared for anything thrown his way.

"Sheriff Hunter, did you ever meet a J. D. Porter, a private investigator?" the prosecuting attorney asked.

"Yes, I did."

"And did he divulge the reason for his meeting with you?"

"Yes."

"And what was that reason?"

"He was looking for a woman," Travis replied.

"Did he say why he was looking for her?"

"Said she had shot her ex-husband and kidnapped their child."

"Did he show you a picture of the woman and child?"

"Yes."

"Is this the picture?" He held up a photograph.

Travis leaned forward to get a better look at it. "Looks like it, but I couldn't be sure."

"When Mr. Porter explained his business, why didn't you tell him you knew Mrs. Sinclair?" the attorney demanded.

Travis smiled ever so slightly. "Because I didn't know her."

The other man exhaled a frustrated breath. "Are you saying under oath that you didn't know the defendant?"

"No, I'm saying that I didn't know a woman named Anne Sinclair," Travis clarified.

"Then the defendant was using another name?"

"Yes."

"When you discovered who she really was, why didn't you call the proper authorities?"

"I don't believe in jumping the gun until I have all the facts. All Porter did was ramble on about a bloodthirsty woman and a big reward. That kind of talk doesn't go over very well with me."

His adversary swaggered. "Is that why the townspeople lied to Mr. Porter, claiming they never saw her, either? You must run a pretty tight town."

Travis's gaze hardened. "I told you before, we didn't know her by that name."

The prosecutor consulted his notes. "You accompanied Mrs. Sinclair back to Houston, am I right?"

"Yes."

"And you are sharing a house with her?"

"Correct."

"Are you sharing a bed?"

"Objection!"

"Your Honor, I'm trying to prove that this man would lie for a woman he has had intimate relations with," the attorney argued, then smilingly backed off. "But if that offends my colleague, I can take a different tack. Are you in love with Mrs. Sinclair?"

Travis didn't hesitate. "As soon as this farce is over, I plan to marry the lady. Is that what you wanted to know?"

"More than enough. Thank you."

By the time the day was finished, Anne was exhausted. As Dave drove them to the house, she leaned back her head and closed her eyes.

"They made her sound like a cross between Lucrezia Borgia and Mata Hari," Travis grumbled from the back seat.

"And I was able to come back at them every time," Dave countered. "They're out to prove Anne deliberately shot Lloyd. I intend to show that it was strictly self-defense."

"It was!" Anne argued.

"I believe you, but we have to get them to believe us, okay?" he soothed.

"I should have killed him that night."

Both men fell still at the low-voiced statement.

"You're talking crazy, Anne," Travis said angrily.

"I agree. That's not the kind of thing to say in public," Dave added firmly. "Besides, if you had killed him, you wouldn't have a chance in court, and you know it."

Once they reached the house, Dave reminded them to either let Rosa answer the phone or allow the answering machine to pick up the calls, since he feared the media would soon find them. So far they had been lucky, but they all knew their luck was running out.

After a dinner they hardly touched, Anne and Travis retired to the den to just sit and share each other's closeness.

"It's all starting to close in," she murmured, laying her head on Travis's shoulder. "Lloyd seems to win a little more every day."

"Maybe so, but we're not going to let him win without a fight."

ANNE'S HEADACHE escalated as the day wore on. Dave admitted that his witnesses for the defense were few, since Lloyd's ex-girlfriends refused to testify to his violent nature. The nurse he had located was his first witness, and the woman calmly explained that she had looked after Mrs. Anne Sinclair when she was admitted for a concussion and broken ribs.

"Now Ms. Palmer, how can you be so sure the broken ribs and bruises Mrs. Sinclair sustained were a result of a beating from her husband?" the prosecuting attorney asked with a knowing smirk.

"I never said I was absolutely certain, but she cried all night, begging Lloyd to stop hitting her, and some of the bruises were definitely the shape of a man's fingers," she explained.

"Certainly such behavior could have been a result of painkilling drugs," he pressed. "It's been known to happen."

She shook her head. "She refused all but aspirin, and drugs aren't allowed when a patient has a concussion."

"After all these years, how can you remember one patient so clearly?"

The woman smiled briefly. "It wasn't difficult. We talked about our daughters, who happened to be the same age, and because she once mentioned she prayed to give her daughter a happier childhood than she had."

Dave then called a physician, who attested to Anne's sound mind and declared that he could find no signs of abnormal behavior. Then he called Anne to the stand.

"Mrs. Sinclair, we want to make this as painless as possible for you." He smiled at his client. "But I want the jury to understand a few things. Why did you run away three years ago?"

She spoke in a low but steady voice. "I felt I had no choice."

"Why?"

"Because I knew no one would bother to listen to my side of the story, after what had happened during my divorce." Anne looked up, caught Travis's gaze and gathered strength from it.

"Why did you go to Lloyd Sinclair's house that night?"

She took a deep breath. "He had called me, complaining that Nikki was crying and he couldn't make her stop. He wanted me to come over and calm her down. When I arrived, I found Lloyd and a woman in the living room and could hear my daughter screaming in her bedroom. By the time I finished calming her down, the woman was gone and Lloyd had obviously had a few too many drinks."

"What makes you think that?"

"The signs. Slurred speech, glassy eyes and the usual hostile manner he got when he drank too much. He also held a large glass of whiskey in his hand." She glanced toward the other attorney, seeing he was gearing himself up for an objection. "The smell from the glass was unmistakable, which is why I knew what he was drinking."

Dave nodded. "Did you leave then?"

She shook her head. "No, I wanted to talk to him about arranging for me to see Nikki more, but he refused to listen. In fact, he said that if I wanted to be with her more, I could do something for him."

"Such as?"

Revulsion showed faintly in her eyes. "Have sex with him."

"Did you agree?"

Her hands twisted in her lap, the only sign of nervousness. "I refused."

"And?"

She shrugged. "I also told Lloyd what I thought of him. That he was a sick, evil man who didn't deserve to consort with decent people. I might have called him some other names, but I don't remember exactly what."

Dave appeared to consult some notes on his table. "And what happened then?"

She licked her lips. As she began to remember the night, her face turned pale, and her eyes grew huge and dark.

"Just take your time," he advised softly, noting her shortness of breath.

She nodded jerkily. "He got angry and threw his glass at me. The next thing I knew, he had hit me in the face a couple of times. Nikki came in and tried to get him to stop, and he struck her across the face. I screamed at her to go back to her room, because I was afraid he'd hurt her badly." She paused to take several calming breaths, but her voice still came out unnaturally high-pitched. "I fought back, but he's a great deal larger than I am, so I didn't have much luck. The next thing I knew, he had me bent backward over his desk and his hands were around my throat." Anne paused, the glazed expression in her eyes conveying that she

was reliving the horror. "And all I knew was that I wa
going to die unless I could somehow get him off me.
groped around, hoping to find something. One of the top
drawers was open, and I guess I grabbed the gun from
there. After that I don't remember what exactly happened
I heard a loud noise and when I came to my senses, Lloy
was lying on the floor bleeding, and Nikki was crying in he
room. I knew I had only one choice—to get out of there
and take my daughter with me. I called 911, told them
heard gun shots and then ran." Her voice faded.

Dave's manner was gentle. "Anne, did you shoot you
husband deliberately?"

"No, I did not."

He again consulted his notes. "One more thing. Wh
didn't you go to your own family for help?"

She drew in a deep breath. "Because they wanted noth
ing to do with me after I divorced Lloyd."

When the prosecuting attorney approached, Anne knew
what she was in for, since Dave had prepared her.

"Mrs. Sinclair, you said that your ex-husband struck you
that night. Now, couldn't that have been in self-defense?"

"No." *Don't offer anything. Just answer the questions*
Anne.

"You said he had been drinking. A man in Mr. Sin
clair's position might drink occasionally, but you're trying
to say he's an alcoholic. Aren't you exaggerating just a lit
tle?" he insisted.

She looked him squarely in the eye. "No, I am not."

He looked a little frustrated. "What about you? Do yo
drink?"

Anne held on to the image of Travis in her mind to keep
her calm. "Very little."

"What do you consider a little?"

"A glass of wine on special occasions."

He showed disbelief. "No more than that?"

"My system can't tolerate a lot of alcohol. It tends to make me very ill," she explained.

The man nodded, clearly not believing her. "Now, your ex-husband must have been upset that night and might have batted at you if you had lost your temper with him, but nothing that would leave bruises, as you claim he did."

Anne didn't like the man, but she knew she couldn't show her revulsion. "What he did to me was more than batting."

"If Mr. Sinclair was so cruel to you, why did you stay with him? Why didn't you go to his family or your own and tell them what was going on?" he demanded, all pretense of affability now gone.

"I stayed with him because I was stupid enough to think he might change. Also because I had no one else to go to. And when I told his family, his father said that all women needed to be knocked around a bit to keep them in line," Anne said in a hard voice. "And as for my own family, my father had started beating me when I was six and didn't stop until I grew older. I knew I wouldn't get any sympathy from either party. I was told by both sides that I was to bear it silently, that my husband could lose his temper if I served him rice instead of potatoes for dinner, and that I was to look the other way if he wanted to have girlfriends. I soon grew up and realized that I was also a human being, and that there was no reason for me to put up with such humiliation any longer."

The attorney was taken aback, clearly not expecting such a strong reply.

"I move that Mrs. Sinclair's answer be stricken from the record, since most of what she has said is hearsay," he stated, recovering quickly.

By the time Anne left the witness stand, she felt like a strand of overcooked spaghetti. She was relieved when the noon recess was called.

"I blew it," she said with a sigh as they left the court
house for a nearby restaurant, where they could be assured
privacy.

"Don't worry," Dave soothed. "Actually you came
across so strong that you did more good than harm."

Anne looked up, her gaze temporarily snared by two
pairs of coldly condemning eyes across the room. "I don't
think my parents will agree with you."

Travis studied the older couple, who were staring dag
gers at their table. "How can parents be so cruel?" he
murmured.

Dave shrugged. "When you've been involved with di
vorce and custody cases for as long as I have, you get used
to everything."

Travis shook his head. "I couldn't. Give me our little
town anytime, where the worst is Wilma going after old
Zeke with her shotgun. At least I know I can take it away
from her without getting shot up myself."

"Dave, what exactly is going to happen?" Anne asked,
knowing that her nerves were rapidly fraying.

"I'm hoping first to show that you had just cause for
what you did, then to call for a new custody hearing," he
explained. "I may not be able to get all the charges
dropped, but I'm going to work for your getting proba
tion." The realization that the verdict might not go that way
hung heavily between them.

When they left the restaurant, Anne felt her head prac
tically splitting wide open, even with the extrastrength as
pirin she had taken after her meal.

"It's all nerves," she told Travis when he expressed con
cern.

"How much longer is this going to be?" he demanded of
Dave in a low voice, taking the other man aside. "She's
tearing herself apart inside."

"It would be a lot easier if we could get some of the old girlfriends to talk," the attorney replied. "But everyone is afraid of the Sinclairs."

"Except me," Anne mused. "I'm the first person to stand up to them, and because of that, they're going to make me pay for it."

Chapter Seventeen

"Hey, sleepyhead, time to get up so we can slay some more dragons."

Anne opened her eyes. When they'd returned to the house the night before, she had taken a long hot bath, eaten lightly, then decided to lie down, hoping to banish her headache. That she had fallen asleep wasn't surprising. That she had slept all night was. She smiled and held out her hand. Travis sat on the edge of the bed and grasped her fingers. She looked up at a man who had asked little but to be with her. He had slept beside her every night, offering quiet-voiced assurances, but nothing else. It was an unspoken agreement that any further development in their relationship was to be put on hold until Anne could call her life her own again. Still, it was as if they both knew that the next step would be permanent.

"What did I ever do to deserve someone as wonderful as you?" she asked softly, lacing her fingers through his.

He smiled, gently squeezing her hand. "It was your lucky day."

"I shouldn't have allowed Nikki to attend Susie's birthday party. Then you would still have your money for your bull, and you'd be living a normal and carefree life, instead of being embroiled in a bitter court case," she murmured.

Travis shook his head. "Wrong. I still would have pursued you because I'm so stubborn. We were meant to be together." He leaned down and brushed his lips across hers. "That's what counts. Now, why don't you put on something a bit more substantial than that skimpy nightgown of yours? Of course, you'd really impress the jury in that little number."

Anne sighed as she sat up. "The way things are going back and forth, I could use it as an edge."

"Nah, wear a short skirt instead, so you can show off those great legs of yours." He pulled her to her feet.

She placed her hands on his shoulders, moving them upward to frame his face. "You've made me whole again, Travis," she said quietly. "Without you, I don't know if I could have gone as far as I have."

"You're wrong, you know. You'd still be in there fighting," he assured her. "Now, get dressed. We're running late today, since I let you sleep a little longer. You needed it badly," he said, showing his concern for her wan features.

"It doesn't seem fair that you know all my secrets and I know so few of yours," Anne grumbled as she put on her makeup.

Travis stood in the doorway watching her. "Ask my mother, and she'll be more than happy to fill you in. Except I don't think I know all of yours." He grinned. "I don't remember ever seeing that star-shaped birthmark Dave was talking about."

"Ah yes, the infamous birthmark," she said dryly as she brushed on mascara. "Amazing I never noticed it, isn't it?" She turned. "Travis, I want you to go back."

His body stiffened. "Not funny, Anne."

"If it goes against me, I don't want you here," she said with a sense of urgency. "And if it comes down to my having to return Nikki to Lloyd, I want you with her. Please understand."

"I do, but she has Maude and Susie to keep her safe. Right now, it's just you and me, kid." He flashed her a loving smile.

"If you weren't so damn stubborn, I could handle this better," she grumbled.

Anne felt as if she was drifting through the days. She missed her daughter, whom she hadn't been able to talk to for the past couple of weeks. She thought longingly of Dunson with its gently rolling hills, of Maude's witty tongue, talking with customers at Lorna's and being with Travis.

"I want life to return to the way it was," she murmured. "All this is a bad dream. Every morning I wake up hoping we'll be back in Dunson."

Travis straightened and walked over to Anne, pulling her into his arms.

"Soon," he soothed, rubbing her back in long, calculated strokes. "We'll even go on a hayride, just the two of us."

She smiled. "Hayrides are meant for more than two people."

"Not the kind I'm planning."

TRAVIS LOOKED over to where Anne sat with one of Dave's associates. While her manner was composed, he knew she was tied up in knots inside.

"You're looking pretty cheerful today," he growled at Dave.

The lawyer smiled. "I have good reason."

Travis's interest sharpened. "Why?"

Dave looked around the courtroom, as if seeking someone in particular. "You'll see soon enough," he murmured.

The minute the court was called to order and Dave stood up, he looked even more self-assured than usual.

"I'd like to call Cynthia Mason to the stand," he announced in a clear voice.

Travis looked at Anne, who paled.

"My God," she whispered. "What is happening?"

"Who is she?" he demanded in a low voice.

She gazed straight ahead. "One of Lloyd's ex-girlfriends." She glanced toward her ex-husband, noticing how his body tensed at the name and seeing the black expression on his face before he turned to speak to his attorney. "Obviously things aren't going the way he thought they would," she murmured.

A brown-haired woman in her early twenties, wearing a simple yellow dress, walked forward to be sworn in. She first faltered when she saw Lloyd's threatening manner, but quickly regained her composure. Dave led her through the first questions, establishing her background and relationship with Lloyd Sinclair.

"Miss Mason, will you please tell the court why you came to me?"

She took a deep breath, keeping her gaze away from Lloyd. "I wanted people to know he isn't as good as he claims he is," she said in a low voice.

"Could you speak up, please?" Dave requested.

Cynthia nodded and managed a weak smile. "Well, when Lloyd—"

"When you say Lloyd, do you mean Mr. Sinclair?" He smiled in an attempt to reassure her. "How long have you known Mr. Sinclair?"

She shrugged. "Maybe six, seven years."

"Now, as to what you know about Mr. Sinclair," he prompted.

"Yes, sir. When Lloyd drank too much, he would talk a lot about how he was fooling his wife, and when he got her back, he was going to teach her a lesson she'd never forget."

"When did he say this?" Dave asked, glancing down at the file folder he held in his hands.

She thought for a moment. "Oh, about a year ago."

"And why should the jury believe you, Miss Mason?" Dave asked.

"Because I have his journal, in which Lloyd commented on how he was going to get back at his wife," she replied.

"How did you happen to have the journal in your possession?" he asked amiably.

Cynthia shook her head. "Lloyd used to keep it in my nightstand drawer and write in it after we made love."

"What was written in it?"

"Stories about what he did to her and what he wanted to do to her. That she'd never see her little girl again, because he'd send her away to some boarding school." She looked apologetically at Anne.

"No!" Anne's mother cried out, standing up. "He would never do that! He loved Nicola!"

"Madam, sit down!" the judge thundered.

Mrs. Williams sat down, digging through her purse for a handkerchief.

Anne could only sit there, feeling the cold seep into her bones. "I had no idea he hated me that much," she breathed.

Dave held up the journal and handed it to the woman on the stand. "Is this the book, Miss Mason?"

She glanced at it. "Yes, sir. It is."

Dave then entered the journal as exhibit A. "I also want to enter in three separate reports from certified graphologists that the handwriting is indeed Mr. Sinclair's."

Anne sneaked a glance at Lloyd. He stared straight ahead, looking at Cynthia Mason as if he wanted to kill her.

"Miss Mason, would you read this particular page in the journal to the court?"

She hesitated as she looked it over. "Anne said she wanted a divorce, which is the last thing I'd do. The old man would kill me. He's on my back more and more for a grandson, but she barely lets me near her. I guess I'm just going to have to force her to get pregnant again. It's pretty much what I had to do before. I'll knock that divorce idea out of her head pretty quickly. It's just a shame she bruises so easily. There's no way she can go to the opera this week. I'll have to tell the old man she's sick again." She looked up.

Lloyd was on his feet by this time, his face flushed. "You bitch!" he screamed. "I'll kill you! Who do you think you are?" He started toward her with murder in his eyes, but the court bailiff quickly intervened and dragged him away.

Anne slumped into her chair, feeling as if all her bones had turned to water.

After the outburst Dave had no trouble in obtaining a recess. The expression on his face signified that he felt success was definitely on their side.

"I wish it hadn't happened this way," Anne said on the way back to the house.

"Don't be sorry for him, he brought it upon himself," Dave told her. "They already are talking deal, but I'm going to hold out for as much as possible. I'm going to make sure they'll never bother you again," he promised, as he parked in the driveway.

"I can't believe she would come forward to help me," she mused.

"She told me he always promised to marry her, but she finally got smart and knew he only said that to keep her dangling. She's decided to move to another state and make a new life for herself, and doing this was the first step. She didn't want Lloyd to win if the journal could help you," Dave explained. "I wouldn't worry any longer. You won, Anne."

"Think he's right?" Anne asked Travis as they entered the house.

"Lloyd blew it today, so there's a good chance, but then I'm not a lawyer. Dave knows what he's doing." Travis switched on a light. He patted his pockets. "Great, I'm out of cigarettes."

She turned around. "You really should quit."

"Nah, I've got to have one vice." He grimaced. "You going to mind if I drive over to that convenience store?"

"Only if you don't bring me back a Butterfinger," she teased. "In fact, bring me two. I need my vices, too. No wonder you wanted a rental car. You wanted it for last minute runs to the store for cigarettes."

He kissed her. "I'll bring you a whole box, if it will get you smiling like that. Be back in a few minutes."

Desiring a shower, Anne called out to Rosa, asking if she would make a pot of coffee, and went into the bedroom to change into a robe. When the doorbell rang, she left the room.

"What did you do, forget your keys?" Her teasing smile disappeared when she identified the man standing on the doorstep.

"Sorry, it's not your hayseed lover," Lloyd sneered, pushing his way past her. "But then maybe it's a good thing he's not here, so we can talk in private."

"We have nothing to talk about," she replied grimly, crossing her arms in front of her.

"Oh, we have a lot to discuss. I want you to return Nikki to me tonight and I'll drop all charges. Otherwise, tomorrow we're going to tear your reputation in shreds," he threatened, standing close to her.

Anne's head reeled from the alcohol fumes that emanated from him. "I think the position has been reversed as of today. Your attorney certainly made that clear when he told you to forget about ever getting Nikki back. Or did you choose to forget that part?"

"I fired that jerk. I'll even throw in a hundred thousand dollars for the kid."

"You lost the case, Lloyd. Give it up and get out." Her voice grew hard and cold.

He grabbed her arm in a punishing grip. "Look, Anne, don't make it any harder on yourself."

She snatched her arm away. "Lloyd, you are so low it's pitiful. Get out of here before I call the police."

"Why did you do it?" he demanded. "I gave you everything a woman could want. A name, plenty of money, beautiful clothes. We went to all the right parties, saw all the right people. You had it made. What was so wrong?"

She looked at him, realizing that he sincerely believed he had done nothing wrong. For all those years she had felt hate mingled with fear for this man, now she could only feel pity.

"Lloyd, if you don't know, I don't think I could explain it to you," she said quietly. "But clothes and parties aren't everything."

His features sharpened. "Didn't our marriage mean anything to you?"

She smiled sadly. "At one time it meant a great deal to me, but not any longer, because you killed those feelings. All you cared about was your precious money and social contacts. You never cared about me or Nikki. All you've ever cared about was yourself."

His eyes narrowed. "What you're saying is you'd prefer living with that backwoods sheriff than trying with me again."

Her laughter was bitter as all her anger spilled out. "Try with you again? Lloyd, I lived with fear and pain for most of my life. Since then I've learned not all men are like you.

You lost the battle. Go on with the life you prefer, and let Nikki and me live in peace.''

He shook his head. ''You're a fool.''

''If so, that's my problem.''

Lloyd headed for the front door, but before he could place his hand on the knob, the door flew open and a dark-faced Travis rushed in.

''What the hell are you doing here?'' he demanded.

Anne quickly crossed the room to stave off what she knew could turn into a physical battle. ''He's just leaving, Travis.'' The hard look in her eyes as she gazed at Lloyd indicated that he was to do just that. ''Goodbye, Lloyd.''

The man looked at Travis with murder in his eyes, but did nothing except brush his way past.

Travis swung around, taking Anne into his arms. ''Why did you let him in here?'' he muttered, pressing her close.

''To release all the ghosts,'' she whispered, wrapping her arms around him and allowing his warmth to seep into her suddenly cold body. ''Why did you come back so soon?''

He shook his head, holding her close, as if he would never let her go. ''A feeling. I just knew I had to get back here in a hurry.'' He kissed the tip of her ear. ''What happened?''

''He's convinced he's still the wronged party and that we could get back together again. He refuses to face the truth. I don't know, maybe he honestly believes he did nothing wrong during all those horrible years. I should still hate him, but I can't, Travis. He's a man to be pitied.''

''I sure as hell don't feel sorry for him,'' he rumbled. ''Not when I've gained all that he lost.''

She wrapped her arms around his waist and laid her head against his chest. ''It's still not all over, Travis.''

He fell still. Was he losing her just when he'd found her? ''What do you mean?''

"I want Nikki and myself to have some counseling, so we can settle all our past fears once and for all."

"Where would you get that help?" he asked cautiously.

"I'm sure Montana has excellent therapists to deal with this kind of problem." She tilted her head back to look up at him. "And I wouldn't mind a proper courtship into the bargain. You've been patient with me and I love you for it. I just hope you can hang on a little while longer." Her eyes pleaded with him to understand. "I want to be a whole woman for you."

A heavy sigh of relief rippled through Travis's body as he realized she wasn't going to leave him. "Lady, you're going to have the kind of courtship a woman dreams about. Fair enough?"

Anne flashed him the kind of smile that made his knees buckle. "More than fair."

H A R L E Q U I N
American Romance®

COMING NEXT MONTH

#313 GETTING EVEN by Beverly Sommers

Ellie Thomas wanted only revenge on her two-timing soon-to-be-ex-husband. She left him, in search of the good life. But the only thing setting records that summer was the heat. Then into her life came Sam Wiley, intrepid explorer and filmmaker. He slept in a hammock and was afraid of the subway—but he made one charming, albeit rumpled, white knight.

#314 WEDDING OF THE YEAR by Elda Minger

In the midst of planning the society wedding of the year Alexandra Micheals found the man of her dreams. Sean Lawton simply devastated her senses. He was perfect in every way, even ready to exchange his jet-set life for the simple joys of home. There was only one problem: Sean was the groom, and she'd been hired to cater his wedding.

#315 FLIGHT OF MAGIC by Jacqueline Diamond

What was the quintessential businesswoman doing with a laid-back cartoonist who'd lampooned her in a syndicated comic strip? Beth Macon was at her best when closing a deal—and at a total loss when it came to romance. Then why was she suddenly wondering what it would be like to fall in love?

#316 LOVE THY NEIGHBOR by Jacqueline Ashley

Emma Springer admired her new neighbor Hack's dedication to police work. But sometimes even Jack took his responsibilities to extremes. His overprotectiveness didn't faze Emma—she simply charged ahead. When Jack posed as a male escort, she secretly signed on as a client. And discovered how perilous—and romantic—police work could be.

JAYNE ANN KRENTZ WINS HARLEQUIN'S AWARD OF EXCELLENCE

With her October Temptation, *Lady's Choice*, Jayne Ann Krentz marks more than a decade in romance publishing. We thought it was about time she got our *official* seal of approval—the Harlequin Award of Excellence.

Since she began writing for Temptation in 1984, Ms Krentz's novels have been a hallmark of this lively, sexy series—and a benchmark for all writers in the genre. *Lady's Choice*, her eighteenth Temptation, is as stirring as her first, thanks to a tough and sexy hero, and a heroine who is tough when she has to be, tender when she chooses....

The winner of numerous booksellers' awards, Ms Krentz has also consistently ranked as a bestseller with readers, on both romance and mass market lists. *Lady's Choice* will do it for her again!

This lady is *Harlequin's* choice in October.

Available where Harlequin books are sold.

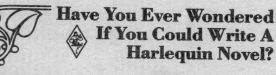

The series that started
it all has a fresh new look!

HARLEQUIN
Romance

The tender stories you've always loved now feature a brand-new cover you'll be sure to notice. Each title in the Harlequin Romance series will sweep you away to romantic places and delight you with the special allure and magic of love.

Look for our new cover wherever you buy Harlequin books.